Educating Emily

MONA PREVEL

DIVERSIONBOOKS

Also by Mona Prevel

A Kiss for Lucy
The Dowager's Daughter
The Love-Shy Lord

Diversion Books
A Division of Diversion Publishing Corp.
443 Park Avenue South, Suite 1008
New York, New York 10016
www.DiversionBooks.com

For more information, email info@diversionbooks.com

First Diversion Books edition April 2014.
Print ISBN: 978-1-62681-678-7
eBook ISBN: 978-1-62681-270-3

For the women who have played a part in shaping my life, my mother, Dora Higgins, and my good friends Sally Mirsky and Thelma Karagines.

I would also like to express my appreciation and gratitude to the members of my critique group for their love and encouragement, with special thanks to our mentor, Jane Toombs. I owe Wilma Counts big time for so generously introducing me to our wonderful literary agent, Jane Jordan Browne.

One

Home! The towers and turrets of Northwycke Hall were silhouetted against a moonlit sky. James Garwood leaned forward in his saddle in anticipation. Tarquin, his sturdy bay hunter, readily picked up his master's mood and, in spite of the arduous trip he'd made from London, quickened the pace.

Personally, James was contented with the country life afforded by his estate in Surrey, but his mistress, Althea, Countess of Brookhaven, preferred city life. He was thankful that London was a scant two and a half hours away from Northwycke Hall, if one had a sturdy mount. Even so, it was damned inconvenient.

Granted, Althea Cross had hair the color of ripe corn, and eyes large and blue enough to foster envy in an angel's bosom. But such charms, in and of themselves, were not sufficient to lure him to London. Many a country phyllis could lay claim to such beauty. He sighed as he thought of the young widow's boudoir skills. She had ways to satiate a man that would turn a courtesan green with envy.

His reverie was broken by a piercing scream, a high, crystal note that brought him crashing down to earth. At first he thought it was an animal caught in a poacher's cruel trap. The sound came from a copse to the left side of the road, home to a large number of plump partridges he laid claim to.

Then he heard the sound of male laughter, cruel and taunting, and a woman called out, "Unhand me, sir!" in a voice high-pitched and tinged with hysteria.

Unhand me? James mused. Pure melodrama.

He had thought it to be a group of young bloods making sport of an unfortunate village girl. Now he wasn't so sure. Either way, he could not countenance such behavior; the people of Northwycke village were his responsibility. He wheeled Tarquin around and headed for the copse.

A series of shrieks rose to ear-shattering heights. He pulled a Manton, one of a matching pair of pistols, from his belt and held it in readiness. On reaching the edge of the copse, he dismounted and quietly proceeded.

An agonizing scream stopped him in his tracks. This voice was decidedly male. There was no doubt at all in James's mind as to which part of the man's anatomy had suffered a grievous blow. He marked up a point for the damsel in distress but gave an involuntary wince all the same.

The price of bravery came high. The hard crack of flesh against flesh was followed by an ominous silence. The female screamed no more.

A man's voice drifted in the air. "I say, Bertie, I rather believe you've killed her. Shame, really. Underneath all that demned mud was a fine looking piece. Shocking waste, old fellow."

He spoke with the studied drawl of a dandy, one of those young bloods whose affected manners set James's teeth on edge whenever he had the misfortune to share their company at a soiree.

"You worry too much, Algie; granted she's muddy. Old Northwycke lives in a bloody quagmire. It may not be quite such sport, but the gel is still breathing. Toss her petticoats if you are so inclined, and be quick about it. I must admit that the blow she dealt me has cooled my ardor somewhat."

"That is a scabrous statement, even for a bounder such as yourself, Bertie Smythe-Jones." James's voice held suppressed annoyance, adding a certain threat to the delivery. The "old Northwycke" remark really rankled. Nine and twenty was not such a great age—was it?

Algie, the smaller of the two miscreants, motioned to draw his weapon. Bertie pushed his hand aside. "Idiot! You don't go up against Northwycke unless you are shriven and ready to meet your Maker. He is a nonpareil with both sword and pistol, and a bloody Peninsula hero to boot."

He addressed his next remark to James. "Nothing to get

excited about, Northwycke old chap, the girl is but a cheap trollop holding out for more coin. She deserves what she got, trying to play her betters for the fool."

"Lord Northwycke, to you, Smythe-Jones. You overstep yourself," James snapped. "And making a fool of you should not be too difficult. You manage a good job of that yourself. However, I take you for a lying knave. Far from negotiating a little commerce, the unfortunate female was, in truth, fighting for her honor—and evidently willing to lay down her life to that purpose."

He grabbed the youth by the collar and gave him a contemptuous shove. "For your sake, that had better not be the case, or I'll see both you and this idiot son of Lord Crestwood's hanged."

When they had cowered and trembled enough to satisfy him, James put away his pistol, then scanned the undergrowth, searching for their victim. The moon may have been full, but the copse was dark and shadowy.

Then he saw her, a limp form sprawled atop a dense bramble. The nature of the shrub he learned when thorns tore at his hands as he lifted her up. She moaned and gave a slight whimper. James held her closer, feeling the tenderness one might feel for a wounded kitten.

While he was thus occupied, Bertie and Algie sidled to their mounts. A forceful, "Stay, sirrahs! You have not yet been dismissed," stopped them in their tracks.

"My father shall hear of this." Algie blustered.

"Algernon, do not be such a paperskull," said James. "I should imagine one more escapade such as this will get you remitted to the colonies. But then, I hear the social life in Australia is most elegant. I doubt you'll miss the London season at all."

Algie cringed.

"Now that I have your attention, listen well. If either of you sets foot in St. Cuthbert's Parish again, you will live to regret it. Now get out of my sight."

With more prudence than valor, Bertie and Algie were

mounted and away with amazing dispatch. James shook his head, then laughed, a deep rolling sound that started somewhere in the pit of his stomach to erupt from his throat like a volcano. The girl stirred, stiffened in his arms, then with a stinging blow to his nose, cried out, "Put me down, you villain." Then she promptly burst into tears.

He felt the blood course from his nose to, he assumed, his fine, broadcloth coat. Why not? he thought; it is already ruined by the mud from her clothing. But he did not loosen his hold on the girl, even though she pummeled his shoulders with remarkably sharp knuckles.

"Damn," he muttered, then out loud said, "Stop. I beg of you, miss. I mean you no harm. I have sent those dastards on their way. There is nothing more to fear."

"Then put me down!" She punctuated this command with yet another barrage of blows to his shoulder.

He did so while keeping a firm grip on her; he didn't want her running off into the night. Lord knows what harm this headstrong female would come to.

Having left the shadows of the copse for the brilliant moonlight, he took her measure. She barely reached his shoulder. This did not make her small, for he was a man of great stature. Her hair was midnight black, the curls tumbling and disheveled.

He couldn't make out the color of her eyes, but they were dark and stormy. Definitely not your typical English rose, he decided. Part Gypsy, perhaps? James dismissed that thought. Even in the moonlight, even though her cheeks were mud-bedaubed, he could see that her skin was as fair as the finest cream in his own dairies, but more to the point, she had the soft, rounded features of a young girl.

Then he saw the bruise fast purpling on her jaw, and his grip tightened on her shoulders. "Those miserable bounders," he muttered.

"Please, sir, you are hurting me. Have pity, I beg of you."

There was something about her voice that struck him as quite odd. Some of her words were spoken in a country brogue, and others were uttered with such refinement, she could have

8

moved in the finest of circles. A lady's maid aping her betters, he decided.

"Forgive me," he said, then released her. He was relieved when she didn't make a bolt for it. He took a handkerchief to his injured nose to staunch the blood, then added, "Allow me to introduce myself. I am James Garwood, Marquess of Northwycke. And you are?"

"Er—Bessy, sir. Bessy Sykes. Yes, sir. Bessy Sykes. Much obliged to you, sir. Now if you don't mind, I'll be on my way." This rapid delivery was punctuated by a great deal of bobbing and curtseying. Another one of the curls adorning the top of her head came tumbling down.

She turned to run, but James was ready for her. He held her just by the authority of his voice. "One moment, miss. You are hurt and require attention. My housekeeper will see to your needs, and after you have had a good night's sleep we will help you to your destination, if you so wish."

She turned to face him but kept her distance. "I declare, Lord Northwycke. A most improper suggestion. And you led me to believe you were not that kind of man."

She gave her head a haughty toss. "Ouch!" The outburst lessened the drama of her gesture.

James laughed. "Bessy Sykes, you really are cork-brained. Every man is that kind of man. However, most of us do not force ourselves upon innocent young girls. Certainly not one who looks as if she's fallen in a pig wallow."

"*Oh!*"

She was sufficiently deflated. At least James thought he'd cut her down to a size where she could be dealt with. He mounted Tarquin and offered her his arm, and with just a moment's hesitation, she allowed herself to be hoisted into the saddle.

At that moment a cloud scudded over the moon, followed by an ominous roll of thunder. "Hang on, Bessy," he said. "If luck is with us we shall be safe and snug in Northwycke Hall before the storm gets here."

Alas, it was not to be. Ten minutes later he handed a wet and even more bedraggled Bessy Sykes over to his housekeeper,

Mrs. Thatcher, who quickly ordered a tin bath and hot water to be sent up to the servants' quarters. Then she whisked away her charge with pursed-mouth disapproval.

Without even uttering a word, Simpson, James's valet, had plenty to say about the state of his master's clothes. He removed the muddied and bloodied outergarments as gingerly as if he were stripping a plague victim and, without so much as a by-your-leave, departed James's chambers with an indignant swish that left the lord of Northwycke Hall shivering from the breeze it created.

Miss Emily Walsingham pulled the quilt over her shoulders. The attic room was cold and drafty, the nightrail allotted to her, harsh and scratchy to her skin. She turned over on the lumpy mattress and winced. The puncture wounds on her derrière were very sore indeed. She yawned and a pain shot through her jaw, causing her to yelp like an injured puppy. Emily had never felt so wretched in all seventeen years of her life.

"What is to become of me? How could things have taken such a bad turn?" Startled by the sound of her own voice, she fell silent.

The beginning of the end had coincided with her come-out, which to dwindling family fortunes was a modest but acceptable affair. A legacy from her deceased mother's family had provided her with an adequate dowry.

Her father had expired in the same carriage accident that claimed the life of her mother, and as the new head of the family, her brother, Miles, had been entrusted with her fortune.

On their arrival in London, Miles fell into bad company and developed a fondness for gaming. Emily learned of this after several young men who paid her court ceased to call.

It was her friend Cecily Tyndall who enlightened her. Miles had squandered her dowry and she was no longer eligible for a brilliant match, no matter how pretty she was. The best she could hope for on the marriage mart was a country squire.

And now, she thought, not even that. Running away, and

being apprehended without so much as an abigail on hand to serve as chaperon, had ruined her reputation beyond redemption.

"And I would do it again," she muttered.

It hardly seemed a mere two days ago Miles had burst into her bedroom, waking her from a dream only to plunge her into a nightmare. With the change in her circumstances it seemed a lifetime ago.

"It is all arranged," he said. "You are to be married by special license next Saturday."

At first, she thought the dream she was having had taken an ugly turn, but then she smelled the spirits on his breath. The odor was too real for any dream. She bolted upright, banging her head on the carved headboard in the process.

"Now see what you made me do." She rubbed her head and sniffed. "Go away, Miles. You are foxed." A statement, not an accusation.

"Indeed I am, sister dear, otherwise Lord Ruysdale would not have beaten me at cards."

"Miles, you really should not play. You cannot be very good at it, as you seldom win." Tears welled in her eyes. "What will become of us? I know Papa would be grieved."

Miles leaned over and wagged a finger in her face. "Watch your tongue. I'll have no impudent Bath miss talking to me in such a manner." Then he swayed and hiccupped.

"You would not dare subject me to such ill usage if Mama and Papa were alive." She gave an involuntary sob. "I miss them so. Where will it all end? What is there left to wager, except the roof over our heads?"

"You." Miles grinned inanely, with the unfocused stare of one who has quaffed too much brandy. "I wagered you, plus Ruysdale promises to forgive all of my gambling debts. Look on the bright side, sister dear: as Lady Ruysdale, you can deliver the cut direct to all of those presumptuous whelps who spurned you for lack of fortune."

Emily leapt out of bed, her fists flailing. "No! No! I will not marry that beast. I would rather die."

Miles pushed her away. "For goodness' sake, Emily, pull

yourself together. You would put a Fulton fishwife to shame. You are going to marry Ruysdale on Saturday, so be reconciled to the fact."

Emily detected a touch of hysteria in his voice—or was it desperation? She could not be sure, but it firmed her resolve to resist his plans for her.

"You cannot make me marry against my will."

"You will marry whom I chose. As head of the family it is my duty to make an advantageous alliance for you. Even princesses have no choice in such matters. Besides," he added, flicking imaginary lint from his lapel, "no one else has offered for you."

Emily shook with rage. "And whose fault is that, pray tell? Two of the most eligible young men of the *ton* paid me court until they found out you had squandered my fortune." She stamped her foot. "How could you, Miles? I am quite undone."

"Lower your voice. Such behavior is unbecoming. Men like their wives to have gentle, compliant dispositions, and I don't suppose old Ruysdale is the exception."

"*Old* is right. For pity's sake, Miles, his lordship must be sixty if he's a day, and—it may be indelicate to say it—the man *smells*. I doubt he's been properly bathed in a month of Sundays." She wrinkled her nose in distaste.

"Consider his advancing years to be an asset. Take care to produce an heir, and erelong you will be a ravishing widow—rich and still beautiful. Well able to take any lover you so choose."

She shuddered. "How horrid of you, Miles, to speak to me so. In any case, the man has an heir, his grandson, and I doubt he will change that for the child of a second marriage."

"No matter," said Miles with an expansive gesture. "Ruysdale has a personal fortune apart from the earldom, and would see to it that you were well dowered. His pride would demand it."

"Do you think his money would make a difference? The man is odious." She turned her back on him and folded her arms. "I would throw myself into the River Thames before I would marry such a foul creature."

Miles shook his head. "Tut, tut. You will have to abandon those missish ways, sister. You can no longer afford them. A girl either marries or resigns herself to a life of poverty. Marriage to Ruysdale will provide you with a very well-feathered nest."

His tone took on a cajoling air. "Take a leaf out of Althea Cross's book: being a beautiful young widow can be very rewarding."

"It will be for naught." Her voice was hollow. "In no time at all you will be in the same sorry fix, and then what will you do? You have no more sisters to barter."

Miles scowled. "If you want to lead a pleasant life, Emily, you must learn to bridle that sharp tongue of yours. The most tolerant of husbands would be inclined to beat you for such insolence. You *will* marry Ruysdale on Saturday. That is my final word."

Emily's shoulders sagged. She was barely seventeen and her whole world had come tumbling down, her dreams of romantic love crushed in the ruins. She was tired. Very tired. Nothing she could say or do would change her brother's resolve, so she nodded her assent.

Miles beamed and, patting her back, planted a kiss on both cheeks. "That's my girl," he crooned. "All is for the better, you shall see."

He hiccupped once more and staggered out of her room, cursing under his breath as he bumped into various pieces of furniture along the way.

Emily closed the door, glad to be rid of him, then with her back firmly pressed against it, whispered, "No, Miles. *You* shall see. I will never marry Lord Ruysdale. I would rather die first."

That night she had not returned to her bed but paced the floor, making feverish plans to steal away as soon as her brother departed the house later in the morning for the social round. For once she was glad that, drunk or sober, Miles was a superficial creature, one who took others at face value. How else could he have been so easily gulled by one he had scathingly dubbed a "Bath miss"?

A gust of wind rattled the window, bringing her back to

the stark reality of her present plight. The room seemed colder. Maybe not fit surroundings for Miss Emily Walsingham, but certainly adequate for Bessy Sykes.

She drew the quilt up to her chin. In spite of her present plight, her only regret was that with her fall from grace she had forfeited any right to happiness—a fact that hadn't bothered her until she had become conscious once more in the arms of the large man with hair almost as dark as her own.

She remembered the warmth and strength of his arms. His clean, masculine scent, which mingled with that of fine soap and even finer horseflesh. And upon seeing his face clearly for the first time in the well-lit reception hall of Northwycke, her heart was truly lost.

James Garwood's face possessed such strength of jaw and chiseled planes, it took all of Emily's self control not to run her fingers over its contours. The rain glistened on his crisp, dark hair, an unruly lock of which tumbled across his forehead with Byronic abandon.

She still remembered the assessing look he had accorded her with deep, brown eyes before giving her what she deemed to be a reassuring smile.

She pounded her pillow in despair. When he gazed into her eyes, she had fallen deeply and irrevocably in love with her knight in shining armor, James Garwood, Marquess of Northwycke. Quite the most handsome man she had ever seen in her life.

Early the next morning, directly after James had partaken of a substantial breakfast, Mrs. Thatcher, still stiff with outraged virtue, begged an audience to discuss the "young person" he had left in her charge.

"Begging your pardon, my lord, but what am I supposed to do with her?"

"First of all, how is she? The girl suffered terribly at the hands of two young scapegraces who should have been horsewhipped for their trouble."

He went on to describe the previous night's encounter, painting his assessment of Bessy's character in glowing terms. Mrs. Thatcher's attitude toward the matter did a complete

14

about-face. "What a brave girl, risking death to save her honor. It explains the horrible bruise on her sweet face, and the—er—other injuries to her person. Bramble thorns can be so cruel, poor, sweet lamb."

"Bessy Sykes seems to have found a champion in you, Mrs. Thatcher, but before we make any decisions as to her future, I would like to have a talk with the girl. It would be prudent to find out more about her, hear her side of the story. Besides, Bessy may have plans of her own. This much I have learned: the girl is no one's pawn."

That afternoon, James was in his library enjoying the pleasure that goes with standing with one's back toward a roaring fire, when with a discreet rap on the door, Hobbes, the butler, ushered the girl they knew as Bessy into the room.

Her traveling dress had been cleaned and mended, but nothing could hide the fact that even before her mishap it had been a very shabby garment indeed. That notwithstanding, she was a pretty young thing, hovering on the threshold of glorious womanhood.

It occurred to James that this would be to her detriment, for without sufficient supervision, she was going to fall prey to any rutting young buck who crossed her path. He motioned to a tapestry armchair. "Sit down, Bessy."

With a nervous bob, she complied. He noticed that she arranged herself on the seat with the grace and deportment of a lady.

He remained standing. "Tell me, Bessy, how came you by those two young rogues. Do you not know better than to talk to strangers?"

Emily was about to offer a retort but remembered her "place" in time. One did not sauce one's betters. "I did not talk to them, sir. I was asleep at the inn when they entered my chamber and carried me off with a blanket over my head. Lawks! Gave me a fair turn, it did."

"Yes. I should imagine so." There she went again, although now she sounded like someone born within the sound of Bow Bells. A Londoner, not a country girl. A very impressionable young thing was Bessy, soaking up sundry backgrounds like a sponge.

"Might I ask what you were doing roaming the countryside, frequenting inns unescorted? It would lead most men to conclude that you were no better than you should be."

Emily demurred.

He silenced her with a gesture. "I am not condoning those two. I am most adamant in the belief that in such matters there has to be mutual consent, but really, child, one should exercise a little common sense."

She kicked the carpet with the toe of her boot, her head hung low. Then she braced her shoulders and stared him in the face. Her eyes are hazel, he noted. Hazel, with wondrous flecks of green and darkly rimmed irises. A man could drown in such eyes, he thought, then mentally flailed himself for harboring such notions about a girl whom he deemed to be scarcely more than a child.

"I had no choice, sir."

"Hmm?" Where had his mind gone?

"No choice but to be abroad the countryside alone."

"You were turned out of service?"

"No, sir. I was not willing to do what was asked of me."

James felt a rising indignation. No doubt the master of the house or one of his pimply-faced sons had been making overtures of a sexual nature toward the unfortunate young girl. "What exactly was your position in the house?"

"Lady's maid, my lord."

Hah! He knew it. Hence the gentlewoman's hand-me-downs. "I am not telling you what to do, Bessy, but if you wish it, I am willing to offer you a similar position in my own household. On a trial basis, you understand."

"Yes, thank you, my lord. Shall I be tending to Lady Northwycke?"

"Certainly not. You are far too young to suit to my mother. You will be taking care of my sister, Lady Maude. She will be sixteen next year. That will give you time to learn her ways before her come-out. A good lady's maid can make the difference to a young girl's success in society."

"I should imagine the size of her dowry would have more bearing on that."

James raised an eyebrow. He was beginning to doubt the wisdom of taking such an outspoken chit into his household. Then he was moved to attribute her untoward remark to frayed nerves brought on by her ordeal. He determined not to tolerate such behavior in the future. At best, Bessy Sykes's position at Northwycke was probationary. An unbidden sense of loss flooded his being, followed by one of irrational anger.

"That will be all, Bessy," he snapped. "Have Mrs. Thatcher find something to keep you busy until Lady Maude returns from London."

Emily executed a vigorous bob and several unruly curls escaped their pins. Clutching the nape of her neck, she fled the room.

James shook his head. The girl cannot even take care of her own toilet, he thought. Of what earthly use could she possibly be to my sister?

Two

"Really, Bessy. You make a very sorry chambermaid. Very sorry indeed. The sheet corners must be done so. You've been here a week; how many more times must I show you?"

Emily winced, and kneaded her right shoulder. She had been put to one task after another since early dawn, and thus far, it seemed that dusting furniture was the only one that the housekeeper had failed to criticize.

"I'm sorry, Mrs. Thatcher. I'll try to do better."

"It's not your fault, Bessy. It's plain as a pikestaff you're a stranger to hard work. It's to be hoped that you make a better lady's maid; otherwise, I don't know what's to become of you."

Emily sighed. Her future looked very grim indeed. Her initial plan had been to go to her Aunt Hermione in Kent, and seek her aid in finding her a position as a governess. She knew the kindly dowager would not countenance the future her brother, Miles, had planned for her. Or would she? Emily wasn't sure of anything anymore.

In any case, the subject was now purely academic. Her maid, Bessy Sykes, had seen to that. It had seemed such a clever plan to change roles with her maid. No one would be looking for a runaway bride with bright red hair, and Emily had doubted that anyone would deign to notice her in the guise of a servant. To most of the *ton*, such creatures were invisible.

In less than one day her plans had unraveled. While they were eating a supper of stringy boiled lamb and watery cabbage at the Rose and Crown in Northwycke village, pert-faced Bessy had caught the eye of an amorous young gentleman. She had countered his stare with a dimpling smile.

While Emily was outside visiting the necessary, Bessy had

departed the inn with the man, taking her mistress's portmanteau of clothes with her. Fortunately, Emily had not entrusted her purse to the feckless maid, so she was able to pay for the meal and a night's lodging.

To make matters worse, she felt betrayed by the girl. Bessy's parents had both been in service to the Walsinghams, and she was often called upon to play with Emily when there were no children of Emily's class on hand to do so.

Being trained as Emily's abigail had been a step up for the girl, since her mother had been a lowly scullery maid. Now she had ruined it all for herself and would have no hope of securing another position. A young gentleman was liable to tire of such a girl at a moment's notice, and then where would she be?

In spite of the pickle in which Bessy's abandonment had left her, Emily still cared for the girl and worried about her. She feared the feckless creature would likely end up starving in a gutter.

Emily soon became aware of her change in status when denied a decent room. "Those have to be kept available for the Quality, my girl," the innkeeper's wife said, not unkindly, but merely imparting a fact of life.

She ushered her into a small cell behind the taproom. It boasted nothing save a small straw pallet and a couple of coarse, horsehair blankets. Emily asked for some water to wash herself.

The woman stiffened. "If you want water, my girl, there's a pump in the courtyard." She flounced away muttering, "Water, indeed. Such airs and graces—for a serving wench!"

Performing one's ablutions in a public courtyard was out of the question. As it was, the room lacked a door, the entryway merely covered by a piece of sacking.

An involuntary sob escaped her throat. She had never felt so wretched and afraid in her life, but it had been a long day, and being tired, she lay down on the pallet. It was not long before she was sound asleep.

Emily shuddered at the thought of the rude awakening she had suffered … was it only a week ago? She looked about Lady Maude's chamber, its wallpaper decorated with rosebuds and apple blossoms, and the soft carpet at her feet. It seemed such a safe haven after her experience at the Rose and Crown, and for the first time in her life, she knew what it was like to envy another human being. She wished that the bedroom, along with the life that went with it, might be hers, not Lady Maude's.

"Heaven's sake, girl. I hope you aren't coming down with the ague."

"Hmm?"

"The ague. It's knocking them over like skittles below-stairs. You're shaking like a leaf."

"No, Mrs. Thatcher. I was thinking about those dreadful men."

"That won't do, Bessy. Won't do at all. Servant girls cannot afford such sensibilities. Life is hard, and you have no choice but to get on with it."

"Yes, madam."

The housekeeper gave the room a final inspection.

"'Twill have to do. 'Tis unfortunate that Lizzy had to be turned off. What with Meg and Joan being poorly 'n all."

"Lizzy?"

"One of the chambermaids. She was a good worker, but she got in the family way and was sent home. The second girl this year that's happened to. Really made us shorthanded. Terrible reflection on Northwycke Hall. Neither one of them would say who the father was. Little trollops probably don't even know."

She gave Emily a brief pat on the shoulder. "That's why I'm hoping you'll prove to be satisfactory. His lordship said you were willing to die for your honor." She flicked imaginary dust from the gleaming surface of a clothespress with the corner of her apron. "I'm tired of training girls only to have them get in the family way."

She surveyed the room, a small frown creasing her brow. "That takes care of Lady Maude's chamber, the sweet lamb. Now for Lady Northwycke's rooms. Hurry, girl. They should be arriving soon."

Emily was at a loss. Seven days prior, she had been a carefully sheltered young lady of quality—one who only a short while ago had aspired to a brilliant marriage with an eligible young lord. Happily, one who would be amiable, handsome, and hopelessly in love with her.

Now, she realized that the loss of her fortune had plunged her into a sordid world indeed, starting with her brother's solution of selling her into a life of debauched servitude as the wife of Lord Ruysdale, and ending with the grim reality of life below-stairs at Northwycke Hall, with talk of trollops and exhortations to work harder.

Even so, she thought as she staggered after Mrs. Thatcher, laden with dustmop, broom, and polishing cloths, cleaning other people's bedchambers was preferable to the sharing of one, no matter how magnificent, with the odious Lord Ruysdale.

Lady Northwycke's carriage arrived at the Hall just as the first clap of thunder heralded a relentless downpour. James hurriedly ushered his mother and his sister, Lady Maude, inside.

Later, he joined his mother in her sitting room at her invitation, ostensibly to partake of tea and dainty slices of simnel cake; however, he knew that the real reason was to indulge in the exchange of small talk and gossip, a pastime she truly enjoyed.

"What is the latest chitchat in Town, Mother?"

Lady Northwycke visibly brightened and leaned forward. "Ruysdale is supposed to marry the Walsingham girl this Saturday."

James shrugged. "So I heard. That story was being bandied about all over London before I left."

"Oh." His mother looked decidedly put out by his prior knowledge of the affair, but not one to be daunted by such a setback, she added, "That is not the end of it. There is talk that the chit has run away. Not that I blame her; I fear I would done the same. I cannot imagine what young Walsingham was thinking of, agreeing to such a match. Admittedly the girl has no fortune, but even so, a respectable country squire would have been preferable to that depraved old man."

She cupped her hand to her mouth and in a conspiratorial

tone whispered, "The *on dit* is that he is in the latter stages of the pox. I suppose that would account for his eccentricities."

James laughed. "Really, Mother. I am shocked. Is that the way the ladies of polite society talk when they leave the gentlemen to their brandy and cigars?"

"Fiddle-de-dee!"

"You are quite right, darling Mater, although I will deny ever saying it. Cannot have the old chap calling me out, now can I?"

Lady Northwycke giggled like a schoolgirl. "No fear of that, my love. The man is strange, not raving mad."

"You evidently have not heard the rest of the story."

"There is more?"

"Quite. I am surprised it has not been noised about at one of your whist parties. Seemingly not much is sacred to the ladies."

"Now you are being tiresome. Pray continue."

James, amused at his mother's impatience, delayed the telling and watched her mounting agitation. His timing was off and the lady rapped his ear soundly with her silver lorgnette.

"I said to continue, you wretch."

"Very well," he said, rubbing his ear. "You are a hard taskmaster, my lady. The rumor is that Walsingham lost his sister to Ruysdale in a game of cards."

"Well, I declare!"

"Ruysdale has played Walsingham like a trout ever since he set eyes on his sister at the beginning of the season. Last week the young fool was finally reeled in, too green to know that he was being cheated all these months."

"I say! Are there not laws against that sort of thing?"

"That sort of thing, as you put it, is hard to prove, especially with a slippery old cove such as Ruysdale. He would let the boy win often enough to allay suspicion, but the outcome was the same. Total ruin for the young puppy and his sister. And now, you say the little bird has flown the nest?"

Before she could reply, the storm raging without gathered intensity and the shifting wind caused the rain to beat a tattoo against the mullioned windowpanes. James put down his teacup and strolled over to the window to survey the desolation outside.

A dreary day among a whole string of such. But then, he thought, that more or less seems to sum up my life in general. He pulled up short. Where did that ridiculous thought come from? Before he could look any deeper, his mother's voice broke into his reverie.

"Yes, by all accounts."

"Pardon me, Mother—you were saying?"

"Where is your mind? I was saying that the girl has run away."

"Of course. The Walsingham chit."

"I feel so sorry for her. Such a singular beauty." Lady Northwycke heaved a sigh before continuing. "I quite liked the gel, and I think you would have too, darling. I was sorry you did not meet her. All the other young hopefuls of this season paled by comparison."

"I will take your word for it, Mother. I cannot abide the company of simpering young girls fresh from the schoolroom, and I especially despise their scheming mamas. They are all so transparent. I cringe for them."

"I dare say," Lady Northwycke retorted. "Rather than choose a wife, you prefer to let yet another season's crop of suitable young hopefuls be snapped up by others. You would far rather dally with a strumpet, who might be well-seasoned, but has seen far too many seasons to make you a suitable wife."

"Mother, you go too far. The Countess of Brookhaven is a delightful woman, but she has no intention of submitting to the will of a husband. Marriage to old Eustace Cross cured her of that notion."

"I should not wonder. Bad-tempered old curmudgeon. But have a care, my son. You are not Brookhaven. Althea Cross will protest her aversion to matrimony right up to the very moment she clamps the leg shackles on you."

James was relieved to see his sister enter the room. Maude was a tall, willowy girl, still at that awkward, gangly stage. A real thoroughbred, he thought, looking with approval at her carefully coifed auburn hair and her clear, brown eyes. Give her a year or two to fill out and she will bring the young bucks to their knees. Then he quickly dismissed the last thought as too uncomfortable to contemplate.

"Ah, Maude, you are looking rosy. Fairly bursting with rude health."

Maude put a hand to her face. "I wish it were so, James. My face is merely chapped from the inclement weather."

Lady Northwycke frowned. "Tut! Have you not been using the almond ball I gave to you?"

"I forget, Mama. Such things are so tiresome." She espied the cake and went over toward the table. "Mmm, simnel. I quite adore it."

Her mother patted the settee. "Sit down, child, I will serve you."

She complied and was handed a slice of the cake on a delicate porcelain plate. "Would you care for some tea to go with that?"

"If you please, Mama."

James observed his sister as she nibbled daintily on the cake with a small silver fork; it seemed such a short while ago that she would have addressed the morsel with more enthusiasm than decorum.

Lady Northwycke frowned. "You really should take more pride in your appearance, Maude. You look as ruddy as a peasant." She turned to James. "It is time to get your sister her own maid. Nanny Bartlett is just not up to the task. Although I must say, her hair is dressed in a most becoming manner, for a change."

"Yes," he replied. "I rather thought so. In any case, I have a surprise for you both. I have taken it upon myself to procure a maid for Maude. Subject to your approval, of course."

Lady Northwycke's cup rattled in the saucer as she placed it on the table. "Really, James! How could you? That is most presumptuous."

"Now, Mother, I said subject to your approval. If you do not care for Bessy, that will be the end of it."

"Bessy?" Maude literally jumped from the sofa, sending

her teacup crashing to the floor. The cup did not break, its fall cushioned by a thick Aubusson carpet, but its contents pooled across its surface, marring the delicate pinks and blues with an ugly splotch of brown.

Maude gestured to the stain. "I am truly sorry."

"Really, child," Lady Northwycke remonstrated, "try to show a little decorum. This leaping about like a clumsy colt just will not do."

Maude's lower lip quivered.

James felt her distress. "It is nothing that cannot be rectified, Mother. Maude did say she was sorry." He went over to a wall niche and tugged at a velvet pull.

"Yes, I am truly sorry," Maude reiterated. "Is not Bessy the chambermaid who tended to me this morning? It took her a while, but I quite like the way she dressed my hair; and she herself is most amiable—and quite refined for one of her station."

"So you have met the young woman, and like her? Good. I rather thought you might."

At this last exchange, Lady Northwycke rose to her feet and puffed out her bosom like a pouter pigeon preparing for mortal combat. "Stop! Am I the only one in this room who has not gone stark raving mad? A chambermaid? Really, James. What can you be thinking?"

Fortunately he was spared a response by the appearance of Hobbes, the butler. "You rang, my lord?" His voice was deep, the tone solemn. James always got the impression that between his duties, the servant resided in some dank, dark sepulchre.

"Yes, Hobbes." James pointed to the offending stain. "Please have it attended to."

The butler viewed the spill with a slight tightening of his nostrils. "Very good, sir." He accorded James a bow and departed.

"Brrr," said Maude. "Hobbes is a most forbidding personage. He gives me goose bumps."

Lady Northwycke snorted, reminding James of Tarquin in full pursuit of a fox. "You have an overactive imagination, Maude. The result of your unfortunate choice of reading material, I fear. Hobbes serves your brother well, as he did your own beloved father. There is great comfort in continuity." She removed a lace-trimmed handkerchief from her reticule and gave her eyes a perfunctory dab.

James always felt uncomfortable at such emotional displays. He attributed this to the fact that, while his father was alive, his parents had ignored one another, rarely exchanging any more words than were neccessary to keep their social obligations functioning smoothly. He was relieved when she returned the dainty square to her reticule.

His father had died while Major Garwood was fighting with Wellington's army in northern Spain at the decisive battle of Vitoria. With Napoleon's troops soundly defeated and on the run, James resigned his commission in order to assume the responsibilities of running his estate in Surrey. His primary consideration was now the welfare of the people of Northwycke village and his mother, Lady Geraldine, and fifteen-year-old sister, Maude.

Presently, Mrs. Thatcher entered the room followed by a footman carrying a bowl of water and some toweling. Under her tutelage, the young man restored the carpet to its former glory.

"Will there be anything else, my lord?" she inquired.

"I do not believe so, Mrs. Thatcher."

"One moment, please," said the marchioness. "I have a request. Kindly send this Bessy person to us. I think it is high time I evaluated her suitability. After all, I cannot allow just any chit to take care of my daughter."

"Quite right, your ladyship. But Bessy seems to be a good girl. She was willing to die rather than lose her virtue. Cannot say that about too many of the wenches in service these days."

Mrs. Thatcher gave a quick bob and backed out of the room. Lady Northwycke raised an eyebrow and turned to her son. "What on earth was the woman raving about?"

"Not now." He shot a warning glance in his sister's direction. "Later."

"Oh."

A knock on the door brought the return of Hobbes.

"Bessy Sykes, your lordship, as requested." He turned to

present her, but she had not followed him in. He frowned. "Be quick about it, my girl. Her ladyship must not be kept waiting by the likes of you."

Emily walked slowly into the room, her head hung low and her gaze riveted to the carpet. James got the impression that she was loath to be there.

"Come over here, young woman. I want to get a good look at you."

She complied.

Lady Northwycke circled her, lorgnette held firmly to her nose, as if inspecting a museum piece. "Hmm, yes. How old are you Bessy?"

"Seventeen, my lady."

"A very young-looking seventeen, I would say. I understand you wish to be my daughter's abigail? I am not so sure I approve. We shall see."

She removed her lorgnette from her face, snapped it shut, and tapped Emily on the shoulder with it. "Yes, indeed. We shall see. In the meantime, kindly accompany Lady Maude to her chamber and assist her in a change of attire before that spilled tea sets on her gown. I assume you know how to treat a stain of that nature?"

Emily nodded.

At the departure of the two young girls, Lady Northwycke wheeled sharply to face her son. "Suppose you explain to me what that was all about?"

"What do you mean?"

"Do not be obtuse, James. It does not become you. I am referring to all that 'death before dishonor' nonsense Thatcher was babbling about."

"Very well, Mother. The whole thing happened right at our very gates. It involves Algie, that goose-brained son of Lord Crestwood, and that young mushroom, Bertram Smythe-Jones. Vulgar family—made their money in textiles, I believe."

"Well I declare," she gasped when he finished the story. "What a dreadful affair! Absolutely dreadful." She took his arm and, with a piercing look, added, "Are you sure that is exactly what happened?"

"Of course I am. Why should I lie?"

"I know you would not lie, darling. I just meant that are you sure you arrived on the scene before she was—how can I put this without sounding indelicate?"

"I do not think there is a delicate way of putting into words what you are implying, Mother, and I cannot for the life of me fathom why you would bring up such a matter." In fact, for some reason he himself couldn't quite understand, he felt an irrational anger toward his mother for what she was suggesting. "The only injuries the girl sustained were some bramble scratches and a bruised jaw."

"You are absolutely sure?"

"I would stake my honor on it. Rest assured, those two rogues did not have their way with her. She fought most gallantly. In fact, the blow she dealt Smythe-Jones has probably cooled his ardor for some time to come. The young woman has my admiration."

A mischievous smile played across his mother's face. "I sincerely hope you will come to harbor more than a feeling of admiration for her, my son."

He stared at her dumfounded, fearing she had descended into an early dotage. "What on earth do you mean? You are not making sense."

She laughed. "But you are wrong. I am making perfect sense. I believe your next step will be to procure a special license. You, my darling, are about to marry the gel."

"Marry Bessy Sykes? Really, Mother. That remark is lacking in both taste and humor. Besides, it demeans both Miss Sykes and myself."

"Pish-tosh! When did you become so pea-brained? Call her what you will. Miss Sykes or Miss Walsingham, it matters not. Before this week is out, it will behoove you to get her to the altar."

Three

At first, James resisted the idea of marriage to Emily Walsingham. Then his mother pointed out that the longer he delayed marriage, the greater the discrepancy in the age between himself and any prospective bride.

"I think the Walsingham girl is an excellent choice. She is not given to giggling. Knowing how you despise silly young girls, that should be a point in her favor."

He shook his head. "Dammit. I hate being pushed into a marriage that is not of my choosing"

"Fiddlesticks." His mother tossed her head. "You said you admire the girl. You have yet to say the same for any other."

"Mother, let it rest. I have to think on it."

She tapped his shoulder with her lorgnette. "Do not think too long, lest some other man snatches her from under your nose."

For some irrational reason, the thought of Emily being wed to another did not sit well with him. "I told you I would think on it, Mother. What more do you want?"

Lady Geraldine did not reply but excused herself, leaving James to pace the floor. An hour later, he summoned Hobbes. "Please fetch Miss Sykes to me immediately. I wish to speak to her."

Emily wondered what she could have done to warrant an interview with the master. She feared the worst. No more demands for her services had been made since the assisting of Lady Maude earlier in the afternoon. Even Mrs. Thatcher had refused her offer of help.

Not being recognized by Lady Northwycke had been a great relief, but it would be of no consequence if she was about to be dismissed. There was only one way to find out. She took a deep breath and knocked on the door.

"Please to enter."

It was James Garwood's voice, deep, sonorous, and infinitely masculine—a quality that sent shivers down her spine every time she heard him speak.

He was standing with his back to the fire once more, evidently a favorite stance of his. Not that Emily found fault with that; it had been her experience that most country houses, however grand, were wretchedly drafty.

He waved her forward. She took a few tentative steps but kept her distance.

"Come over by the fire, miss, it is deucedly cold today."

Emily complied, halting gingerly on the edge of a thick hearthrug. "You wished to see me, sir?"

"Yes. We have a great deal to discuss."

"W-we do?"

"I am afraid so."

"Afraid? I suppose that means I am not to be Lady Maude's abigail after all, and since Mrs. Thatcher says I make a very sorry chambermaid, I expect I shall be leaving in the morning. Alas, there is no other position for which I qualify."

"You are wrong, my dear. There is one position for which you are eminently suitable." He raised her chin with just a forefinger and gave her a searching look, seemingly well pleased with what he saw. She found it pleasurable to be admired by the handsome Lord Northwycke, but she was prudent enough to realize that therein lay great danger.

Brushing his hand away, she said, "For shame, my lord. I would rather starve to death than countenance such an arrangement." She covered her mouth with both hands, shocked by her own temerity, and awaited his wrath. Serving girls simply did not have the luxury of lashing out against their betters.

To her surprise, Lord Northwycke seemed to find her outburst amusing. In any case, he laughed.

"A most admirable virtue, for which I commend you. If it were otherwise, would you find me so repellent?"

She shook her head. "No, sir. You are a very handsome gentleman, as well you know, but what is more important, I considered you to be a just and honorable one, qualities I hold in far higher regard than fine looks. I meant no offense, sir."

"None taken. I find much in your character to admire. I would not dream of suggesting that you become my mistress. As with domestic service, I do not think you are up to the position."

"Oh?" Emily wanted to slap him. "Then just what position are you offering me? I do not sew well, and though I am good with children, I perceive your nursery to be quite empty."

"Yes, it is. But I am pleased to hear that you fare well with little ones. Eventually, I would like you to help me remedy the situation of an empty nursery."

"I would be gla—what did you say? Are you making sport of me, my lord?" She looked at his face for any sign of amusement, but could find none.

He put both hands on her shoulders. "In my clumsy fashion, my dear, I am asking you to become my wife."

She pushed him away. "I may be only a serving girl, sir, but I do have feelings. It is a cruel jest you play. Gentlemen simply do not marry their chambermaids."

"No, they do not. But whereas Bessy Sykes is a most unsatisfactory chambermaid, I am thinking that given time, Miss Emily Walsingham could become a splendid Marchioness of Northwycke."

Emily gasped, wide-eyed with surprise, then with a look of fury exclaimed, "Why, you wicked, wicked man! You stuck me in that horrid garret and let me make a cake of myself, carting those brooms and mops around. Look at my hands; they are covered in blisters."

He took her wrists in a firm grasp, then kissed the palms of her hands. She exhaled. The sensation of his lips against her skin took her breath away.

"I am truly sorry for that, Emily. Serving girls do not have an easy time of it, I agree, but I pride myself on being a fair and humane master. I had no idea who you were until my mother enlightened me. She recognized you right away, of course."

"Of course." What a goose she was to think otherwise.

"Then it is settled. I shall hie to London to obtain your brother's consent, and we shall be wed as soon as I return."

Emily shook her head. "I think not, my lord. I am mindful of the honor you do me by the asking, but my answer must be no."

He lifted her chin once more, and said most earnestly, "Then answer me this, and do me the kindness of speaking the truth. Had I paid you court during your come-out, would you have considered my suit?"

She gave the question considerable thought, then said, "I believe so. You are a caring, honorable man, and not hard to look upon, but had you bothered to attend all the assemblies and looked over all the possible hopefuls, I doubt you would have chosen me."

He rubbed his chin and grinned. "You are still young enough to be painfully honest, I see. Why would I not have chosen you, pray? My mother says you were the pick of the crop."

"Lady Northwycke is too kind. Granted, I attracted my fair share of admirers, but as soon as they perceived me to be penniless, they melted away like snowflakes on a summer's day."

"And you think I would have done likewise? I assure you, my dear girl, your fortune or lack thereof is of no consequence to me. My own is more than sufficient. I have no need to marry some simpering goose-brain, however well dowered."

"As I see it, my lord, marriage is not an estate to which you aspire at all, and I certainly have no wish to marry any gentleman who offers for me out of a sense of obligation. It would not be a felicitous arrangement."

"At last there is something on which we can both agree."

"Sir?"

"A marriage should be a felicitous arrangement, which is why I have been slow to wed. My mother has her own reasons for encouraging this alliance, but I would not give my name to a woman unless my regard and esteem went with it."

Ah, to be that most fortunate of creatures, Emily thought. "Well, there you are." Even to her own ears, her voice sounded overly bright and brittle. "You offered for me. I declined. Honor is satisfied and you need no longer concern yourself over the matter."

He raised a brow. "You think not, Miss Emily? Well, think again. Did you not say that had we met under different circumstances you would have accepted my offer?"

"I will not be married out of pity."

"Nor would I offer out of such." He shook her by the shoulder. "Listen carefully, Emily. I want to marry you because you have qualities I admire, and I think our union could have that aforementioned felicity. Granted, you are much younger than I would have liked, but time will solve that problem. Thank heaven you are not typical of the gaggle of silly geese society turns out every year, although I still wonder about you, roaming the countryside all alone."

"I protest. I am not completely witless. I traveled with my maid...."

"Bessy Sykes?"

"Yes, Bessy."

"And you changed places with her? She played the lady, and you the maid?"

"Yes. But how did you know that?"

"That was not too difficult to deduce, my dear. Even your feckless brother would not have you go about dressed in such a sorry fashion. Incidentally, what became of Bessy? Was she also carried off by some rascal?"

"No, she went of her own accord, taking my clothes with her. Even so, I hope she has not come to any harm."

He caressed her cheek. "What more surprises do you hold for me? You are incredibly brave and, without a doubt, the most honorable young lady I have ever encountered. My offer of marriage could solve all of your problems, yet you choose a more difficult path. Now you express concern as to the comfort of a faithless maid, thereby adding compassion to your list of virtues."

"Bessy and I grew up together, my lord. It is only natural that I should worry about her."

"Please call me James."

"James."

"I like the sound of my name on your sweet lips. By the way, did I happen to mention that I consider you to be most beautiful?"

Emily smiled, running her fingers through a wayward ringlet. "No. The subject never arose."

"Most remiss of me." He bent down and kissed her cheek.

In response, she reached up to his cheek and exchanged his kiss for one of her own.

"Mr. Walsingham is not at home to anyone at the present, sir."

Standing on the threshold of the Maxwell Gardens town house in the borough of Marylebone, James gave the portly butler a freezing look. "Kindly inform your master that the Marquess of Northwycke is at his door and he *will* see me, even if I have to tear this sorry establishment apart brick by brick."

"But my lord, Mr. Walsingham is indisposed."

"Suffering the consequences of imbibing too much brandy last evening, more likely. For God's sake, man, grant me entry. I am not accustomed to being left standing on the doorstep."

The butler gave him a surly look, then complied, compounding his insolence by moving at a snail's pace, causing James considerable irritation.

Once ushered into a small reception room, he turned to the servant and with an imperious sweep of his arm, said, "Please summon your master and be quick about it, Hotchkiss. You *are* Hotchkiss, are you not?" With a look of distaste, he added, "You fit the description Miss Walsingham gave."

The mention of Emily energized the slothful servant, and without so much as an honorific in deference to the visitor's station, he blurted, "You have news of the young mistress, then?"

Incensed by the man's behavior, James gestured toward him with his walking stick, coming perilously close to whacking the man on the shins with it.

"My business is with your master. I wish to see Mr. Walsingham, and I wish to see him *now!*" He punctuated this request by bringing his cane down to the floor with an ominous swoosh.

The plump little man exited the room with a speed that, in earlier times, would have earned him a laurel wreath. James watched his departure with mild amusement.

As he surmised, Miles Walsingham lost little time in presenting himself. Once rich and of some consequence, the Walsinghams had seen their fortunes dwindle over the generations, but it had taken Miles and his fondness for gaming to reduce the family estate to penury. He was in no position to make an enemy of a richer and more powerful man. James was determined to use this fact to his own advantage.

Miles stumbled, rather than walked, into the room. His clothes were badly in need of a sponging and pressing, and his cravat was arranged in a slipshod manner.

He peered at James from bloodshot eyes. "Hotchkiss says you have news of my sister." His speech was slurred.

I'll be damned, James thought, the young rakehell is as foxed as a sailor. He probably rolled home just ahead of me. Out loud, he said, "Hotchkiss takes too much upon himself. Personally, I would not countenance the fellow."

Miles remained silent for a moment, then asked, "What have you done with Emily? You will answer for this. You must be the reason she balked at marrying Ruysdale. Fortunately the lord is eager to wed my sister. I believe if discretion is exercised, he need not learn of this little escapade."

James grabbed Miles by his cravat, and for a moment he had an urge to strangle him, but common sense prevailed. He contented himself with merely pushing him away. The man was beneath contempt.

"I say!" Miles exclaimed, making a big show of righting his rumpled linen. "A trifle excessive, what?"

"Keep quiet, man. For a moment there, I was about to strangle you. I still might."

He regarded Miles with distaste. This creature, he thought, is about to become my brother-in-law. A thoroughly daunting prospect that evoked a shudder.

"I find it hard to reconcile the fact that you spring from the same roots as Emily," he said. "She is an honorable young lady, and you, sir, are as vile as they come."

Miles puffed up his chest. "I will not be insulted under my own roof, my lord."

"Keep quiet then and listen. Through circumstances I will not go into right now, your sister has become my charge. She is a lady of considerable virtue and deserves better than being sold off to a pox-ridden old wreck such as Ruysdale; therefore, I am prepared to marry her myself."

A gleam of hope came into Miles's brandy-shot eyes, then just as quickly faded. "Ruysdale will not take kindly to such an idea."

"And you are in his debt."

"You heard about that?"

James stared at him for a moment. "Of course I have. It is the talk of the town. He wanted your sister, so he deliberately ruined you to that end."

"What are you saying?"

"That you were a country cabbage, green and ready to be harvested, and, being a cheat, Ruysdale obliged you."

His words had an amazing effect on the younger man. Walsingham's shoulders sagged and he shriveled like a pricked balloon. He dropped into an armchair of faded green brocade and motioned to James to be seated in its equally shabby mate. Then he bowed his head and covered his face with both hands.

James took the seat, totally fascinated by the metamorphosis taking place before his eyes. He waited for Miles to speak, but for what seemed to be an eternity, the younger man just sat there, his face obscured by his hands.

James was about to speak when Miles's body started to shake, and from behind his hands came the sound of muffled sobs. James remained silent. He had never seen a man cry before, and under different circumstances, he would have made a discreet exit, but he was determined to see his mission accomplished.

He rose, went over to Miles, and gave his shoulder a gentle shake. "Pull yourself together," he said. "As your brother-in-law,

I will not let you go under. This matter can be resolved."

Miles looked up and wiped his tears with the sleeve of his coat. James handed him a linen square removed from a pocket hidden in his own sleeve. The distraught man gave his nose a hearty blow, then to James's relief, secreted the handkerchief in his own sleeve.

Miles got up and said, "I must apologize, sir. I should not have subjected you to such an unseemly display. It has been too much for me, and contrary to what you might think, I have been worried sick over Emily's disappearance."

"Yes," said James. "I should imagine losing your last asset would be a trifle upsetting."

For a moment, he thought Emily's brother was about to burst into tears again.

"On the face of it, I suppose I deserve that remark," Miles admitted. "But in truth, I would like nothing better than to see my sister married to an honorable man such as yourself. Alas, that cannot be. I am well and truly in Ruysdale's clutches."

James made a fist, sorely tempted to pop the other man's cork, but refrained from doing so. It was more important to sort out the coil they were in.

"*You* are in Ruysdale's clutches, as you put it, but why did you see fit to drag your sister down with you? She owes the man nothing."

Miles wrung his hands. "If only it were that simple. Do you not think that I would boil in oil if it would spare Emily? That's the rub. He threatened her life as well as my own. I have been in London long enough to know he would make good on the threat. There are enough cutthroats in this city that would murder their own mothers for less than a guinea."

James found himself pitying the youth. His lack of power and rank had made him easy prey for an unscrupulous lord whose riches and power were only exceeded by his capacity for evil.

He put a steadying hand on Miles's shoulder. "You must leave everything to me. I will make it very clear to his lordship that his cheating at cards renders your debts null and void, and that any further nonsense of his will not be tolerated."

Miles shook his head. "It will not deter him from his purpose. I doubt even the aegis of your illustrious name would keep him from my sister. The man is mad."

"Up to a point, I grant you, Miles. Up to a point. But if I were to suggest that such behavior would result in his being separated from his raddled manhood, I think he will see reason."

Miles beamed, appearing taller and lighter. "Words seem inadequate, but I do thank you, my lord. I am most grateful that my sister will have the protection of the Garwood name. Lord knows, I made a sorry mess of it. I am in your debt, and you have my undying loyalty."

Then, to James's consternation, he found himself trapped in a bearhug. He disentangled himself from Miles's embrace and exclaimed, "I say. Steady on, old chap. No need for that!"

Four

Patting his breast pocket, James departed the Archbishop of Canterbury's office in Doctor's Commons. In the pocket was a special license with which to marry Emily Walsingham; juxtaposed, a small jewelry box containing a pair of diamond-and-sapphire earrings—a parting gift for Althea Cross.

Althea. The feel of the jewel box in his breast pocket reminded him he had not given her another thought since attempting to call on her earlier that morning. It then occurred to him that it was usually the stirrings of desire in somewhat tight trouser pantaloons that brought her to mind at all. Nothing more. The necessity to end the liaison came with no regrets.

He pondered his indifference. Could it be attributed to a certain lack in his emotional nature? Indeed, was he capable of harboring an abiding love for any woman? He was almost thirty, and not once had he felt anything but relief at the ending of an affair.

Althea had not been at home, and since the breaking off of a relationship required going through the proper motions to make the act more palatable, he had decided to postpone the event until his return to London. God willing, this would be before the news of his marriage leaked out.

Emily's brother was waiting for him in the cobbled courtyard, mounted on a dappled gray gelding. Tarquin stood beside him. Miles's cheeks and nose were cherry red from their exposure to the elements.

"Brr, it's deucedly cold out here. What took you so long?"

"Sorry, Miles. Those clerics have nothing better to do than plague a fellow with inconsequential details. We had better get going if we hope to make Northwycke Hall by dusk."

He mounted Tarquin and headed for the highway. They rode in silence, each lost in his own thoughts. At the outskirts of the city, James spoke. "I am glad you decided to attend the wedding. It will mean a lot to Emily."

Miles looked doubtful. "How can you say that, the way I treated her? Granted, I was trying to save her life, but I would not blame her if she banished me from the church."

"That remains to be seen. Let us hope she lists a forgiving heart among her many virtues. I must warn you, from what I have learned of your sister's nature, I think she would have chosen death over marriage to that bounder."

"That is what I fear. You seem to know her better in a week than I do after a lifetime. Are you sure you want to be leg-shackled to my sister? She is liable to prove a most unbiddable wife."

James threw back his head and laughed. "I have had no trouble in managing the little poppet thus far. It has been my experience that women are rather like kittens. Pet them, play with them, tell them they are beautiful, and they will sit on your lap and purr all day long."

Miles shot him an admiring glance. "The devil you say. So that is your secret?"

"Hmm?"

"When tales of your swordsmanship are bandied about at White's, more often than not, they are not referring to your stint on the Peninsula."

"Exaggerations," said James airily. "People have nothing better to do with their time than make wild conjectures."

"I do not believe that for a moment. I suspect you are too modest by half. A nonpareil has no need to boast. Most men would sell their souls to the devil for your purported boudoir skills."

Up to that point, James's eyes had been focused on the road ahead, but suspecting mockery in such extravagant praise, he turned his head sharply in Miles's direction. He was about to rebuke the youth for his insolence when he saw the look of intense hero worship in his eyes. It was all he could do to keep from laughing.

At that precise moment, he warmed toward his future brother-in-law. He realized that in many ways, Miles was less mature than his sister, Emily. His naiveté appealed to James's protective nature. He would make it his duty to school Miles in the ways of the world. Besides, it was awfully hard not to like a fellow who considered one to be a demigod.

As they made their way into the heart of Surrey, James mused on recent events. He had made good use of the past two days and had not only obtained the wedding license, but had also managed to secure the services of two abigails who came highly recommended—one for his future bride and the other for his sister. Both were seeking new employment due to the deaths of their previous mistresses.

He had decided to confront Simon Fishberry, the Earl of Ruysdale, *after* the wedding, when any objections he might put forth would be purely academic.

On their arrival at James's country seat, both men were somewhat taken aback by Emily's reaction at the sight of her brother. She gave a sharp little scream and darted from the living room with unseemly haste.

Coaxing her out of her bedroom, James learned that she had mistaken her brother's arrival as evidence that rather than being married to the Marquess, she was about to be handed over to the odious Lord Ruysdale. It took assurances on James's honor that such was not the case. Miles told his story. James was right. Emily claimed yet another virtue by forgiving her brother amid hugs and copious tears.

Later, James awaited Emily at the bottom of the great staircase in order to escort her to the dining room. When she finally made her descent with a natural grace that no amount of tutelage could achieve, he watched her progress with undisguised admiration.

She wore a gown of fine, white muslin with a spencer jacket of watered silk in the fashionable shade of jonquil yellow. Her lustrous black ringlets were adorned by matching ribbons of the same sunny color.

He had seen his sister, Maude, in the same dress from time

to time, but it was not the same. Not at all. Emily filled out the bodice in a most disconcerting manner.

James had stopped breathing from the moment she had appeared at the top of the stairs and did not draw another breath until she was close enough for him to catch the fragrance of her perfume. A delicate blend of roses and lily of the valley.

She placed her gloved hand gently on the arm he offered her and smiled, making no attempt to mold her lips into the pursed rosebud that was the ideal of feminine beauty of the day. Her mouth was unfashionably full, her lips naturally rosy, the gift of good health and youth.

The desire to kiss that delectable mouth was overwhelming. He was taken aback, startled by his emotions toward a girl scarcely out of the schoolroom. Throughout dinner, conscious of Emily's close proximity, he breathed in her perfume and drowned in her smiles, scarcely containing the urge to throw down his knife and fork to take her in his arms and kiss her in front of his family and servants.

Beads of perspiration formed on his forehead at the mere thought. He drank deeply from a water goblet. No more wine for him that evening. He was overheated enough.

To his dismay, he was wondering how soon after the ceremony on the morrow he could bed the sweet young thing who had set his blood on fire. James Garwood, Marquess of Northwycke and swordsman extraordinaire, was completely and utterly in lust.

St. Cuthbert's dated back to the time of the Vikings. Indeed, the north wall of the church tower had to be rebuilt after a particularly enthusiastic onslaught by those savage marauders. But now, with its rose-covered lychgate leading to a serene graveyard, those times seemed but a dream.

And it was in a dreamlike state that Emily walked down the aisle of St. Cuthbert's on her brother's arm. She knew she looked beautiful. She was wearing yet another dress of Maude's. A lovely white silk confection, all quilled and beribboned, with dainty pink rosebuds adorning the sleeves. A veiling of tulle, held by a coronet of white roses culled from the orangery, adorned her hair.

Smiling at her, Miles gently squeezed her elbow and whispered, "Be happy, little sister."

Emily returned the smile. How could she not be happy? To think otherwise would be absurd. Was she not about to marry the most prodigiously handsome gentleman in the realm? A gentleman she loved, and who loved her back? There was no doubt in her mind as to this. She had seen the way he had looked at her as she descended the staircase the previous evening, and the way he continued to regard her at the dinner table. No other gentleman had ever looked into her eyes quite that way before. Not with such intensity of feeling. It had been a very heady sensation.

Of course he loved her. It would be a glorious marriage. He would adore her and constantly kiss her on the cheek in the delightful manner he had displayed when he proposed to her. He would feed her strawberries with his own hands and dance with her at the assemblies. She would be the envy of every woman wherever they went.

In her innocence, her dream did not invade the boudoir. She had no conception of what took place in such a chamber, and no inkling of the interplay between the sexes or the establishment of one's role in a marriage—that along with the strawberries and kisses, some needs were unmet, and dreams could be unrealized.

Oblivious of such matters, she proceeded down the aisle, convinced that she was the most fortunate of creatures to be marrying her knight in shining armor.

James watched her starry-eyed progress toward the altar. The girl had such natural grace and beauty, he mused. Who would have thought Bessy Sykes would turn out to be a diamond of the first water? Do clothes make the person? She had always been pretty, but not being one to take advantage of those in his employ, he had not allowed himself to dwell on her charms. He regarded his own clothes: exquisitely tailored blue tail coat paired with light gray breeches and sheer, black hose. His valet did an excellent job of putting him together. He doubted he would cut quite such a dash garbed as a lowly gardener, for instance.

Not one for lasting humility, he dismissed the thought and held out his hand to his beautiful bride. With a tremulous smile, she placed her hand in his, the tapered fingers first lightly touching his palm, then firmly clasping it, warm and soft to the touch. She shyly bowed her head, at the same time giving him an upswept glance, her green-flecked eyes aglow with love.

This sweet young innocent actually loves me, he thought. He was overcome by a feeling of guilt. Granted, he greatly esteemed her courage and highly developed sense of honor. He could even admit to a growing affection for her—but love? He was not even sure he was capable of such an all-encompassing emotion.

All-encompassing—that was the rub. He had no desire to surrender his control over his own destiny, and such a love would demand it. What happiness would there be for Emily under the circumstances?

It was too late. He was suddenly aware of the vicar's voice solemnly intoning the words of the wedding ceremony. I will make it up to her, he vowed. I will see to it that she is showered with every kindness and consideration.

He gave her hand a gentle squeeze and was rewarded with a radiant smile. He felt reassured. Keeping such a lovely creature content should be a pleasure.

After the wedding breakfast, Emily changed into a carriage dress of a corbeau green superfine, trimmed with black epaulets and frogging. Her matching silk bonnet adorned with black egret feathers completed a most becoming ensemble, compliments of her mother-in-law, now called Lady Geraldine, since Emily had assumed the title of Lady Northwycke.

James had also changed into clothes more suitable for travel. Not that they were going very far. They were bound for London. Emily was sorely in need of a wardrobe that would befit her new station in life as wife to one of the richest men in England. And although James cared little for the London season, he wanted her to savor the social triumphs that were her due.

A servant had been dispatched to the house on Maxwell Gardens to collect Emily's clothes, and they would be waiting for her at the Northwycke mansion on Mayfair Court. But as Emily put it, they were not the *dernier cri* in style or particularly elaborate.

With a reassuring pat of the hand, James told her there was no cause for embarrassment; he was sure her clothes would suffice until new ones could be obtained.

On seeing the Northwycke carriage, Emily let out a little gasp of admiration. "Such a lovely shade—bottle green, would you say?"

"Yes, I suppose," James answered, taken aback by her enthusiasm. The carriage was just a convenience to him. He suddenly saw it through her eyes, and yes, it was a very imposing vehicle, with the family crest, a fierce-looking black eagle rampant on a field of gold, emblazoned on the door.

After waving good-bye to the family and retinue of servants lining the driveway, the bridal couple settled into their seats. James noticed Emily took special care to arrange her skirts to assure the least amount of wrinkling. It did not occur to him that she had never worn such a grand carriage dress before.

Miles rode alongside the carriage on his gray gelding. For the first mile or so, James was painfully aware that he and Emily had nothing to say to one another. That they were total strangers who had just been joined in the most intimate of unions. He finally broke the ice by taking her hand and kissing the gloved palm. She rewarded him with a diffident smile.

"You made a beautiful bride," he said.

"Thank you," she replied, then shyly added, "You were exceedingly handsome in your blue tail coat."

He squeezed her hand by way of reply and held it for the rest of the journey. He made no further overtures except to point out places of interest along the way. James realized that a bride so young and innocent required special handling, and he had no intentions of ruining his wedding night.

Miles parted company with them as they approached Hyde Park, Maxwell Gardens being farther north. When the carriage finally arrived at Northwycke House, the whole place was in a flurry of excitement. On their entering the reception hall, as if on cue, a large retinue of servants lined up to bow and curtsey to the new mistress.

Later they were served an intimate dinner in James's private rooms—a small, unpretentious little meal, featuring a shrimp soup, delicately flavored with sherry wine. Squab, roasted and stuffed with a sausage dressing, was served with succulent baby vegetables imported from Jersey in the Channel Islands. This was complemented by a hot, crusty cottage loaf and a crisp Chablis wine, the latter smuggled from France and chilled to perfection.

Afterwards, James went over to a huge armchair situated by a fire crackling in the hearth and beckoned his bride to join him. He patted his knee in invitation, and when she approached, he pulled her onto his lap.

He had dismissed her maid for the evening, fully intending the pleasure of undressing her for himself.

She put her arm around his shoulder and nestled close. He looked into her eyes. They bespoke innocence and trust. Her mouth, curving with happiness, radiated a special joy. James was convinced she was all set to purr. Maybe her initiation into the rites of Venus would not be so difficult after all.

On a small table beside the chair, two silver bowls, one filled with ripe strawberries culled from the orangery and the other with clotted cream, gleamed in the firelight. He nuzzled her ear and, on hearing her sigh, caressed her silken shoulder with one hand while swirling a large strawberry into the thick cream with the other. He then coaxed the juicy morsel between her lips. A sweet symbol of a far more intimate gesture, which had yet to fail him in such matters.

"Oh," Emily murmured, closing her eyes she rolled the berry over her tongue.

Elated by her response, James ate the rest of the strawberry himself, then swirled yet another in the cream and offered it to his bride. This time, she gazed impishly into his eyes while she slowly ate the tidbit.

This was a little game he played because it pleased the

ladies, and they knowingly went through all the moves, from little flicks of the tongue to more sensuous symbolism, while he watched their little ploys with detached amusement, wondering if it would be a six-strawberry affair or if the whole bowl would be polished off before he got around to removing their garters and other lacy delectables. Emily did not play the game. She ate of the fruit with the innocence of a child; then with a delighted little gurgle she parted her lips in anticipation of the next cream-dipped morsel.

He had yet to feed this adorable young innocent her third strawberry, and it was all he could do to refrain from tearing off her clothes. This was not supposed to happen. James liked to be in control at all times. Then, to his surprise, Emily leaned over and took a strawberry from the bowl, swirled it in the cream, and offered it to him. He bit on it, then watched as she put the rest into her own mouth. The red juice ran over her lower lip, and in all innocence, she retrieved it with the tip of her tongue.

With a groan, he pulled her head to him and crushed his lips to hers. The flavor of the strawberries mingled with that of her own sweet essence, and he was eager to sate himself at such a sensual banquet with so delightful a partner.

Emily's reaction shocked him. She sprang from his lap, and with a look of horror rubbed her mouth with the back of her hand, as if to erase the kiss. "You beast!" she gasped. "How could you have so little regard for me?"

James rose almost as quickly and tried to take her hand, but she recoiled from his touch.

"Compose yourself, Emily. Of course I have regard for you. Would I have given you my name if it were otherwise? I must say, I find your behavior hard to comprehend." He threw up his hands in confusion. "I know you lost your mother when you were but fifteen, but did she not tell you anything about love and kisses and what they lead to?"

"Of course. Mama warned me, and she was right."

"Warned you? With what nonsense did she fill your head?"

Emily jutted her chin, and with eyes sparking with indignation declared, "Do not talk about my dear mama in such a fashion. She made it quite clear that I should never allow a gentleman to kiss me on the lips, that such behavior lends itself to all manner of disgrace."

James was tempted to laugh, but he saw that behind the anger her eyes glistened and her lips trembled, and she was perilously close to tears. His heart softened, and he opened his arms to her.

"Come, my dear. You are my wife and have nothing to fear from me," he murmured.

She slowly walked toward him, seeming to gain courage as she neared him. Then he gathered her close and gentled her with soothing pats with one hand, while he pulled a bell rope with another.

Presently there was a knock on the door, and at his invitation Susan, Emily's new maid, entered. He gave her a wry smile. "Kindly help Lady Northwycke prepare for bed."

With a final pat on Emily's shoulder, he bowed and departed for the library, where he poured himself a large glass of brandy. There he sat and pondered his situation, scarcely able to believe his wedding night had taken such an unexpected turn.

When he finally entered his bedchamber he was surprized to find that Susan had seen fit to assign his bed to Emily. Her hair spilled over the pillow in a tangle of curls, the abigail having omitted the customary nightcap.

Desire flooded his being once more. Confident that his wedding night had been salvaged from disaster, he retired to his dressing room and quickly donned his nightshirt, eager to joined her in his bed.

Alas, she no longer seemed a delectable feast awaiting his pleasure. She lay on the edge of the bed hunched in a fetal position, cutting such a wretched figure, his desire plummeted at the sight.

Compassion replaced passion. He reached out to her and, with a reassuring pat, took her in his arms and cuddled her as one might a child. Gradually the stiffness left her body, and not long after he could hear the steady rise and fall of the breathing of one in a deep sleep.

He lay awake for a while, wondering how he might deal with Emily's irrational fears. Should he go through the motions of a slow seduction? Or should he have his mother educate her in such delicate matters? He dismissed the latter thought. His parents' marriage had been no shining beacon of marital bliss.

It occurred to him just before he fell asleep—and it offered no comfort—that for the first time in his life he had failed to make a woman purr.

Five

When Emily awoke the next morning it took her a moment to realize where she was. She had been in so many strange beds of late. She noticed the rich lace adorning the sleeves of her nightrail, then became aware of the plain gold band on her finger.

It had not been a dream. She was James Garwood's bride, but he was not with her. She patted the other side of the bed and found it to be empty and cold, so he had been gone for some time. For a moment she felt abandoned. Perhaps her new husband had not found her pleasing to his taste.

But such thoughts were absurd. Mama was right. A lady *must* maintain certain standards if she wished to be honored and respected. Her resolve firmed. After all, such regard was to be desired above all else.

She stretched, got out of bed, then wandered over to a chest of drawers that contained her new husband's toiletries. She picked up his beautiful hair brush, which was fashioned in an intricate Georgian design of the finest silver.

She replaced it when her gaze alighted on a small velvet box, and with no sufficient consideration as to the propriety of such an act, she opened the lid.

Nestled on white satin were a pair of the most beautiful diamond-and-sapphire earrings Emily had ever beheld. She gasped in delight and held them up to her ears. "'Tis a most wondrous gift," she exclaimed. "Dear, dear, generous James. I must remember to act surprised when he gives them to me."

With a pang of regret, she returned the jewels to the box, knowing that the happiness of receiving them would be somewhat diminished by the prior knowledge of their existence.

A knock on the door heralded the arrival of Susan,

bearing a freshly ironed morning dress. "The Master awaits you downstairs, your ladyship, and wishes you to join him for breakfast," she told her.

"Then we must make haste," said Emily, still elated over finding the earrings. "It simply will not do for me to keep him waiting."

James kissed her on the cheek when she entered the morning room, and with a breezy "Good morning, darling," escorted her to the breakfast table.

She was most relieved by his cheerful countenance, but it only confirmed what her late mother had drummed into her head: a gentleman should be put in his place if one wished to be well regarded.

Later she was somewhat crestfallen when, rather than suggesting a carriage ride in Hyde Park for the both of them, James mentioned some errands he had to run. He promised to join her later that evening for dinner.

The first item on James's agenda was a visit to Althea Cross's establishment. The lady lived on the next square, and he usually walked to her house, but directly after meeting with her, he had yet another unpleasant task to perform—that of rendering Lord Ruysdale harmless. He rode over on a bay gelding, sibling to his beloved Tarquin.

On arriving at Althea's town house, he was ushered into a small reception room, an exotic-looking place furnished in the Chinese style—a mode too alien to appeal to James. He preferred the comfort of familiar English furnishings.

"James, darling!" Althea trilled, as she swept into the room, greeting him with outstretched arms.

He winced at the sound of her voice. It was high-pitched and piping, full of false gaiety. He wondered why its timbre had not bothered him before. Emily's softer, more musical voice echoed in his mind. An infinitely more pleasant prospect if one had to listen to a woman for the rest of one's life.

He took a step backward and with both hands held out,

palms facing her, warded off her embrace. "Sit down, Althea, my dear, there is something I have to say to you."

Instead of complying with his wishes, she pirouetted around him, then, in a flurry of muslin and lace, spun into his arms and cooed, "Say no more, my darling. It is all over town, and although I had no intention of doing so, you have quite worn me down. I can do no other than say yes. Yes. Yes. I will marry you."

And having said so, she sealed the avowal by planting a kiss on his lips, evidently mistaking his open-mouthed shock for an expression of passion.

He gently but firmly disentangled himself.

Marry Althea Cross? At seven and twenty, her face was already puffy and coarsened by late nights of debauchery and a fondness for gin. The heavy application of rouge on her cheeks, meant to emulate the bloom of youth, merely looked garish in the merciless morning light, and the decolletage of her dress rendered her full, blue-veined breasts lewd rather than alluring. He could not for the life of him remember why he had ever considered her beautiful.

When had she become so vulgar? he mused, and why had he not noticed? Every day better-looking courtesans were turned out of brothels with no other choice than to haunt the alleyways of St. Giles—or even less salubrious places—in search of sordid commerce.

Marry Althea Cross? Known for her love of men and good horseflesh, and famous for her prowess at riding both? The woman must be mad!

He gestured toward the chair. "Please sit down, Althea dear, I beg of you. There is something we must discuss."

"Very well," she said with a coy glance. "I suppose you should not be denied the pleasure of the asking." She dropped abruptly into the chair, causing her dress to billow like a cloud.

Such a lack of grace, James thought. How unlike Emily. Probably the result of spending too much time in the stables. With a sigh he sat down next to her.

"Althea, there was no talk of marriage between us."

"No, there was not, you sly boots. But your secret is out. You were seen leaving the Archbishop's Chambers with a special marriage license. La. Such a wild, impetuous devil. You quite take my breath away."

She leaned forward and squeezed his knee, her ample breasts coming dangerously close to escaping her bodice. The muscles of his thigh stiffened at her touch. This was going to be more difficult than he could possibly have imagined.

He coughed in embarrassment. "Althea, I am truly sorry. Charming as you are, my duty lies elsewhere."

At first she looked blank; then as his words sank in, she clutched her throat and said, "I do not understand. What are you saying?"

Finding it impossible to look her squarely in the eyes, his gaze dropped to his boots. "Miss Emily Walsingham and I were married yesterday."

"M-married?" Her eyebrows shot up in surprise; then her face contorted with fury. "You beast! Married, you say? And to Emily Walsingham, of all people? You could have warned me! This is complete humiliation!"

"I tried to warn you, Althea, but you were not at home, and it's hardly a thing one leaves in a note on a calling card salver. If it will make it easier, tell everyone you ended our liaison. I certainly will not gainsay you."

She stood up and gave him a withering look. "Do not be absurd, sir. What would you have me do—place an announcement in *The Times?* A lady does not admit to having had an affair, much less bandy about its ending to all who are willing to listen," she said coldly.

"Quite," he said, reddening at his uncharacteristic *gaucherie*.

"Kindly leave my house, sir; your presence is an affront to my sensibilities. How could you prefer that scrawny little schoolgirl over me? She is nothing but a penniless little nobody, whereas *I* am both the daughter *and* the widow of an earl."

Not wishing to stoke her anger, he did not fly to Emily's defense but instead, carefully choosing his words, said, "I am mindful that you are a great lady, Althea, and I wish that circumstances could have been otherwise. But alas, certain duties arise."

He removed the jewel box from his pocket and quickly opened it to reveal its contents. "Therefore, I wish you would kindly accept these as a token of the esteem and regard in which I hold you."

Before she could refuse his gift, he thrust the box into her hands. There was a momentary gleam in her eyes, then her expression became veiled.

"I am not a demimondaine to be fobbed off by a bauble," she snapped. Nevertheless, she did not return his gift, but placed it on the table beside her chair. "Now, you will oblige me by departing my house."

James bowed. "As you wish, madam. I shall trouble you no further," he said, then quickly made his departure. It could have been worse, he thought, as he reclaimed his mount from the livery boy. Althea could have orchestrated a full-blown scene, awash with tears and recriminations. He had been let off quite lightly, thanks to her aristocratic pride.

His visit to Ruysdale was quite tame in comparison. On hearing of the marriage between James and Emily, Simon Fishberry merely shrugged. "I suppose I will have to look elsewhere," he said. "I was so taken with the Walsingham chit, I did not really look further. Still. One gel is more or less the same as another, providing you let her know who is master."

The man sniggered, his ruddy cheeks creasing into furrows, and his potbelly quivering like pâte in aspic. A fleck of saliva shot from his mouth and landed on James's highly polished boot. James did not try to hide his distaste at the desecration of fine leather, but his host seemed not to notice.

"Then the threats you made to Miles involving bodily harm were empty in intent?"

"Good heavens, yes. What do you take me for—a bloody lunatic? The young fool was so easy to gull, he quite took all the sport out of it."

The man roared with laughter, evidently overcome by his own wit, his body rippling like water on a disturbed pond.

James was fascinated by the spectacle. As heavy as Ruysdale is, he mused, the man scarcely seems solid. One could imagine him draining away into a gutter, until all that remained was that idiotic guffaw of his.

James coughed. "There is the small matter of the money that exchanged hands."

"But of course. There is a bank draught all in readiness. I was going to return every penny as soon as I married the gel. I have no need of the poor fool's money. It will be sent over to your establishment first thing. Mayfair Court, is it not? Seem to remember attending a crush there one time or another."

James nodded. "I will be expecting your messenger on the morrow."

"Good, good," he replied absently, a response that James interpreted as dismissal.

"Then I bid you good day." He bowed to his host, then hesitated at the door. "Incidentally," he tossed out. "If for some reason those threats against Lady Northwycke and her brother do have some substance, let me assure you, Ruysdale, that you will be making no visits to the marriage market, as I will see to it personally that you are separated from what is left of your manhood."

The large man reddened with anger, his jowels shaking like turkey wattles. "I will not be intimidated," he bellowed.

"I beg to differ," James replied, not in the least perturbed. "If I should meet with an unfortunate accident, I have several good friends who would gladly see to it that my dying wishes in this matter are fulfilled." He punctuated this remark with a wicked grin and departed the mansion, chuckling to himself.

Emily passed the next few days being escorted by James to the various emporiums dealing in dresses and furbelows for ladies of quality. Ackermann's for outerwear. Clark and Debenham for hosiery and fine laces. She was dizzy with excitement at all the things presented for her inspection, and awed at the amount of purchases James deemed necessary for her position in life.

It was on the third day that he took her to a small shop just off Bond Street, owned by a Madame Dupres, daughter of French émigrés and known for its high fashions and even higher prices. Any lady fortunate enough to attend a ball wearing one of Madame's creations was guaranteed to be shown to full advantage.

With the sapphire earrings in mind, Emily gravitated toward a particularly fine silk of the same color, but James shook his head.

"Brilliant blue would not show your eyes to advantage," he said and pointed to a bolt of emerald green silk.

"Milor' is most discerning," Madame Dupres gushed. "Madame will be *tres ravissante* in the green."

Emily was confused. If blue was not her color, then why had her husband bought her sapphires? And if they were not for her—then for whom? Lady Geraldine?

The green silk was decided upon. Madame Dupres suggested an overtunic starting just under the bosom, of a transparent gold tissue.

At a questioning glance from James, Emily nodded her assent.

"Have it ready in time for the Fotheringhams' ball."

"But Milor', *c'est impossible!*" she wailed. "That is to take place next Friday."

Emily was crestfallen.

"Nonsense," James replied. "Hire some more girls. I will pay you double your fee for your trouble."

The offer of more money worked miracles. In a scant three days, Emily had her first fitting, and the final touches to the dress were executed the day before the ball.

Lady Geraldine accompanied Emily for her final fitting, having made the journey up to London also to attend Friday's ball.

She had intended to leave Maude behind at Northwycke hall, where her governess was doing what she could to add the finishing touches to the young girl's education before she came out the following season. But seeing how crestfallen Maude had appeared over the matter, Lady Geraldine had not the heart to deny her the trip.

When Emily emerged from behind the Chinese lacquer screen in Madame Dupres's fitting room, Lady Geraldine brought her lorgnette to her eyes and graced her daughter-in-law with a sweeping glance. "Oh *my,*" she murmured. "Yes, indeed."

"Madame approves?" asked the proprietess, hovering anxiously in the background.

"Yes, 'Madame' approves," Lady Geraldine replied. Her next remark was addressed to Emily. "My dear, I feel quite sorry for all the other young beauties who will be attending the Fotheringhams' ball. You will bloom like an orchid amid a bed of daisies."

Emily blushed with pleasure at such extravagant praise, and at that moment, she began to form a liking for her outspoken mother-in-law.

Later that afternoon, Emily and Maude took advantage of a late-breaking sun to stroll in the rose garden for which the mansion in Mayfair was famous. It was a myriad of arbors and bushes—unfortunately not yet in bloom, it being too early in the season. However, this did not lessen the pleasure of the two young girls as their laughter pierced the crisp spring air.

"They seem to get along very well, thank goodness," said Lady Geraldine as she viewed them through the library window.

"As well they might," James replied. "They are certainly of an age for such frivolity."

His mother gave him a sharp look. "So you find her too young then?"

"I did not mean to imply such. Really, Mother, you blurt out the strangest things."

"Pish-tosh. You were always so transparent. At least, to me. Out with it, James. Perhaps I can be of some help."

He gave her a rueful smile. "Perhaps," he said, then gazed out of the window before continuing. Emily and Maude were on the lawn, tossing a bright blue ball to one another.

Finally he spoke. "This is a very delicate subject; I really do not know how to begin," he said, with great diffidence. "To be perfectly frank, my wedding night was a bloody fiasco."

He saw his mother wince at the profanity and was relieved that she chose not to voice her disapproval. It would not have taken much for him to become as close-mouthed as a Clacton clam.

"Do not fret, my boy, most wedding nights are unmitigated disasters," she soothed.

"But I have never had this trouble before. Not to be indelicate, but most females seem to be well pleased with my attentions."

Lady Geraldine responded with a poorly suppressed hoot of laughter. "And rather than receiving your advances with delight, our Emily is shocked by them—nay, absolutely appalled?"

"Strong words, Mother, even for you."

"James, you just lack experience in such matters."

"L-lack experience?" He puffed out his chest in indignation. "I think not. I have never had any complaints before."

His mother laughed and gave him a playful bob on the shoulder with her lorgnette. "You delude yourself, my boy. You are not the Adonis you believe yourself to be. It requires very little effort to woo the light-skirts and strumpets you seem to favor; however, it takes a great deal of finesse to woo a virtuous young girl. A skill you apparently lack—and a point in your favor, I might add." She seemed to reflect on the matter for a moment, then giggled. "I should hate to think you ran about all over the place, besmirching young maidens right and left."

"I am sure this is very amusing for you, Mother dear, but you are of no help to me."

"I am sorry. But there is more humor in what takes place between a man and a maid in the boudoir than you will ever see on the London stage. As I see it, your bride was unprepared for the duties of the marriage bed, and you were too precipitous in the claiming of such services."

"You jump to conclusions. If that were the case, I would put the sorry matter behind me and resolve to do better in the future."

She raised an eyebrow. "Are you telling me that Emily is still a maiden?"

"Very much so. I made so bold as to kiss her on the lips, and she became unhinged. Her mother prepared her for wedlock by telling her that kissing of that nature was taboo." James gave a wry smile. "It seems the woman failed to mention that this rule only applied to suitors, not husbands, and I suppose she died before she could finish Emily's education in such matters."

"Um, yes, I see. A sticky wicket all around. What do you propose to do about it?"

James cleared his throat. "I was rather hoping to get a little help from you."

"From me? How could I possibly help you?"

"Oh, I cannot say exactly, that would be up to you. Perhaps have a little coze with Emily, you know? Explain what is expected of a wife in the marriage bed—possibly play up the pleasurable aspects of such an arrangement?"

Lady Geraldine raised both eyebrows. "The *pleasurable* aspects of the arrangement?" Her voice was filled with disbelief. "Are you suggesting I tell that sweet, innocent child she should find the indignities inflicted upon a woman in the marriage bed *pleasurable?* You must be mad!"

"In that case, I suppose nearly every man in England should be carted off to bedlam. Where does that leave Emily and me?"

"I will explain the duties of the marriage bed to her, if that is your wish, but I am not going to lie to the poor creature. At least once your sister was born, your father made no further demands of me. Being the very soul of consideration, he did what any decent husband would do—he took a mistress."

James almost choked. "The devil, you say."

He decided that anything his mother had to say to Emily on the subject of matrimony could be no more helpful than the poison her own mother had imparted. He suddenly felt sorry for his mother. His father must have been a very indifferent lover to inspire in her such a loathing for the delights of Venus.

"Never mind, Mother, I will see to Emily's instruction myself."

"Try Madeira."

"Hmm?"

"Your father got me through the ordeal of the wedding night with a generous application of Madeira. I can scarcely remember what took place, but I was prodigiously sick afterwards. To this day, I cannot bring myself to partake of that particular wine."

Six

James paced the length of the saloon, a glass of brandy in hand. He glanced at the clock on the mantel, a French confection of bronze and ormolu garlanded with delicate porcelain roses. "It is twenty minutes after nine, Mother. How long should it take for a lady to get dressed?"

"Have patience. I am sure the results will be worth the waiting. Susan had a little difficulty dressing Emily's hair. It is a very elaborate style and took an inordinate number of pins."

Lady Geraldine also strolled the room, vigorously shaking a gold-handled fan fashioned of black ostrich feathers. Her dress, of garnet-colored taffeta with an overlay of black netting, rustled with every step she took.

James felt the breeze of her fan as she walked past him. No one else can handle one of those things with the grace and dexterity of my mother, he thought.

Geraldine Garwood was a woman of imposing stature, usually described as handsome rather than beautiful. She had worn well, having kept her figure, and very little gray sprinkled her fine auburn hair. She smiled as she passed him, displaying teeth surprisingly even and white for her age.

James returned her smile. "You are looking in particularly high feather yourself this evening, Mother," he said. "That is a most becoming ensemble you are wearing. Yes, indeed. Most becoming, if I may be permitted to say so."

The smile he received for his pains was even more dazzling, and as if to show her pleasure, she tapped him on the nose with her fan. Really, he thought, Mother is not happy unless she is swatting someone, be it with her fan or lorgnette. A tiresome habit for which she is bound to brought to task one of these days. On second thought, the person with the temerity to bring his mother to task had yet to be born.

The slight creaking of the large gold-and-white doors signaled Emily's entrance into the room. James caught his breath when he beheld her, a vision in green and gold, her hair a riot of cascading ringlets adorned with gold-tipped egret feathers. On her bosom a magnificent set of diamonds and emeralds nestled, and matching stones of equal grandeur dangled from her ears—a gift he had presented to her in her dressing room a scant half-hour before.

He walked over and kissed her hand, then both cheeks—a social ritual, but for some reason that James could not for the life of him fathom, it seemed to give Emily inordinate pleasure.

"You look very beautiful this evening, my dear. You quite take my breath away."

Emily beamed and fingered her necklace. "Thank you for my emeralds, James. What lady would not look lovely wearing such exquisite things?"

He caressed her cheek, saying, "Nonsense, my darling. You would look beautiful wearing sackcloth," then glanced at the clock once more. "My word, it is almost ten. We had better make haste."

His mother apparently had her own opinion on the subject. "Stuff and nonsense, James. What has come over you? You know full well that these crushes do not get under way until at least eleven, and the thought of listening to the names of the same old people being announced as they arrive is more than I can bear."

Mother is right, James thought. Apart from this year's crop of young hopefuls angling for husbands, and the usual pack of young bloods looking them over, the place will be thronging with over-painted dowagers gossiping behind their fans, and potbellied old war horses, recounting past glories on the battlefields of bygone wars.

So why am I in such a hurry to get to the Fotheringhams? The answer came to him almost immediately. He wanted to show off his beautiful young wife to all of his friends… and, perhaps, especially to his enemies. Good Lord, he thought. Am I that petty?

"Absolutely," his inner voice whispered.

On the carriage ride to Lord Fotheringham's town house, James ran the tips of his fingers over Emily's arm, wishing he could caress her soft skin and not the fabric of her long, white gloves. He ached to explore her charms further, but with his mother present, he was constrained from doing so.

Instead he held her hand, promising that, come what may, whether by his seductive skills or the decanter of Madeira his mother had recommended for the task, this was the night he was going to make love to her.

Fotheringham's butler announced their arrival in stentorian tones. Those who were not dancing interrupted their conversations to turn and stare in their direction.

"By Jove," Alfred Fishberry remarked to Althea Cross. "So that is the chit Northwycke married." He stroked his chin. "I cannot imagine my not noticing such a lovely creature. Perhaps wearing the weeds of a marchioness makes the difference." He chuckled. "No wonder my grandfather is foaming at the mouth over her slipping through his gnarled old fingers."

Althea Cross, who up until that moment had remained with her back to the portals of the ballroom, turned around and gave the Garwoods a cursory glance. Her lip curled in a sneer. "Fine clothes can only do so much for a woman, Alfred. Emily Walsingham is still a scrawny scarecrow."

The Earl of Ruysdale's heir laughed. "Sheathe your claws, Lady Brookhaven. Jealousy for your replacement in Northwyke's affections colors your judgement. Beware, lest the *ton* jump to the conclusion that *he* cast *you* off like last season's pantaloons."

Her eyes glinted with anger. "Watch your tongue, sirrah. You know full well I sent James Garwood packing, not the other way around—and, I might add, he cut a very abject figure. Very abject, indeed. He only offered for the Walsingham chit after I had refused him."

Alfred Fishberry briefly raised his eyes to the cupids painted on the ballroom ceiling, then, covering a yawn with a languid hand, said, "So you keep insisting, my dear."

Her eyes narrowed. "Alfred, you are not only a fool; you are insolent. Not good qualities if you wish to maintain your place in society. The waltz you claimed is about to start, and I have no desire to be kept waiting."

She displayed her displeasure by vigorously shaking a fan fashioned from the feathers of a peacock. Her dress of blue-and-green-shot silk shimmered from the motion, as did the magnificent pair of diamond-and-sapphire earrings dangling from her ears.

He smirked, seeming to derive great pleasure in her discomfort, then gave her a slight bow that bespoke mockery, not the respect due her rank. "At your service, madam," he said, then gallantly offered her his arm, which she took, an angry glare marring her features all the way to the ballroom floor.

While this little drama was unfolding, the Garwoods were running the gauntlet of well-wishers offering their felicitations on the recent marriage of the young couple. Several gallants clamored to be included on the marchioness's dance card.

James held up his hand and laughed. "Gentlemen, I am afraid you will have to wait for that pleasure. The next dance is a waltz, and I fully intend to claim it for myself." He gave the crestfallen swains a flourishing bow. "Now if you will excuse us."

Emily glowed with excitement at all the attention she had garnered, but everything paled in comparison with the thought of dancing the waltz with her husband. Such a handsome man, and such a deliciously romantic dance. As she made her way on his arm toward the ballroom floor, her feet seemed scarcely to touch the ground.

She was painfully conscious of the fact that she had never danced with James before, and she feared she would prove clumsy by treading on his fine silver-buckled slippers. Such fears proved groundless, however, and they sailed over the floor as effortlessly as two clouds scudding a brisk wind. After a particularly well executed twirl, James said, "You dance like a dream. No matter how intricate the step, you have not faltered once."

Emily glowed with pleasure. "You must take the credit for that, James. You are indeed a most masterful partner."

He suddenly pulled her closer and whispered in her ear, "In all things, darling wife, as you will learn ere this night is over."

Intrigued by the intensity expressed in his voice, she looked up into his eyes. They were smokey with desire, and a rush of excitement flooded her being, filling her with a longing for something unknowable, and the vague tinge of apprehension accompanying the emotion merely added to its delight.

The next dance was a quadrille. A young man came to claim it. James surveyed him coldly and said, "Lady Northwycke does not care to dance with you, sir."

The youth blushed and, after an awkward bow in Emily's direction, beat a hasty retreat.

"Damned impudence," James growled.

"I do not understand," said Emily, bewildered by her husband's indignation.

He bent over and whispered, "That, my dear, is Algie Howard, Baron Crestwood's idiot son and one of the blackguards who abducted you."

"Oh!" Emily gasped, covered her lower face with a fan, and peeped over the top of it, horrified.

James squeezed her other hand. "Do not distress yourself, Emily dear, the bounder does not recognize you. It was dark that night, and he is scarcely going to associate the Marchioness of Northwycke with a hapless serving girl."

"I suppose not," she replied, greatly relieved.

Suddenly, a tall young man with a shock of red curls and a handsome set of mustachios stood before them. James's face lit up with a huge smile. "Rodney! So you are finally home from the Peninsula. How marvelous!" He gave the man a hearty slap on the back.

"Ought to be," the man replied laconically. "The war finished last year."

"You took your time coming back."

"I had business of a personal nature to take care of."

James turned to Emily. "I forget myself. Forgive my

rudeness, darling. Allow me to present to you my oldest friend, Mr. Rodney Bonham-Lewis. Rodney, old chap, meet Emily, the new Marchioness of Northwycke." Emily held out her hand, and Rodney bowed over it in a most gallant fashion and, with a sharp, military click of his heels, lightly kissed the air slightly above her fingers.

He then turned to James and said, "I say. It is being bandied about all over town that you married the most beautiful girl of the season, but that is not exactly true."

"Oh?" James raised an eyebrow.

The welcoming smile on Emily's face faded at the unexpected words, to be replaced by a questioning expression.

Rodney laughed. "I think the most beautiful girl to make a come-out in the past decade—that would come closer to the truth. Yes, indeed. Since ought five, to be exact, a young blonde filly, Lady Althea something-or-other, caught herself an earl. Which one escapes me for the moment."

"She married Brookhaven. He departed this vale of tears right after you left for the Peninsula."

"Brookhaven. Of course! It all comes back to me now. His death was to be expected. He had one foot in the grave when he married the gel. It is a wonder he lasted the honeymoon." He grinned, as if relishing the thought. "Do you remember how the ladies' fans fluttered when she presented him with an heir? There was some speculation as to whether the old boy had had some help in the matter, although I do not suppose he delved too deeply into that, having married so late in life."

He was quiet for a moment and then said, "Probably never would have married if he had not unexpectedly come into the earldom. Understand that up till then, the old boy had scarce a farthing." He erupted in laughter. "Then to marry a handful like Lady Althea. I understand—"

"Hrrmph!" James interjected, casting a glance in Emily's direction.

Rodney colored. "Oh I say! I quite forgot myself. Please forgive my indelicate behavior, Lady Northwycke. Most untoward of me. Most."

Emily had been intrigued by the turn the conversation had taken, but society demanded that a lady pretend otherwise, so she responded with a demure nod of her head.

Rodney smiled, apparently relieved by her gracious condescension. "In any case, what I meant to say before I digressed, Lady Northwycke, the—er—lady in question was no prettier than you. I suppose one truly great beauty a decade is all we fellows can hope for, and old James has had the good fortune to win your heart."

Emily blushed with pleasure at such extravagant praise. "How very kind of you to say so, Mr. Bonham-Lewis. But since you are James's dearest friend, you must call me Emily."

He beamed. "Only if you will do me the honor of calling me Rodney."

The two men then launched into a conversation that consisted of, "Whatever became of…?" and "Did so and so ever…?" interspersed with the occasional, "Do you remember when…?" as they rehashed their own experiences in the recent war.

Left to her own thoughts, Emily's mind dwelt on the subject of their previous conversation: the marriage—and subsequent widowhood—of the Countess of Brookhaven. There was something familiar about the topic. Something she should know and was on the verge of remembering.

Then it came to her. Lady Althea was the woman Miles had cited when extolling the earthly pleasures to be enjoyed at the demise of a much older spouse. As if that would have been an incentive for her to marry the odious and odiferous Lord Ruysdale. Miles is such a paperskull, she thought.

The familiar lilt of a cotillion wafted down from the minstrels' gallery, interrupting both her thoughts and James's animated conversation with his friend. Rodney bowed to Emily and requested the dance.

"It is one of the old ones, even I can manage it without calling too much attention to myself."

"I would be honored and am most pleased you asked at this time," Emily replied. "You see, my card is filled for the next few sets."

James laughed. "I had to be sharp about writing in a few dances myself, but I promised this one to dear old Mater, so if you will excuse me."

As Rodney escorted her to the dance floor, he said, "James should not refer to Lady Geraldine in such a disparaging fashion, she is still a handsome-looking woman and can out-dance quite a few of the younger fillies."

"James meant no disrespect, I am sure," Emily replied. "His remark was meant as a term of endearment. He is very fond of his mama, as she is of him. They are both fortunate."

"My friend James most certainly is a lucky fellow, having found such a fiercely loyal wife. And you are quite right, of course. He exchanges confidences with Lady Geraldine in a manner I quite envy. I could never be that honest with my mother. For one thing, she would never speak to me again."

The next few moments were taken up in finding a square to join. Once accomplished, the set proceeded with much gaiety, and she tackled the dance with *élan*. As Rodney had remarked, the dance was fading in popularity, being rapidly superceded by the quadrille; but it was one of the first dances she had been taught by the dancing master she had shared with her friend Cecily Tyndall, and thus, she always took pleasure in it.

As she crossed hands with a pale-faced young man participating in her square, she had the feeling she had met him before, but his name escaped her. One encountered so many strangers in the course of the London season, she thought. The next time he came into her orbit, he gave her a searching stare that made her feel most uncomfortable. It was only on being escorted back to her seat that she remembered why he seemed so familiar, and the knowledge gave her a sense of foreboding.

Rodney had promised the next dance to another lady, so he thanked Emily and took his leave. She found waiting for James to return his mother to her coterie of friends barely tolerable, and when he finally returned to claim the next dance, she clutched his arm and said, "Pray tell me, James, who is the young man talking to Lord Fotheringham?"

"You mean the portly gentleman, or the one with the

impossible-looking cravat?"

"The latter."

"It is Alfred Fishberry, heir of your old friend, Lord Ruysdale." James was silent for a moment, then laughed. "Good Lord! Do you realize you were within an inch of becoming his grandmother?"

Emily gave him a sharp rap on the arm with her fan, tearing its delicate fabric in the process. "That is scarcely amusing."

He grinned. "I found it so. Why do you ask about him? He is not the sort of chap you should be interested in. He is fast becoming as big a bounder as his not-so-illustrious grandsire."

Emily was dismayed. "Then I am quite undone, my husband. Albert Fishberry is the young man I told you about."

"Hmm?"

"You know, the one who lured my maid, Bessy, into goodness knows what sort of downfall."

"The devil, you say. I should not worry too much about it, my dear, I hardly think he paid you too much attention, seeing as he was taken with this Bessy Sykes."

The remark was scarcely flattering to Emily, but in this case, she hoped her husband was correct in his assumption. She attempted to cool herself, but the fan had been rendered useless.

"Seems you destroyed your fan. A pity. It is so deucedly crowded in here, the heat is intolerable. If you do not mind, I think we should forgo this dance in favor of my getting us some punch. I know I shall be the better for a glass of something or other."

She watched him deftly weave through the crowd, comfortable in the knowledge that she could sit there without fear of being considered a wallflower. One of the wonderful advantages of being a married lady.

At the beginning of the season, she had not lacked for dance partners, but later on, when word got around that Miles had squandered her dowry, there was a thinning of the numbers among those willing to dance with her. A most humbling experience.

She viewed the young women as they danced by, and

wondered if any, among the fairer ones, could be the Countess of Brookhaven. This pastime was interspersed with the small talk of well-wishers, who would stop in their strollings to offer their felicitations.

During a lull in these social interchanges, she picked out a tall, willowy blonde, then realized it could not be the lady in question, for the girl seemed to be about her own age. The Countess of Brookhaven would have to be ten years older.

Presently the dance came to an end, and James had yet to return with their refreshments. She consulted her dance card to see who that next partner would be. Her brother, Miles. Ordinarily, he would not have been invited to a crush given by any so high in the instep as the Fotheringhams, but being the brother-in-law of the Marquess of Northwycke had added a certain cachet to his social standing.

The orchestra struck up the lively tune of the Sir Roger de Coverley, a dance more at home at country gatherings, but it was a vigorous romp enjoyed by most in whatever milieu.

She and her brother had traversed the floor twice before either one of them spoke. They had never been very close, and the treatment she had suffered at his hands had widened the gap. It was Miles who broke the ice.

"I hope you are having as good a time as I, little sister. I cannot remember attending a more successful ball." He looked about him, seemingly very satisfied with the turn his life had taken. He returned his attention to her with an admiring assessment. "Might I say, Emily, dear, that you are in fine looks this evening. Extremely high in the feather. The married estate must agree with you."

Uncomfortable with the idea of discussing her marriage even on a superficial level with the man who had tried to saddle her with Lord Ruysdale, and remembering the untoward remarks he had uttered toward that end, Emily merely responded with a faint smile.

Miles seemed not to notice the lukewarm reception his words had garnered—not that this surprised her. She had come to realize that her brother did not delve too deeply into any aspect of his dealings with others. In fact, he seemed to lack the depth of character required to do so.

As they were leaving the dance floor, a man put a delaying hand on Miles's shoulder. "I say there, Miles, old chap, Lady Brookhaven and I would be much obliged if you would present us to your charming sister."

It was Alfred Fishberry, the man who had lured Bessy away from the inn. Emily felt the blood drain from her face, realizing by his smirk that he had recognized her.

Her heart sank. Such a creature would spread the scandal of her mad dash from London without the benefit of a chaperon, thereby bringing dishonor down on her head and, what was worse, besmirching the good name of her husband's family—unless, she surmised, it was to his advantage to do otherwise.

The air became heavy with the tension sparking between the two of them, but Miles, blithely unaware, greeted with unseemly enthusiasm the grandson of the man who had almost brought him to ruin.

Emily steeled herself for the introductions, wondering how she would survive the ordeal. "Emily, my dear, allow me to present the Countess of Brookhaven."

Up until that moment, she had been too preoccupied by the predicament she faced to take much notice of the lady seeking the introduction. At first glance, Althea Cross was something of a disappointment. She was still beautiful but somewhat overblown, rather like a cabbage rose about to drop its first petals.

"How do you do," Emily said, acknowledging the countess with a regal bow of the head. It was only when eye contact was made that she noticed the sapphires adorning the other woman's ear lobes.

She was riveted to the spot, frozen with shock. No wonder James did not want me to wear blue, she thought bitterly. It is his mistress's color. The bile rose up into her throat, and she fought the tremor that threatened to overcome her, thus paying scant attention to Alfred Fishberry's introduction and barely remembering to make him a curtsey.

"You seem very interested in my earrings, Lady Northwycke," Althea Cross said, with a malicious little smile. She cocked her head to one side, causing the stones to glint in the light.

"They are very beautiful," Emily replied, fighting to gain control over her feelings. It occurred to her that the woman *knew* that she knew who gave them to her, and she determined to die rather than give the strumpet the satisfaction of seeing her squirm.

"Yes, are they not?" Althea agreed. She gave her head a preening toss. "They were given to me by a man who is *insanely* in love with me, poor thing." She punctuated this with a laugh, then, as if to throw a bone to a defeated adversary, added, "Those are very handsome emeralds you are wearing, my dear."

It was a tactical mistake. Emily was both young and inexperienced, but she was not stupid. She gave the countess a beatific smile and, fingering the largest stone on the necklace, replied, "It is very kind of you to say so, Lady Brookhaven. These were given to *me* by a man who loved me enough to give me his name."

Althea Cross shot her a look of pure hatred and Emily gave an involuntary shiver. With nothing more to be said, the two couples bowed and went their separate ways.

"That went rather well, do you not agree?" Miles said, his face wreathed in a pleased smile.

Emily wondered where his attention had been directed for the previous five minutes. Really, she thought, my brother could witness the end of the world and not know it. Then it occurred to her that it had taken but a moment for her world to come crashing down about her.

Seven

Emily was not given to constant giggling and endless chatter, and for this James was extremely thankful; but on the way home from the Fotheringhams' ball she uttered not one word, unless it was a monosyllabic reply to a question posed to her.

It seemed that between the time he had left to get refreshments and the time he returned to her side, the light had gone out of her. He wondered if she had been subjected to some kind of snub or slight during his absence, but that was absurd. No one snubbed a Garwood. His family belonged to the very cream of the *ton*.

When they repaired to their chambers for the night, he gave Susan sufficient time to prepare her mistress for bed before walking through the dressing room adjoining both bedrooms.

His timing was perfect. Emily was in her nightclothes, seated at a table, having her hair brushed. As Susan applied the strokes to his wife's lustrous hair, it danced and crackled as if it had a life of its own, and his senses quickened at the thought of possessing her.

He motioned with a slight gesture of his head for the servant to leave. Once he had Emily to himself, he clasped her by the shoulders and bent over to kiss the top of her head, watching her face in the mirror to see if she was receptive to his advances.

He was shocked by the anger reflected there. Releasing his hold on her, he stepped back, hurt and confused.

"What have I done to inspire such displeasure?" he asked. "Heaven knows, I try my best to make you happy."

He began to pace the floor, his agitation and frustration growing with each step he took.

"Do I not accord you every kindness and consideration?

Am I not the most patient and generous of husbands? Yet nothing seems to please you."

He gestured toward the table. "Those emeralds you have so carelessly tossed aside, for instance, cost a king's ransom."

She rose, picked up the necklace and turned to face him, her eyes glinting with anger. "Then I suggest you give them to your countess," she cried, throwing it at him. It struck his chest before falling to his feet.

For a moment he was frozen with shock; then he was beset by a cavalcade of thoughts. First came the realization that she had found out about his liaison with Althea. He wondered who, that evening, would have had the effrontery to tell her. But most of all, he was appalled by her behavior. Such a display of bad temper and so little self-control. It was beyond the pale.

He bent down and picked up the necklace glistening at his feet and, without a word, put it in his dressing gown pocket. He received a look of scorn for his pains.

"Well done, sir. I am sure the Countess of Brookhaven would welcome yet another bauble to flaunt in my face." Her lower lip quivered. "She took great pleasure in letting me know the sapphires were the gift of some poor fool insane with love for her."

She paused for breath. "An apt description, would you not agree? A man would have to be mad to love such a vulgar creature."

James winced. All claim to gentle breeding had been thrown aside like a gossamer veil as her voice reached full decibel. Suddenly she crumbled, her bravado gone, the outraged woman giving way to the hurt child. She stood in silence, tears coursing down her face.

Doing his best to ignore what he considered to be emotional excess, and wishing to get to the bottom of the matter, he said, "And from that, you deduced that it was I?"

"No. I saw the jewelry box on your chest of drawers," she sobbed. "I opened it without thinking."

"You go too far, madam." His voice was icy. "Furthermore, I would be obliged if you would conduct yourself as befits your position as mistress of this house. By now, the lowest scullery maid below-stairs has heard your unseemly outburst."

He waited for her reaction, hoping that the rebuke would make her more biddable, but her eyes widened with an expression that could only described as disbelief.

"You do me the sorest grievance, sir, and all you can do is worry about what the servants think?" She gave an involuntary sob. "This is not to be borne."

He handed her his handkerchief. "Compose yourself. There is no talking to you while you are in this state." He paced the room once more, allowing his sense of outrage to build, then whirled around and shook his finger at her. "It is I who have been grievously used. How *dare* you pry into my things? It was most ignoble of you, madam."

He watched her twist the handkerchief through her fingers and wondered how she would justify her bad behavior. He was surprised, for instead of contrition she displayed indignation.

"You gave that notorious creature the means to cause me great humiliation, and then you turn it around so that somehow this whole sorry affair is my fault?" She raised her chin. "You, sir, are the most devious of villains. And it is my misfortune to have thrown in my lot with yours."

That settled it for James. He threw up his hands in frustration. "Emily, I bid you good night. There is no advantage in continuing this conversation. There is nothing to be gained by trading insults." He bowed and exited through the dressing room to his own chamber.

Desire having fled, he tossed in his bed, extremely upset over the turn his marriage had taken. Priding himself on his own sense of honor, it was a trait he prized most in others. Emily's seeming abundance of the virtue was the thing he had admired most, even above her beauty. Now he had to face the fact that she had pried into his personal things. He was sadly disillusioned.

The next morning, breakfast proved to be a solitary meal for Emily, as no other member of the family was present. A servant piled her plate with eggs, smoked fish, and several rashers of gammon, but she refused an offer of fried kidneys. He bowed and left the room.

She had no appetite and merely played with the food until it was cold and congealed on the plate. It was a relief when Lady Geraldine poked her head around the door and said, "Good, I see you are up and about. I trust you slept well?"

"No, Mother, I did not."

"Hmm. I cannot pretend to be surprised. Disagreements can be so unsettling."

"James told you what has transpired?"

"No. He left the house before I rose this morning, and according to Hobbes, he will not be home for a few days."

A feeling of hopelessness came over Emily. Her affairs were not going well. Without a happy marriage her future would be very bleak indeed. A woman's husband and family defined who she was.

Lady Geraldine looked hesitant for a moment, then added, "No one had to tell me the two of you had a disagreement; you could be heard all over the house."

Emily flushed with embarrassment. "I am most sorry, but I was sorely provoked."

Her mother-in-law sat down in the chair next to her and patted her hand. "Would you care to tell me what my son did to turn such a sweet girl into a raving madwoman?"

Emily sheepishly told her about finding the velvet box on James's chest of drawers.

Lady Geraldine shook her head. "That was not well done of you, my dear. Such lapses in propriety generally lead to personal disaster. You did James a grievous disservice."

"But the sapphires were for that dreadful woman," Emily remonstrated.

"The Countess of Brookhaven? Yes, you are right, she is a most dreadful creature."

"You mean to say you *know* about her?"

"But of course, my dear. Every one does, except perhaps, innocents barely out of the schoolroom, such as yourself."

Emily fought rising indignation. "Then why did he marry me if he has a *tendre* for her?"

Lady Geraldine put an arm around her shoulder. "My dear, rest assured you are first in his affections. Althea Cross was merely a convenience. Gentlemen have—er—certain needs, you know. You may be sure that she is no longer a part of his life."

"You must be mistaken. Why else would he have given her those earrings? She made a point of telling me that they were a gift from a love-sick admirer. Those were not her exact words, but her message was clear and she took great pleasure in the telling."

"I am sure she did," Lady Geraldine replied, her mouth set in a grim line. "Those are the words of a woman whose beauty is fast fading. It must be driving her to desperation." She tilted Emily's face by the chin. "Whereas you, my dear, are at the very peak of your youth and beauty, and you did something that, try as she might, she was unable to manage."

"Oh?"

"You are the one my son married, thank heavens."

"Yet he bought her sapphires."

Lady Geraldine threw up her hands. "But of course he did, you silly child. It is *de rigueur*. The castoff mistress is always given a bauble to soften the blow. In Althea Cross's case, since she is a countess, not an adventuress kept in a discreet little house somewhere, it had to be a particularly expensive parting gift."

Emily pushed her plate aside. "I find this all very distressing. You mean to say that there are rules to follow in such matters? That polite society condones such perfidious behavior?"

Lady Geraldine laughed. "Condones? Not exactly. But acknowledges its occurrence, gentlemen being what they are. These affairs are usually conducted in a civilized manner."

She gestured with her right hand. "The feelings of the parties concerned have to be considered." She gestured with her left hand. "The least amount of damage has to be wrought, so that on the inevitable day when one of the little baggages is sent packing, there will be no recriminations. So do not begrudge the lady her sapphires, my child; they came with her marching orders."

"Then what she implied was all a hum?"

Lady Geraldine rolled her eyes. "Is that not what I have been telling you?"

She wagged a finger at Emily. "It all comes back to your prying where you did not belong. If you had had no knowledge of the jewels, she would not have been able to hurt you."

"She did not get off scot-free," said Emily with a sly grin. "When she condescended to admire my emeralds, I told her they were from a man who loved *me* enough to bestow his name upon me."

Lady Geraldine raised her brow. "Did you, indeed? So our little kitten has claws! It was a point well taken, but I hope you will be more circumspect in your future dealings with the *ton*. One gathers enough enemies over the years without going out of one's way to find them."

James sat in the library of the Bonham-Lewises' town house, drinking port with Rodney. A fire was glowing in the hearth, and since it was his second glass, he had a glow of his own and was feeling decidedly better.

"It was deucedly kind of you to talk me out of staying at White's. This is infinitely more pleasant than being inveigled into frivolous wagers as to the way other people's peccadilloes will go."

"Not at all," Rodney replied. "Besides, my parents are abroad, sunning themselves in Italy."

"I thought I had had enough of the sun blazing down on me during the war in Spain, but one winter back in England makes a jaunt to Italy sound most attractive."

Rodney took a sip of wine, then said, "You should take Emily there. Begin anew. Try to make up for the bad start you both seem to have had."

James raised a brow. "I would rather not discuss it, if you please."

"Do not play the pompous lord with me, James; I have

known you far too long. How else are you going to sort out this pickle you are in, unless you talk it out? That is what old friends are for: to listen, console, and advise and then, perchance, forget what was said."

James managed to smile. "You are right of course, but I find it very difficult to accept that Emily pried into my things."

"You make too much of it, my friend. Women are as curious as cats. You were a damned fool for leaving the jewels in sight. Besides, the gel told you she opened the box without thinking."

"She displayed a shocking temper when she confronted me over it. Most excessive—I was absolutely appalled."

"But do you not see? You may perceive two truths from that. First, she must care for you deeply if the thought of you with the other lady drove her so wild. Second, such magnificent fire as she displayed could be quite pleasant at certain times. Preferable to being shackled to a cold fish, eh?"

"You really think so? That she harbors a *tendre* for me?"

"Absolutely, old chum. Not that I am reneging on my offer of hospitality, but I think you should be home right now, negotiating a reconciliation. You are obviously in love with your wife, for I have never seen you in such a state over a female."

"Pray do not talk such drivel. I am not so sure I even believe in love. At least, not that romantic claptrap."

Rodney looked skeptical. "Come now. I find that hard to believe. Neither a warmer hearted fellow nor truer friend walks this earth."

"Granted, I have affection for those near and dear to me, but I cannot say I have ever been potty over a female. I should imagine it could get quite sticky. Have you ever suffered in that way?"

"But once. And you are right, it is not all moonlight and roses. But when it is, my friend, there is not another emotion in this world comes close to the happiness it brings."

"And you are as yet unmarried."

"There was a girl in the Peninsula: Elena. She was warm and beautiful, and not a day goes by that she is not in my thoughts." A look of incredible sadness washed over Rodney's face.

"How did you meet her? Those grandees keep a close watch on their daughters, as I recall."

"Her father was a shopkeeper, not a grandee, but I am sure she was carefully guarded. Unfortunately her whole family was killed by the French, and she sought revenge by becoming a liaison between our regiment and the resistance fighters."

"Well, that explains a lot. However, much as you may have loved her, it would have been a most unsuitable match."

"On the contrary. I would have been honored to have her for my wife. Unfortunately it was not to be. We were ambushed by the French and she deliberately took a bullet meant for me. So do not tell me our marriage would have been unsuitable, my friend. No other woman could possibly measure up to my Elena."

"I am deeply sorry, Rodney. You have been through hell."

"One could say that. But the point is that I also experienced a joy that few are privileged to know. Do not be afraid to love your sweet Emily. Kiss and make up. Life is too short to be wasted over a silly spat."

"I have to think the matter through. In any case I think I will stay away a while longer. Give Emily pause to reconsider her behavior. I cannot have her thinking that every dispute can be won by throwing a temper tantrum. It just would not do."

Rodney nodded. "Oh, quite. One has to maintain the upper hand in such matters. But you have to look at it from her viewpoint—it must have been a terrible shock to see some baubles she thought were for her dangling on the ears of the most notorious woman in society."

"I say. That is a harsh thing to say about my erstwhile mistress," James replied playfully, eager to inject a lighter note into their conversation. "After all, we were together for almost a year."

Rodney grinned. "Do not trouble yourself over the matter, James," he said, swirling the contents of his wineglass. "You know full well that by now Althea Cross has found another to take your place. From what I gather, she has been known to change lovers more than some of us change our smallclothes."

"But even so, under the circumstances a gentleman should display a certain amount of gallantry. After all, the lady was very devoted to her duties as mistress." He chuckled. "*Passionately* devoted."

Rodney smiled. "I am not surprised. No doubt about it, the lady in question is reputed to be as lusty as any man. A most unnatural female. Society as we know it would crumble if all women were like her."

James nodded. "Would you give credence to it? When I went to her house to end the affair, she actually thought I had come to propose? I had the devil's own time getting out of that one with any grace."

Rodney chuckled. "The poor woman must have made a real cake of herself. Mark my words my friend, you have made an enemy for life."

"Nonsense. Nothing so extreme. I think I handled the whole sticky wicket with extreme finesse," said James, smugly examining his fingernails.

"Do not be so cocksure. What you have said clarifies a certain incident for me."

"What are you talking about?"

"Last night after you left, the lady in question was caught in a very compromising position with young Fishberry in Fotheringham's shrubbery."

"Most odd. But I fail to see a connection."

Rodney heaved a sigh. "It is plain as a pikestaff. Until last evening, Althea Cross would rather have been caught dead than be seated next to a Fishberry at a dinner party, much less be tumbled by one in the bushes. At least, that is what I was told."

This gave James reason to ponder. "That is true. No hostess would dare to seat a Fishberry male next to Althea at a dinner party. She expressed her contempt and loathing for both the grandfather and the grandson. I had supposed that it was because even she had her standards. What do you make of it?"

"That the Countess of Brookhaven is up to no good. Tell me James, if you wanted revenge of some sort, would you not seek out the most unconscionable blackguards you knew to assist you to that end?"

"I would do my own dirty work."

"But if you were a woman? What then?"

"I see what you mean." He pondered this for a moment, then shrugged it off. "The Fishberrys would refuse her. The two of them together would be no match for me."

Rodney rose, stood over his friend, and with finger wagging said, "Make light of it if you will. Those blackguards would hardly seek an open confrontation. A stab in the back, preferably in a dark alley and most likely perpetrated by a hired assassin, would be more to their style."

"Perhaps you read too much into last night's incident, Rodney. I think it is just a case of Althea having an overwhelming itch, and the Fishberry spawn just happening to be on hand to scratch it for her."

Rodney threw up his hands. "You are impossible. Just the same, promise me you will keep your wits about you."

"That is not a problem. I always keep a wary eye. I have acquired enough enemies over the years."

Rodney poured himself another glass of port, then turned to James, holding out the decanter. "I will not bring up the subject again. How about another drink before we retire for the night?"

The next day Emily ventured outside. There was a small park in the center of Mayfair Court, a pleasant haven with a square of grass just greening with the advent of spring. A path lined with plane trees and formal flower beds ran through it, now alive with the color of daffodils and tulips.

She gained access through a tall gate of black wrought iron with a key the butler had given her and took a leisurely stroll along the path circling the green. After a while this began to pall, so she sat down on one of the wooden benches dotting the walk.

She fast became lost in thought, idly kicking the gravel on the ground while she mulled over her situation. She was determined to do whatever it took to mend the breach between James and herself. Her future happiness depended on this. She had never felt so wretched and alone in her life.

"Ah. There you are, child. Your abigail told me I might find you here. Do you mind if I join you?"

She gave the older woman a faint smile, and without answering, she made a place for her on the bench. Lady Geraldine straightened out her skirts before sitting down.

"I do not think it is wise for you to be out here alone, Emily, my dear. Granted the gate is locked, but any footpad determined enough could find a way in."

"I carry no purse."

The older woman shook her head. "You have other treasures a man might risk the gallows for."

"I do not understand."

"No. I do not believe you do. A more naïve young lady never walked the earth. It is a pity your dear mama departed this world before she could educate you in such matters."

Emily blushed, feeling the heat diffuse her face. "I am not unmindful of this, Mother. I fear my ignorance of the world has wrought grievous damage to my marriage, and I would truly like your help in rectifying this matter."

Lady Geraldine patted her shoulder. "I am most heartened to hear this. Where would you like to begin?"

Emily was silent for a moment. It took all of her courage to continue. "This business of mistresses, for instance. You say they fill certain needs?"

"Er—yes."

"You mean like sitting on a gentleman's lap and being kissed?"

"It would be part of it."

"On the lips?"

Emily studied her closely, waiting to see her reaction to such a shocking question, and was surprised to see a fleeting smile cross the older woman's face.

"I suppose so, from time to time. Kissing is one of the more pleasant things that take place between a man and a woman."

"But my mama told me—"

"Your mama did not tell you enough."

Emily bridled. "What do you mean?"

"It is all right for your own husband to kiss you on the lips—in fact it is his right to do so."

"But Mama—"

"Your mama was warning you against would-be seducers. Had she lived long enough she would have told you that husbands must be obeyed in all things. Do you not remember your marriage vows?"

"Oh, dear. I had no idea I was making such a promise. In that case, I suppose it would be proper for him to do such."

"It would be a start."

Emily raised a brow, suddenly out of her depth. "A start? You mean there is more?"

"Of course there is. How do you think babies are born?"

"I had thought by the kissing on the mouth, in which case I realize I was wrong to react the way I did on my wedding night. My mother gave me such dire warnings as to the consequences of such behavior. I never really thought the matter through. Now I am confused."

"An understatement if ever I heard one. Listen, child, it gives me no pleasure to be the one to tell you this, but have you not wondered why men and women are different, not only in character but in form?"

"Men are the protectors."

"And what do you think they protect, pray tell?"

"Their wives and children."

"The children of their seed. Their one claim to immortality. Contrary to what you might think, babies are not made by kissing, neither are they brought by the stork, found under gooseberry bushes as my mother once told me, nor are they the result of an immaculate conception. Only God fathers children in such a fashion. No. A baby must be planted the same as any other growing thing."

"But how?"

"I can tell you no more, save trust your husband. However,

I should warn you that as the mother of his children, a husband places his wife on a pedestal and expects her to conduct herself in a pure and chaste manner. Mind you, it is quite proper to show pleasure at being kissed, in fact, a husband finds this most gratifying, but for heaven's sake, there must be no unseemly display of base passions."

"B-base passions?"

"You have no idea of which I speak, do you? It was rumored a few years ago, that after years of submitting to her wifely duties in a becoming manner, the late Lady Brimstoke went quite mad one night and behaved with the abandonment of the most debauched of strumpets."

"Oh dear," Emily murmured, thoroughly convinced that the married estate held more pitfalls than she could possibly negotiate. "What became of Lady Brimstoke?"

"No one knows for sure, because she was never seen again in polite society. It was rumored that her husband locked her away in the north tower of the castle for the rest of her life."

Emily gasped.

"You do well to be shocked. Usually, only women of the lower orders behave in such a disgusting fashion. The gentlemen expect this of the low creatures they keep for such purposes, but not from their wives."

"R-really?" Emily was desolated at the thought of James being with such a woman.

"It is hard to believe, I agree. Gentlemen find this necessary in order to protect their lady wives from their animal lusts. A wife is considered to be the pure vessal sacrificed for the continuance of the family line."

"S-sacrificed?" At this point, Emily experienced pure, unadulterated terror.

Lady Geraldine nodded. "Rest assured, no gentleman would subject his wife to such indignities if there were any other way."

Emily's lower lip quivered.

Lady Geraldine patted her shoulder. "There, there, Emily, you love my son, do you not?"

Emily nodded.

"Then I repeat, trust him, obey him in all things and, God willing, by this time next year you will have made me a grandmother."

Eight

Rather than waiting a few days, James returned to Mayfair Court the next afternoon. He missed Emily. In the short time they had been together he had grown to like her company. Sharing breakfast with Rodney was not the same.

Was he developing a *tendre* for her? The kind of love Rodney found so exalting? He discounted this idea almost immediately, coming to the conclusion that he was a very shallow sort of chap who merely liked to bask in the adoring glances Emily sent his way.

Having a young, impressionable girl for a wife was not entirely a bad thing. Then he recalled the way she had viewed him the last time he had been in her company, her face flushed and eyes sparking green fire—angry enough to want his guts for garters.

She had been magnificent in her fury—a wild, passionate creature—and it occurred to him that most of his anger had stemmed from frustration. He would have gladly forfeited ten years of his life to have possessed her then and there on the carpet. On his return to Mayfair, he found her seated in the small drawing room his mother favored, demurely plying a needle to a small embroidery frame.

She put it down when he entered the room and half rose from her chair as if to greet him. Then, seeming to think better of it, she sank into the cushions once more with a dejected expression on her face.

He quickly came to her side and kissed her cheek by way of offering an olive branch. "Good afternoon, my dear," he said in his most urbane manner. "I trust you are feeling better today."

"Yes, thank you, James." She brightened momentarily, then

looked diffident. "I owe you an apology. I fear my behavior last evening was beyond the pale. Your mother explained the situation and made me realize that most of my distress was brought on by my own ignorance of such matters."

This was prettily said, with her head lowered and a ring of sincerity to her voice. He felt the last vestige of resentment toward her disappear. He pulled her to her feet and enfolded her in a warm embrace, his senses taking in the texture and perfume of her lustrous hair.

"You are such an innocent," he murmured. "How were you to know?" He nuzzled her throat, his desire for her rising. "We shall put the whole thing behind us, darling, and make a fresh start."

"Oh, yes, James. That would be most agreeable," she said, then to his surprise, kissed him on the mouth. It was a mere peck, but this was a big step for her to take, and his heart beat faster.

"I do not know how much more of this I can stand," he replied, his voice thick with desire.

"I want what you want," she whispered, but even as she spoke the words, there was fear in her eyes.

He cupped her chin and put his lips to hers, taking care not to frighten her. She entwined her arms around his neck, then closed her eyes. He showered her eyelids with butterfly kisses.

A tiny moan escaped her throat and she grew limp in his arms. Taking this to be a sign of sweet surrender, he crushed his mouth to hers.

At first she held her lips firmly pressed together, as if to ward off the intrusion, then gradually they opened like a bud coming to flower. His passion flamed beyond all reason.

He ended the kiss and pulled back, shocked by the emotions raging through him. The wiles of even the most skilled of paramours had failed to send such a fever raging through his blood as did an innocent kiss shared with this most chaste of women.

He grasped her shoulders and searched her face for any sign she might also be caught up in the moment. She glowed with excitement, her lips parted, ripe for the taking. With the utmost finesse, he brushed the palm of her hand with his lips, then tenderly kissed each tapered fingertip. She gasped, encouraging him to devote his attention to her lovely mouth once more—first with tiny nibbles on her lower lip, followed by sweet intrusions into her mouth with the veriest tip of his tongue.

She mewled like a kitten.

"You want what I want?" he murmured, an undercurrent of urgency in his voice.

She nodded, her face rosy from his attentions.

"Are you sure? For heaven help me, there shall be no turning back."

"Yes, James. I want this."

Without another word he led her out of the room. Side by side they climbed the wide staircase, and once safely out of view of the footmen, he swept her into his arms and carried her to his bedchamber.

Wishing to give the young lovers every chance to start their marriage on a firm footing, Lady Geraldine wisely departed for Northwycke Hall the next morning. She took Maude with her, thus affording James and Emily the privacy needed to deepen their intimacy.

Later that afternoon the newlyweds sat in front of a roaring fire in the library, listening to the rain beat on the window-panes—a sporadic tattoo, with occasional increases in intensity, depending on the gusting wind.

"This must be the wettest spring in a long time," James remarked.

"I quite agree," Emily replied, looking up from the book she was reading. "I cannot recall a wetter one."

She quickly returned her attention to the book.

James regarded her with a jaundiced eye. They had been exchanging meaningless small talk all afternoon, both of them seeming loath to carry the conversation to the next level.

The consummation of their marriage was very much on his mind. Initially, their lovemaking had been warm, with Emily showing signs of responding to his attentions most favorably, when suddenly she grew limp and just lay there with both hands clenched to her sides.

Her maidenhead had already been breached, so he completed the act, hoping that sometime in the process she might show some signs of life. Apart from a slight gasp toward fruition she might well have been a rag doll.

He was despondent. His inability to make his bride's initiation into physical intimacy a memorable one filled him with dismay. Heaven knows he had brought every erotic nuance he knew of the art of love to bear in the hope of giving her pleasure. Alas, to no avail.

He shuddered at the thought of his marriage turning into the sort of alliance his parents had endured. After their children were born he did not want to be pushed into the arms of a paramour by a wife who would deem it the gentlemanly thing to do.

Unable to sit quietly by the fire any longer and be plagued by such disquieting thoughts, he got up and wandered over to the window. The garden was filled with desolation. The trees were bending against the wind, the spring flowers beaten flat to the ground.

Emily looked up from her book, it seemed to her that his restlessness denoted a certain discontent. Her whole being flooded with despair. Perhaps she had not been as successful in masking the base, animal passions his lovemaking had roused in her as she had hoped. If so, she deserved his contempt. She certainly did not measure up to Lady Geraldine's description of the pure, chaste, wife.

She had tried so hard to lie quietly as her husband took his pleasure. At least she assumed he found it pleasurable if his cries of passion were anything to go by. Perhaps a sign that James suspected her own wanton nature if he used her with what she assumed to be such wild abandon. It seemed that no part of her body had been taboo.

James turned away from the window. "God, I hate the city when it rains," he muttered.

Emily brightened. The bad weather was the reason for his discontent. She determined that in future she would try even harder to control her passion. The thought of losing his good regard was not to be endured.

"If you find the city odious, then why not return to return to the country?"

"I would not want to deprive you of the pleasure of attending the Routledges' ball next Saturday. It is the event of the season. I hear the Prince Regent will be attending. Madame Dupres is working her assistants' fingers to the bone making sure your new gown will be ready for the occasion."

She got up and joined him at the window and leaned her head against his shoulder. "Somehow it is no longer important to me." She gave a little shiver. "Brr. What a dreary day. Rain adds to the grayness of a city, yet in the country it has the opposite effect. Everything becomes alive and green, as if God had cleaned the canvas of a vast painting."

James smiled. "That is a unique way to put it, but I quite agree. If you really do not mind, I should like to leave directly after the ball."

"Pray do not stay in London on my account. It is of no import to me who will be attending the ball. I too, would like to return to the country." She sighed. "I had thought it would please me to attend such lofty affairs and mingle with exalted personages, but alas, it seems such is not the case."

"Oh?" He raised a brow. "Go on. I would like to hear your reasons. Surely disillusion has not set in at such a tender age?"

She looked distressed. "James, darling, I did not mean to sound like an ingrate. You have accorded me every kindness, and I am mindful of my good fortune in having you for my husband...."

"But..."

"But?"

"Yes. Pray continue." He stroked her cheek. "This promises to be an improvement over anything else we have discussed today. Including the weather—a topic regarded as sacred by every right-thinking English lady and gentleman."

She gave him a playful push. "I declare, sir, you are a dreadful tease. I was going to say that certain members of the *ton* do not hold up well under scrutiny. They are petty and spiteful, and I fear some are even dangerous."

His ears pricked up at the last word. He grabbed her arm and pulled her to face him. "Dangerous? What a thing to say. If anyone has threatened you, I'll—"

"No, no. Pray do not trouble yourself. It was a poor choice of words. I should have told you right away, but that silly argument we had drove it right out of my mind."

"For goodness' sake, Emily, get on with it. Let me be the judge as to any danger there might be."

"That young man recognized me."

"Who? Algie? Do not fret over it. He is hardly likely to admit to abducting a lady. His father would remit him to the colonies forthwith."

"No. The other. The pasty-faced one with the silly-looking neckcloth."

"Fishberry's spawn." James punched his fist into the palm of his other hand. "Damn!" He checked himself before alarming her further and with a reassuring smile said, "Pray do not give it another thought, darling. Alfred Fishberry is just a little pipsqueak of no consequence. A word of warning to his grandfather should keep him in check."

She exhaled. "That is such a relief."

"Do you still want to leave London, my love?"

Her face lit up. "Oh, could we?"

He smiled, his heart warming. She was such an adorable little poppet, he thought. Perhaps in time he would unlock her passion; meanwhile, she was a most pleasing companion.

"We shall depart on the morrow, weather permitting."

He was rewarded with a hug. He chucked her under the chin and prayed that the poppet he had taken to wife would become a woman erelong.

• • •

On rising the following morning, Emily peeked through her bedroom drapes to ascertain how the weather was fairing. She smiled. The sun was out, and below, several gardeners were busily restoring order to the storm-ravaged gardens. They would be leaving for Northwycke Hall as soon as breakfast was over.

They had been comfortably settled in the country for over a week when Mrs. Thatcher knocked on the door of their private sitting room, seeking an audience.

"Begging your pardon," she said with a nervous little bob. "I hate to intrude, but there are things going on below-stairs that should be looked into."

James frowned. "Whatever the problem, I am sure it can be taken care of by Mr. Hobbes or, failing that, the steward, Mr. Rainey, without bringing Lady Northwycke and myself into it."

Mrs. Thatcher pressed her lips together and took a deep breath before continuing. "That is as may be, sir. But those two make light of the matter and it's me as has to deal with the consequences. It's getting as no decent family will let their young 'uns come to work at Northwycke Hall."

"'No decent family?'" James put down the newspaper he had been reading.

Emily watched her husband with interest, having an inkling of what was about to be disclosed from her own brief experience as a chambermaid. It was obvious that Mrs. Thatcher now had his full attention, and she wondered how he would handle the domestic crisis the housekeeper was about to put on his shoulders.

"'No decent family?'" he reiterated. "Out with it, Mrs. Thatcher. There had better be a good explanation for such a preposterous statement." His voice took on a very stern tone. "I will not tolerate divisiveness below-stairs. Such a thing is ruinous to the smooth running of a house."

She gave another nervous bob and began twisting the strings of her apron. "Y-yes, my lord."

Emily was troubled by the poor woman's distress. She knew that the housekeeper's livelihood depended on James's grace and favor. After all, had not Emily been in that same unenviable position just a scant fortnight ago? She gave Mrs. Thatcher an encouraging smile.

The woman seemed to take heart from the gesture; in any case she found the courage to continue. "Begging your pardon, my lord, but I have just sent Polly back to her family. She was sick several mornings in a row."

James frowned. "That was reason enough to terminate the unfortunate girl's employment? Really, Mrs. Thatcher."

The woman shook her head. "No, my lord. But the reason for her sickness was, so's to speak. Polly is in the family way— the third chambermaid in as many months, I might add."

"The devil, you say. Who is the father? The rogue must be made responsible and marry the girl, if he does not already have a wife."

"That is the problem. Four girls in all over the past year have been sent back to their families in disgrace, and not a one will divulge the name of the swine responsible."

James stroked his chin. "Really? Why have I not been informed of this matter before now?"

"It is not for me to say, my lord. That was Mr. Hobbes's prerogative. He takes the attitude that if a girl is foolish enough to make free with her person she has to face the consequences, but I do not agree, sir. As I see it, the loss of a girl's wage and an extra mouth to feed is a big burden on a family. It's small wonder the village people would as lief their daughters went elsewhere to work. And where does that leave me, I ask? Everyone having to do the work of two. This cannot go on."

By now the good woman displayed a highly agitated state. She continued to roll the ends of her apron strings with increasing rapidity and with a furrowed brow began to gnaw on her lower lip.

Emily went over to her and put an arm around her shoulder. "Please do not distress yourself, Mrs. Thatcher." Her voice was soothing. "Rest assured that his lordship will get to the bottom of this puzzlement and everything will be all right again."

"Lady Northwycke is correct. I *shall* get to the bottom of this disgraceful situation, and mark my words, the miscreants will be held accountable. The best thing you can do, Mrs. Thatcher, is to go to your kitchen and have a nice cup of tea."

As soon as the door closed on the housekeeper, he turned to Emily and said, "What do you make of it?"

Emily flushed with pleasure at having her opinion deemed worthy of consideration. "In the first place I find it rather odd that all four girls would keep quiet as to the father. It leads me to believe that they were frightened into silence."

"Great heavens. Is that not a little melodramatic? I mean to say."

Emily shook her head. "There was a time I might have thought so, but not now."

"Go on."

"A servant's world and ours may only be separated by a flight of stairs, but after being at the bottom of that flight looking up, I can assure you they are vastly different."

"By Jove, Emily, were you mistreated? If so—"

She shook her head. "Of course not. But the fate of a servant is entirely in the hands of his or her master. If by some chance they displease that master, or even any other servant with greater authority, they can be turned off without a letter of recommendation, to starve in a ditch. Such a person lives with fear every waking moment of her life."

He put his arm about her and kissed her forehead. "My poor darling, I had no idea what a profound effect all this has had on you. The lower orders are born into that condition and therefore are inured to it, but it must have been terrifying for a gently nurtured girl such as yourself to have been thrown into such a coil." He wagged his finger. "I have half a mind to thrash that brother of yours."

She shrugged. "You must not blame Miles. He was ill-equipped to handle the responsibilities thrust upon him at the death of our parents. I think my experience has made me a more compassionate person. It did bring us together, James, darling. Do not forget that."

This remark earned her another kiss, this one on the lips. "Of course. How could I forget? I suppose I should be thanking

Miles for his indiscretions."

"But we digress."

"Hmm?"

"You asked me my opinion on the matter."

"Ah, yes, dear wife. And received a dissertation on the fears and perils of life below-stairs for my pains. So you think there is an underlying theme of silence brought on by fear in all these circumstances?"

"I do."

"In which case, they must have been in fear of their lives, or those of their loved ones. I am sure that some of the parents tried to beat the answer out of their wayward daughters. That is the custom."

"How barbaric."

"Life is not easy for these people, and they do not need their misery compounded by some unscrupulous blackguard."

"So you think one person is responsible in each case? A person powerful enough to threaten their lives if they speak out?"

"That is hard to say." He started to pace. "It could be a member of the gentry. A neighbor, perhaps, preying on my household rather than his own."

He shrugged, seemingly unwilling to accept that idea. "But that would have to be someone I know and accept as a friend, and I find that abhorrent. On the other hand, an impressionable girl might be easy to frighten by just about anyone with more authority than herself. As you were kind enough to point out, a servant's lot is evidently fraught with fear."

"Oh, dear," Emily replied, putting her hand to her bosom. "Are you suggesting the villain could be one of the upper servants? That is most unsettling."

"But not improbable," said James, a grim expression on his face. "To think that those poor girls were not safe under my own roof. There will be no more of this perfidy. Rest assured I will get to the bottom of this if I have to question every living soul in this village."

"And these unfortunate girls will have to be provided for."

"Eh? By Jove, I believe you are right. After all, they were

under my protection." He stopped his pacing to caress her cheek. "My ever-compassionate Emily. Lord knows what I ever did to deserve the love of such a sweet angel."

Emily basked in his admiration. "Nay, my lord. It is I who am most fortunate to have found such a caring husband," she murmured, garnering for herself yet another one of his kisses.

Over the next few days, the atmosphere in the house became tense. James systematically interrogated the staff, starting off by giving Hobbes a dressing-down for not apprising him of what had been taking place under his own roof.

Hobbes took to snapping at those members of the staff subservient to him, seemingly singling out Mrs. Thatcher for particular criticism. It was Emily who heard him giving the housekeeper a scathing tongue-lashing, accusing her of disloyalty and of undermining his position at the Hall.

"After all," he had said. "I can hardly be blamed if the little besoms toss their petticoats for every passing stranger. His lordship should not concern himself either. If girls are so inclined, there is no stopping them. What was I supposed to do? Lock them up every evening?"

After a week or so, James's investigation had reached an impasse, and thinking it had come to an end, the servants began to breathe easier and the tension dissipated. Northwycke Hall was a much more pleasant place to be.

Emily pondered the situation, determined that if James could not resolve the matter, she would try to do so. The steward, Mr. Rainey, made a trip to London and acquired not one, but three servants from an employment agency. Mature women, too old to inspire passion in a below-stairs Don Juan and certainly too old to lure any gentleman away from his own estate, yet still capable of putting in a day's work.

There was but one thing to spoil the harmony of the Garwood household. Mrs. Thatcher took to singing while attending to her duties.

> *On Richmond Hill there lived a lass, more bright than May Day morn, whose beauty other maids surpass, a rose without a thorn.*

It was on the second morning, after the third rendition of "Richmond Hill," that James put his foot down and asked Hobbes to suggest to her as tactfully as possible that she confine her trilling to the kitchen garden, out of earshot of the family quarters.

"But the poor woman sounds so happy," Emily demurred.

"Even if she could carry a tune—which, heaven help us, she cannot—the song is hardly appropriate. Can you imagine if the Prince Regent happened to pay us a visit and she burst forth with that particular ditty?"

"I have to agree her voice gives others no pleasure, but why should His Highness object to such a harmless little song?"

"My. They do keep you Bath misses insulated from the world. The 'lass' referred to in the song is none other than Mrs. Fitzherbert. Better known as Princess Fitz, onetime morganatic wife to our dear Prince. She was snugly ensconced in the Richmond Hill district in a gilded little love nest for many years. A little long in the tooth, now, and I suspect our fickle Prince would rather forget her very existence."

"How very sad. I pray you never wish me out of your life. I think I should be desolate."

He took her in his arms and kissed her long and deeply. "I doubt a man could live long enough to tire of you, my darling."

Emily wanted to believe him. But it had not been lost upon her that for all his cosseting, the terms of endearment he showered upon her, and the delicious things he did to her body within the confines of his huge, four-poster bed, not once had he ever actually said he loved her.

Nine

Under the tutelage of her mother-in-law, Emily quickly assumed the duties of mistress of Northwycke Hall. In a scant month she had taken over the reins and was running her household with quiet confidence.

Lady Geraldine informed James that the time was right for Maude and herself to move into the Dower House. She quashed all objections the young couple put forward against such a move, but she took her son aside seeking his support for the action, warning him of the discord that came of having two women living under the same roof.

"Besides," she explained to Emily as they were strolling in the garden. "I have a need to run my own establishment. The Dower House is only half a mile away, on the other side of yonder stand of horse-chestnut trees." She pointed west. "Now that summer is almost upon us it will make a very pleasant stroll."

At first, James was concerned that Emily might miss having Lady Geraldine and Maude as daily companions, but he was relieved to see that she slipped even more easily into the role of mistress of the house when his mother departed for her own residence.

About a week after his mother and sister moved into their own establishment, James invited Emily to accompany him to the stables to look at a new horse he had purchased. It was a beautiful young mare the color of fresh cream.

"She is beautiful," Emily exclaimed. "Does she have a name?"

"Syllabub, I have been told."

Emily petted the horse, and it nuzzled up to her and wickered. She smiled in delight. "Syllabub likes me. Do you think I might ride her?"

"Any time you wish. She is yours."

Emily flung her arms around James. "You are absolutely the most darling man on earth. Do you think we could go for a ride this very minute?"

Amused by her girlish enthusiasm, he signalled a groom to bring out a saddle for the mare. It was a beautiful affair of rich, tan-colored leather, intricately carved and chased with silver. Emily was positively euphoric.

She rode the horse out of the paddock and across the meadow with James in hot pursuit on Tarquin. Emily and Syllabub moved as one. James was pleased with his choice. Whenever the weather permitted, husband and wife took to riding the countryside, at one with each other and the mounts they rode.

Life was not without its responsibilities. As the ranking family of St. Cuthbert's parish, the company of the Garwoods was prized by the local gentry. It was deemed a feather in one's cap to be able to say that Lord and Lady Northwycke had graciously condescended to attend one's soiree, and invitations to dine at Northwycke Hall were imperative to secure one's place in society. Such entertainments helped alleviate the dreariness of the weather.

As if to make up for the bad weather in the earlier part of spring, May came in a burst of sunshine. The hedgerows were fragrant with the scent of honeysuckle and wild roses. In the woods, bluebells vied with sweet violets for attention, and the meadow flowers seemed to bloom more profusely than in other years.

Daisies, cowslips, and primroses dappled the lea, while in the low-lying marshes buttercups made carpets of gold. A glorious celebration of life had begun, orchestrated by nature's symphony—the buzzing and clicking of insects, the croaking of frogs, and over all, the sublime music of the birds as they winged their way over woodland and meadow.

James had always strolled the pastures in solitude, taking in the beauty of the scene and, with the soft breezes caressing his face, reveling in the knowledge that it was Garwood land, and had been since Norman times. Now, as he walked the fields with Emily by his side, his arm around her waist, he felt an even closer connection to the land, for even now—although she certainly was as slender as a reed—she could be carrying his son in her womb.

He had certainly been diligent in his attempts to get her with child, for he had been as randy as a goat of late. He grinned at the thought and stopped in his tracks to bestow a hearty kiss on her lips.

She responded with a playful slap to his shoulder. "That is a most wicked smile, my lord; I fear no good can come of it."

"That depends on what you mean by good," he replied, nuzzling her cleavage. "I know that what I have in mind may not be considered good by some, but the doing of it makes me feel very good indeed."

"James! Not here, for every passing cowherd to see. Can you imagine what the villagers would say?"

"They would say that Lord Northwycke takes his duties as a husband very seriously and Lady Northwycke is to be considered a very lucky woman."

This remark earned him another slap, which in turn gave way to a merry chase, Emily's shrieks rending the air as she hared across the meadow, James following in full pursuit.

He allowed her to stay ahead until she reached the edge of a lake, the jewel in the landscaping of the estate. In its center was a small island, dream-child of the famous landscape artist Capability Brown toward the end of the eighteenth century, complete with a grotto and folly built to resemble a Grecian temple. The latter became the focal point of a plan fast forming in his head to make the rest of the afternoon a pleasant interlude.

He grabbed her around the waist with a triumphant, "Got you! Now what would be a suitable punishment?" He then released her and put his forefinger to his cheek, pretending to ponder the matter, then said, "Aha, I have it."

He led her to a small boat. "I shall row you over to yonder island and keep you prisoner in the folly and never let you go."

"Not ever?" she asked, going along with his game.

"No, never," he replied. "I shall lock the door and make love to you night and day, day and night until you beg for mercy."

"And what if I do not choose to beg?" she asked coyly.

He shrugged his shoulders. "Then I suppose we shall just have to make love until one of us dies."

"Alas," she said, rolling her eyes. "You will be missed, dear husband, but I know I shall look lovely in my widow's weeds."

He slapped her bottom. "Get in the boat, you shameless creature."

James had never made it to the island so swiftly in his life. He pulled on the oars, his muscles straining at the effort. When they finally reached their destination, he carried her up the marble steps and beyond the pillared portals of the summer house. Without any preliminary courtship conversation he proceeded to undress her.

When her beauty was laid bare for his eyes to feast upon, he carried her to a small bed in an alcove embellished with cherubs carved in pink marble, quarried in France when Louis and his Antoinette still held sway.

There he made love to her, paying tribute to her body with his hands and his lips, neglecting no aspect of her considerable charms. She returned kiss for kiss and even ventured a tentative caress of her own, but when he finally came to possess her she became a rag doll once more and just lay there as he took his pleasure.

As was always the case, James felt a certain abasement at the one-sidedness of the act, but heaven help him, with each passing day his desire for her intensified.

The weather remained fair for the next ten days and the young lovers fell into the habit of taking a picnic lunch over to the island. They made it a festive affair, with cold meats and fruits, crusty bread, and a decanter of the contraband Chablis.

Afterward, they would spend the afternoons making leisurely love. In spite of Emily's apparent inability to respond to the fulfillment of their mating, James had never felt so happy in his life.

• • • •

It was on a Wednesday in the second week of May that their idyll came to an abrupt halt. They were departing the house for their afternoon tryst on the island when a visitor rode up—a dark, saturnine man, the sweat glistening on his brow from the heat.

James turned to Emily and, with a shrug of his shoulders, said, "That is Hensley, my man of affairs. I was not expecting him for at least another week; he must have news of my cargo from India. Favorable news, I trust."

"Your cargo?" Emily's voice registered a mixture of shock and surprise. "You are in trade?"

"Of course. A gentleman can no longer rely on his estates to sustain his wealth. It is my duty to the family to secure the fortunes of those who follow. I would not have our children's children sink to a life of genteel poverty, with only their bloodlines to commend them."

"Such as Miles and myself? With the misfortune to be descended from a line of younger sons?"

James could have cut out his tongue at the hurt in her voice. He put his arm around her waist. "I am sorry, darling. That was a thoughtless remark on my part. I intend to change all that for Miles."

"What do you mean?"

"Well, I have shown him the folly of trying to make one's fortune at cards, that there are those with a skill at dealing from the bottom of the deck. He was most enlightened."

"I do thank you for that. I feared to see my brother in debtors' prison."

"I will do better than that for him. I have arranged for him to have a small percentage of future cargoes. His modest investment will serve him well, and he can go from there. There is no reason to doubt that under my tutelage, Miles will one day be a gentleman of substance."

Emily's eyes widened in amazement, the expression could only be described as worshipful admiration. "Oh, James," she said. "You are most prodigiously clever."

103

His chest swelled with manly pride. What was it about the Walsinghams that compelled them to regard him as a demigod? he wondered. In any case it made them most endearing.

By now the rider had dismounted and a footman relieved him of his horse. James descended the large granite doorsteps, his hand extended in greeting. "Mr. Hensley. I trust your journey was not too rigorous?" He regarded the perspiration on the other man's brow. "A trifle warm, I would hazard."

"A trifle, my lord. I cannot remember a warmer May."

"Come, allow me to present you to Lady Northwycke; then we shall retire to the library for some refreshments, and you can apprise me as to the condition of my affairs."

Half an hour later, the two men emerged from the library. Hensley discreetly walked ahead, affording James the privacy of saying good-bye to Emily.

"I am sorry, darling, but I am afraid our little picnic will have to be postponed. Favorable trade winds have resulted in a speedier voyage than anticipated. My ship will dock in London in a day or so, and I would like to be there."

"Oh, dear," she said, forming her lips into a pretty little moue. "How disappointing. But I suppose you must." She rose onto her toes and gave him a kiss. "I do so look forward to our afternoons," she whispered, her voice seductive, making it perfectly clear what aspect of their picnics she found most attractive.

James found this mystifying. If she found their lovemaking so pleasurable, why did she not take a more active part in the process? He had given her every encouragement, to no avail. Emily was the shyest, most constrained woman he had ever bedded and, for some reason that was beyond him, the only one who had managed to get under his skin.

"There will be other days," he whispered back. "The afternoon is yet young. Invite my sister to picnic with you. I am sure she will welcome a break from her studies. One of the grooms can row you over and see to your safety."

Emily visibly brightened. "Yes, I should like that. Perhaps she could stay here until you return. That way I shall not be quite so lonely."

"Splendid idea. I am sure mother will raise no objections." He took her in his embrace for a good-bye kiss. "You go ahead. I shall be leaving just as soon as I change my clothes and a fresh mount can be found for Mr. Hensley."

Emily and Maude made their way across the meadow accompanied by a burly groom from the stables with the unlikely name of Clarence. He seemed to take his duty of guarding the ladies very seriously, offering respectful admonishments if they did anything he deemed dangerous, such as crossing streams on wobbly logs, or getting too close to grazing cattle.

His tone was of the utmost obsequiousness, but from time to time, Emily would catch him staring at her in a most unsettling manner. A strange birthmark close to his right eye added menace to his aspect. She vowed to use another groom if she ever decided to repeat this little outing with her sister-in-law.

Mercifully, he kept his silence while rowing them over to the island. On arriving there, he kept out of their way but was told to remain within earshot while they explored the small island. Emily and James had never made it past the summerhouse.

The girls spent their time picking wildflowers and fashioning elaborate circlets of daisies to wear in their hair. Amid a lot of giggling, Emily regaled Maude with tales of her come-out, describing the antics of society's more eccentric members.

Still laughing, Maude put a buttercup to Emily's throat. "Do you like butter? Indeed you do, dear Emily. The flower sheds its golden hue upon your skin." This was punctuated by another gale of inane giggling.

"There must be a universal liking for the stuff. Buttercups do that to everyone," Emily offered.

"Do not be so prosaic," Maude admonished. "It takes all the fun out of everything." She cast the wildflower to the ground, no longer interested in its butter-testing properties. Instead, they removed their shoes and stockings and waded barefoot along the shoreline of the lake.

After a full five minutes of silence between them, Maude finally spoke. "I wish next year would hurry up and get here."

The significance of her words was lost upon Emily for a moment; then she realized the younger girl was referring to her come-out. "I suppose you do," Emily replied. "The year before one's come-out is most difficult. One is no longer a child, yet everyone refuses acknowledge the fact and continues to treat one as such."

Maude smiled. "I knew you would understand, sister dear. You are the only one in the family save Miles who accords me the kindness of treating me as an adult. Even Mrs. Thatcher still uses me as a child who is underfoot."

Emily found mention of Miles in such a capacity something of a surprise. He did not treat her with such consideration, even though she was now a married lady with a large household to run.

"Do not hurry the process of growing up, Maude. You will probably be spoken for your very first season. Why, this time next year you could be mistress of a large house with all kinds of responsibilities to take up your time."

Maude turned to her. "It does not sound like much fun when you put it that way. Do you not like your life, Emily?"

"Of course I do. But then, I am married to James," she said, as if that explained everything.

Maude gave her hand a squeeze. "It is plain to see that every time you regard my brother, you absolutely adore him."

"Am I so transparent? My mama always told me that such a display put a lady at a distinct disadvantage. That it is preferable the other way around. The husband should be the one who loves the more."

"Then you have nothing to fear," said Maude warmly. "For it is certain that James is equally besotted with you. It is almost embarrassing the way he cannot keep his hands off you. He touches you at every opportunity."

"Oh, dear." Emily gave her hair a pat, setting her chaplet of daisies awry. "What must your mama think?"

Maude smiled softly. "Do not concern yourself with Mama. I think it gives her great peace of mind to know that in spite of your alliance starting out as a marriage of convenience, it has developed into a love match. I think every mother wishes that for her child. I know I want that for myself, and I will not marry without it."

It was Emily's turn to squeeze Maude's hand. "I sincerely hope not, Maude dear. Er—certain aspects of the married state would be absolutely abhorrent if one did not love one's husband."

"I have suspected as much. Mama is always making veiled references to certain outrages ladies have to endure in the marriage bed, without actually naming what they are." Maude bit her lip. "Apart from the greater freedom marriage affords a lady, I fail to see the attraction in the estate, at least up until now. Yet you seem to thrive on it. But I do not suppose you will enlighten me on the subject."

"No, Maude. I cannot. It would be most indelicate of me." Emily blushed. "Besides, I do not think I would know where to begin."

Suddenly a breeze came up and Emily noticed the sun hanging low in the sky. "My goodness. Where has the time gone? The late spring evenings can be most deceiving."

They hurried back into the folly to put on their shoes and stockings, then called out for Clarence to take them back across the lake.

They swept into Northwycke Hall full of the noisy exuberance of youth, their chaplets of daisies wilting on their brows, only to be met by Hobbes, the butler, looking as serious as an undertaker.

"If you please, my lady, Mrs. Thatcher and I should like a word with you." He shot a glance in Maude's direction. "Alone, if you please, madam. What we have to tell you is too indelicate for Lady Maude's ears."

"Very well, Mr. Hobbes. I will receive you in the drawing room." She turned to Maude, who looked just as mystified as she was feeling. "Please excuse me, Maude, darling, I shall join you later for dinner."

Hobbes followed Emily into the drawing room and rang the bell for Mrs. Thatcher. A few minutes later the housekeeper entered the room, redfaced and out of breath, Emily presumed, from climbing the stairs too fast.

Hobbes addressed Emily. "I sent for Mrs. Thatcher, madam, because under the circumstances what we have to impart would be more fitting coming from a woman."

Hobbes then withdrew from the room, leaving Emily alone with Mrs. Thatcher. The woman remained silent for a moment, looking most uncomfortable; then the words poured from her as if a floodgate had been opened.

"You could have knocked me down with a feather, your ladyship. Lubin Thorpe seemed like such a nice young lad. I never would have thought him responsible for all these dreadful carryings-on. I still find it hard to believe, but you never know. As my Yorkshire grandmother always used to say, 'There's nowt so strange as folk.'" Then, and only then, did the woman pause to catch her breath.

"Please, Mrs. Thatcher, slow down, I find it most difficult to comprehend what you are trying to say. Who is this Lubin person and what has he done to put you in such a state?"

"Begging your pardon, madam. Lubin Thorpe is an underfootman, and he was caught in the cellar in a small room where we store the apples for the winter, it being almost empty this time of year—"

"Mrs. Thatcher, you are doing it again. Get to the point, I pray you."

"Eh? Well, yes. What it boils down to is Lubin was caught in the cellar with young May Smith, the tweeny, under very compromising circumstances, if you get my meaning."

"You mean they were…?" Emily did not give name to it.

"Well, not exactly; I believe they were apprehended too soon, thank goodness—who would want to see something like that? But May looked very sheepish, and her not yet fourteen years old." The housekeeper tutted in disapproval.

"And you believe this young man is responsible for the downfall of the other young women?"

"He denies it, of course."

Emily pondered the matter for a moment. "What does May say about the matter?"

"What could she say?"

Emily felt she might as well be talking to a brick wall for all the progress she was making with the housekeeper.

"She could say whether or not she was coerced into such behavior," she said with all the patience she could muster.

"That's the rub. The little besom seems quite besotted over him. It seems he promised to marry her as soon as he got a promotion. Not much chance of that. He is more likely to end up in the colonies, that one."

"But you have no proof he is the man you are looking for."

Mrs. Thatcher shrugged. "What proof do you need? He was caught red-handed."

"But has anyone visited the other girls and asked for any corroboration of this story?"

Mrs. Thatcher puffed herself up. "Mr. Hobbes thinks he's the culprit, and we have no one else as fits the bill. In any case, being found with young May is reason enough to see him off the premises."

"Which, I presume, Mr. Hobbes has seen to?"

"Oh, no, madam. He is being detained until the master returns. If it can be proved he threatened all those young girls, it will be off to the colonies with him and good riddance. The very idea."

Emily was relieved to hear that the matter would be shelved, awaiting James's scrutiny. If this Lubin Thorpe person happened to be wrongly accused, it would leave the real culprit free to ruin the lives of other young girls.

"That will be all for now, Mrs. Thatcher. It seems that Mr. Hobbes has everything well in hand. You will let me know, of course, if anything else comes to light."

"Yes, my lady." Mrs. Thatcher bobbed and departed the room, leaving Emily determined to question the young 'tweenie first thing in the morning. Right then she craved a bath and a good meal. But most of all, she wished James was there to take care of the situation. Without delving too deeply into the matter, it seemed that Mr. Hobbes was awfully anxious to lay the misdeeds at Lubin Thorpe's door.

Ten

The news Mr. Hensley imparted regarding James's ship was of more import than the mere return of the vessel from India. James kept the man well supplied with cash to pay a network of spies in order to keep him apprised of any doings that might have the slightest bearing on his affairs. The practice had paid off handsomely on more than one occasion over the years.

This particular time, prior knowledge could make the difference between acquiring untold riches and a severe financial setback for the Garwoods.

It seemed that a man whose tongue had been loosened by too much grog at a dockside tavern let slip that he and some of his cohorts were being paid handsomely to see that James's cargo never made it to the warehouse. In fact, if both it and the sailing vessel could be destroyed, so much the better.

Disturbing news, to say the least, and James had little doubt as to who was behind the dastardly plot. Evidently Simon Fishberry was not so easily intimidated. James's mouth set in a grim line. He was determined the errant lord would pay for his lack of good judgment.

James rode alongside Mr. Hensley, planning his strategy against the expected foray on his cargo. Mr. Hensley had suggested he used his contacts in Limehouse to round up their own bunch of ruffians to offset the attack. James had agreed to it, but now he doubted the wisdom of the idea.

"I am having second thoughts about hiring the mercenaries, Hensley."

"Oh?"

"If one can talk in his cups, so can others. I prefer an element of surprise. Besides, I think the crew of the *Ocean Queen* would rather earn the extra pay. After a long voyage they will be spoiling for a fight."

Hensley grinned. "A good fight, or a good tumble with a tavern wench."

James chuckled. "They will be able to bed as many wenches as they want with the extra pay they will earn."

That evening he paid a visit to Rodney to apprise him of what had taken place.

"I say, old Ruysdale must be completely around the bend if he thinks he can carry that off without any repercussions."

James nodded. "I gave him credit for more sense than that. The pox must have addled his brain."

"When is the *Ocean Queen* due in port?"

"By all accounts, within three days."

Rodney rubbed his hands together. "Good. That gives us time to plan our strategy. I know Wiffey Carruthers would like a hand in this."

"Out of the question. This is my fight."

"Nonsense. Wiffy is in town, and like me, he's bored to distraction with civilian life. I met him at Boodles a couple of nights ago and he was positively whining about the dull life he is leading."

"Then why did he leave the regiment?"

"Wiffey and I left for similar reasons. With Old Boney being on the run, family duties were brought to bear. Wiffey's old pater threatened to disinherit him if he 'did not grow up and perform his filial duties.'" Rodney grimaced. "I will not begin to tell you what *my* father said. So you see, old chap, you would be doing us both a favor if you gave us the opportunity to crack a head or two."

"But—"

"No 'buts'; leave everything to me. Why risk the fate of your cargo in the hands of a shipload of unruly sailors when a captain and a major of His Majesty's army would be only too delighted to help you run the show?"

James threw up his hands. "I give up. Do what you will. I have known you long enough to know that when you get a bee in your bonnet, nothing I can say or do is going to stop you."

Rodney looked smug. "There's a good chap. Be here early tomorrow afternoon and the three of us can plan a course of action. I suggest you go home now and we'll both get a good night's sleep."

Needless to say, James tossed in his bed most of the night dreaming up one plan after another, only to discard them one by one. Finally he drifted off to sleep, to be awoken around ten o'clock the next morning by a footman as requested. The servant also assisted him with his toilet since Simpson, his valet, had been left behind in the country.

At first James, who was feeling the worse for lack of sleep, was indignant at being rousted out of bed; then the happenings of the previous day flooded back into his consciousness. His anger toward the servant was replaced by a nagging anxiety about what lay ahead.

He forced down a substantial breakfast in spite of a diminished appetite. He reasoned that he would need his strength to get through the next couple of days. By then it was time to go to Rodney's house.

The moment he was ushered into the reception hall of the house on Portman Square he heard the familiar sound of Wiffey Carruthers' distinctive laugh booming through the halls. James took heart. For heaven's sake, he thought, we three faced Buonaparte in Spain with less trepidation than I feel contemplating a sorry band of ragamuffins. What is wrong with me?

Then it came to him. When fighting on Spanish soil he had been a carefree bachelor. Now he was married, with Emily to consider. With his insatiable need to mate with her at every opportunity came the possibility of an heir to provide for. Is this reason enough to come unmanned? he mused. James firmed his resolve, determining to stop at nothing to protect what was his.

On entering the wood-paneled room that the Bonham-Lewises set aside for gentlemen to smoke their cigars and partake of their brandy, he was immediately set upon by Rodney and his other visitor and subjected to having his back slapped and pummeled.

Wilfred "Wiffey" Carruthers, a tall, slender young man whose languid elegance bespoke the courtier rather than the sword-brandishing major, raised a quizzing glass to his eyes and subjected James to a studied scrutiny.

"You seem right enough," he said.

"And why not, pray?" James replied, somewhat irritated by his friend's patronizing tone.

"Heard you were reeled in by a little chit almost half your age and evidently twice as clever. Thought at first she might be one of those bluestockings with a brain three times as big as her bosom, but Rodney set me straight. It seems that your marchioness is most amiable and was this season's beauty, to boot."

Wiffey accorded James a wicked grin and gave him yet another bone-jarring slap on the back. "Well done, Colonel Garwood. If you had to be leg-shackled I am glad it was not to some antidote with a disposition to match her looks."

"Oh, come now," Rodney remonstrated. "When have you ever seen James in pursuit of anything less than a diamond of the first water?"

"I seem to remember a certain innkeeper's wife on the Peninsula. Constanza something or other. Had a heavier mustache than even you, Rodney, old sport." Wiffey roared with laughter, seemingly overcome by his own humor.

"I say," Rodney replied, with ill-concealed amusement, "in all fairness, one has to admit in that instance our friend James was the prey."

James shuddered. "For a moment there I did not think I would come out of that little skirmish alive. It was a case of either being suffocated to death in the passionate embrace of the hirsute and somewhat unwashed *señora* or being hacked to pieces by the rusty saber her irate husband wielded."

"One of the more hellish aspects of war," said Wiffey with a dismissive shrug. "Let's sit down and iron out your present dilemma. As I see it…"

Two hours and several brandies later they left the smoke-filled room in complete accord. Rather than being ambushed on the docks on the morning the *Ocean Queen* was due to arrive, they would take a boat and meet the cargo-laden ship several miles out to sea, where the captain and his crew could be made ready for the oncoming encounter.

Meanwhile, completely oblivious of the life-and-death decisions her husband and his friends were making, Emily secured a chip-straw hat to her head with pale yellow ribands and went outside to sit under an arbor of white roses. By contrast, the riotous hues of the other flowers in the garden seemed somewhat extravagant.

In her lap a slim volume of poetry, the works of William Wordsworth, lay unopened as she sat bemused by the sweet perfume of the flowers and the sound of birdsong wafting on the balmy spring air.

The book was about to slip through her fingers when she was suddenly alerted by the crunch of footsteps along the gravel path. It was her brother, Miles. Jacket slung over one shoulder, he gave her a cheery wave with his free hand.

She placed the neglected book on the bench and ran to greet him, her happiness at seeing a familiar face erasing some of the hurt and disappointment she had felt at the ill-usage she had experienced at his hands.

"Miles, how nice to see you," she exclaimed; then her brow furrowed. "What brings you here—James is all right?"

"I should imagine so; I have heard nothing to the contrary. I did not even know he was in London. Rather thought I should find him here. I must say he could have let me know he was in Town. Not well done of him at all."

She patted his arm. "You must not fret. James left quite suddenly yesterday afternoon—something about a cargo arriving from China. I am sure he would have called on you as soon as he could."

He put his hand on his chin. "Hmm. The *Ocean Queen* was not expected for at least another week or so. Trade winds must have been favorable."

"You would know more about that than I. Until James's

man of affairs arrived yesterday, I had not the least notion that he indulged in such trading, much less owned a sailing vessel that plied all the way to India. I do not know what Papa would have said about such things."

"Papa was too much of a gentleman for our well-being. Our family has sunk far below what is considered to be an acceptable level of genteel poverty. With the guidance of your worthy husband, I intend to rectify that."

Emily put her fingertips to her lips for a brief moment, then said, "Have a care, brother. I am sure that James means well, but what if this *Ocean Queen* is beset by pirates? He might be able to sustain such losses, but your circumstances are different."

He tweeked her cheek. "You underestimate that husband of yours. The *Ocean Queen* is but one of four vessels he owns. I intend to invest a little on all four. That was James's suggestion, by the way. Have you any idea how lucky you are to have made such a brilliant match?"

He put a hand on her shoulder and gave her a supplicating look. "I hope you find it in your heart to forgive my bad behavior. After all, had you not run away, you would not now be Northwycke's wife, nor the future of the Walsinghams quite so rosy. I doubt that Ruysdale would husband the welfare of our family in such a manner."

Emily pulled away. "You make it all sound so horrid, Miles. I married James because I could not contemplate a life without him, and even then he had to convince me that he wanted the marriage, that he was not going through with it out of some misplaced sense of duty. Damn it, Miles, I love him."

He raised a brow. "I believe you, little sister, but I never thought to hear such an epithet pass your chaste lips." He grinned. "I have heard that matrimony can be a coarsening experience for some of the gentler sex. What has old James been teaching you?"

"Miles!"

"Hmm?"

"Hold your tongue before you really give away how big a noddy you are."

"Touché. I was right. I warned James you would be a formidable adversary in the battle of the sexes, but he must be as besotted as you—he married you anyway."

"Miles, I am warning you." She glowered, then burst out laughing. "I give up. You are a most incorrigible creature, but you are my brother and I love you, so I expect you are just a cross I must bear."

"Steady on. Laying it on a bit thick, I would say."

They both laughed and the tension between them dissolved.

When their mirth subsided she became aware that in her position of hostess her attentions toward her brother had been remiss. "Please forgive me, Miles. You must be in need of refreshment after your trip in the heat. Your face looks quite red from the sun. Perhaps some balm would be in order." Linking her arm through his, she led him toward the house.

She sat next to him as he ate an ample platter of cold game pie, ham cured in their own smokehouse, and an assortment of fruit and cheeses, all washed down with a home-brewed ale from a recipe that had been in the Garwood family as far back as anyone could recall.

With a final blotting of his lips with a linen napkin Miles leaned back in his chair, a satisfied look on his face. "I must say, the Garwoods keep an excellent larder. Sign of an exemplary staff from byre to dairy and places in between. Whoever runs the kitchen must be an angel from heaven."

Emily gave him a wry look. "I do not mean to be unkind, Miles, but any household staff has to be superior to the sorry bunch in your employ."

He nodded. "One gets what one pays for. No one worth their salt would work for what I can afford to pay." He visibly brightened and added, "One day that will change. I shall have a well-run establishment presided over by an admirable wife. You will be proud of me. Just you wait and see."

She lay her hand upon his. "I am sure everything will be as you say, Miles dear. Too great a burden at too young an age was laid on your shoulders when our dear mama and papa were taken from us. You did the best you could. Under James's guidance I am sure there will be no limit to what you may accomplish."

He accorded her a grateful smile.

Not wishing to see her brother humbled thus, she affected an air of gaiety. "La. With all this talk of cargoes and treasures I quite forgot to ask you the reason for your being here—not that you have to have a reason," she quickly added. "Is this a long-awaited social visit, or do you have business to discuss with James? Either way I do hope you will stay for a while. We have not seen you since we departed London."

"Nothing of any import, sister dear. Just thought I would spend some time with you—if it is convenient." He cleared his throat before proceeding. "By the way. I have yet to see any sign of the other ladies of the house. Are Lady Geraldine and Maude away visiting? There was some talk of a visit to Bath, I believe."

Emily could sense the effort he was making to sound casual. So that is how it is, she thought. Miles has come to see Maude. She viewed this knowledge with a heavy heart. However much she loved him, she knew that the Garwoods had a much loftier match in mind for Maude. Any suit of her brother's would not be entertained for a moment. The best he could hope for was an alliance with the daughter of a rich cit willing to pay for the acquisition of the Walsingham name for his family.

"It was discussed, but Lady Geraldine and Maude have yet to leave. They have taken up residence in the Dower House."

"Got rid of them, did you?"

"Nothing of the sort," Emily retorted. "Really, Miles, if you were a female you would be labeled a cat. Lady Geraldine quite wisely decided that she wished to run her own establishment. Nothing James or I could say or do would stay her from such a course."

Miles offered no further comment and finished eating in silence. Afterward, when Miles and his valet had been assigned suitable quarters, Emily sent a note over to the Dower House inviting Lady Geraldine and Maude to dinner that evening. Waiting for the footman to return with a reply, she began to doubt the wisdom of involving her in-laws in her plans for entertaining her brother.

That Miles had brought his valet with him was an indication he intended to partake of her hospitality for more than a day or so. She had mixed feelings about this. She welcomed the diversion of her brother's company during James's absence, yet she was fearful lest he presume too much and go out of his way to beguile the innocent young Maude.

Her worst fears were realized. After dinner, Miles offered to entertain the ladies at the pianoforte with renditions in his beautiful tenor voice of several old favorites.

Maude sat by his side on the music bench, ostensibly to turn the music pages for him, but she was apparently so intent on gazing into his eyes that she missed her cue a time or two.

Matters really came to a head when he started to warble,

Drink to me only with thine eyes, and I will pledge with mine.

To Emily's dismay, Maude joined him in harmony with a rich contralto voice. Miles, seemingly encouraged by her participation, continued the lied with increased enthusiasm. At its conclusion they both remained seated at the piano bench, staring into each others eyes.

"Charming, very charming," Lady Geraldine remarked coldly, a frown furrowing her brow.

Her obvious displeasure broke the spell. Maude and Miles quickly rose from the bench in tandem, both betraying their discomfort by a telltale flush of embarrassment.

Emily could have cheerfully strangled her brother for allowing—nay, encouraging—the incident to happen. And when, pray, she thought, did Miles become such a paragon of grace and charm? For that matter, when did he learn to sing in such a seductive manner? Poor Maude does not stand a chance!

"Quite so, Mother." Emily's tone was noncommittal. "Might I now suggest a game of whist? Both Maude and I need to sharpen our skills at cards."

"Thank you, no." Lady Geraldine replied. "It has been a lovely evening, Emily dear, but it is way past Maude's bedtime. The *child* is still growing and cannot afford to miss her sleep."

The emphasis on the word *child* was not lost on Emily.

Its delivery was accompanied by a glare in Miles's direction. Seemingly oblivious to Lady Geraldine's displeasure, he offered to escort the ladies back to the Dower House.

"That will not be necessary," Lady Geraldine replied, her voice cold and distant. "A servant awaits us with a carriage."

On their departure, Emily turned to Miles and shook her head. "That was poorly done of you brother."

He looked surprised. "What on earth do you mean by that? I thought I did a very good job of entertaining your in-laws."

"Do not play me for the fool, Miles. I am not a Bath miss anymore. You are doing your best to make poor Maude fall in love with you. It just will not do."

"And why not, pray? The Walsingham name is a noble one and counts for something." His voice was petulant.

"Why not?" She hesitated for a moment, then took a deep breath and plunged in. "Miles, I do not how to say this without appearing unkind. The Garwoods would never agree to such an alliance. Maude grows prettier every day and, with her fortune, is expected to make a brilliant match."

His shoulders sagged. "You are right, of course."

"There are other young girls, also well dowered, whose papas would leap at the chance to have you for a son-in-law."

He raised a brow. "Now look who is being horrid. I care not for Maude's fortune."

"Then you love her?"

"I believe so."

It was Emily's turn to raise a brow. "You are not sure?"

"Please do not look at me in such a fashion, Emily. It does not help matters."

She was surprised by the distress in his voice. She had thought Miles lacked the depth to display such emotion.

"Forgive me. I did not mean to be unfeeling. Perhaps you would like to discuss it with me."

"I cannot promise to go through with it, but I shall endeavor to explain how I feel."

"I believe it would be helpful."

"I have always had this picture in my mind as to the sort

of girl I would like to marry. Just let us say that I knew Maude before I ever met her. It is so mad, even I have to question it."

"Are you sure you did not allow your ideal to metamorphose into Maude to fill a void in your life?"

"That would be almost as irrational as having conjured her up in the first place, would it not?" He looked perplexed. "Granted, the Garwoods are a strong, close-knit family. They have really taken you to their bosom, and I suppose I *am* on the outside looking in like an urchin with his nose pressed to the window of a sweet shop."

She leaned over and kissed his cheek. "Poor darling. You miss Mama and Papa as much as I do. Please forgive me for not realizing. Of course you are a part of this family. Why else would James concern himself with your welfare?"

A rueful little smile crossed his face. "Why, indeed? James has no reason to regard me with anything but contempt. At best, I would say it is out of love for you, but it is far more likely that he is trying to raise my fortunes in order to make me less of an embarrassment to the Garwoods."

Emily shook her head. "In that I fear you are gravely mistaken. James is very fond of you for your own sake and has a strong desire to see that you have a happy, productive life."

"Short of marrying his sister."

She heard in his voice not only bitterness but an underlying feeling of alienation. It filled her with a great compassion for her brother and a nagging guilt because of her own good fortune.

"Please do not fault him for that. It is his duty to secure the most brilliant match possible for Maude."

"At the expense of her happiness?"

"Of course not. James would not make his sister marry where her heart did not go."

"Go on, say it."

"Say what?"

"Unlike your brother who would have shackled you to one of the most depraved creatures in England."

She grabbed his arm and shook it. "Stop it! That thought did not cross my mind. You were as much a victim as I in the matter. I have forgiven you. Kindly forgive yourself."

He did not reply, but the look in his eyes filled her with despair. Miles would never forgive himself; of this she was certain. She fervently hoped that his sense of guilt would in no way ruin any future chance for happiness that might come his way.

Eleven

"This is an unexpected honor, gentlemen. Indeed, a signal honor."

After having bathed and put on his best uniform, John Walters, captain of the *Ocean Queen*, was considerably more cheerful and effusive. At the unexpected arrival of James and his friends, he had smelled little better than the men under his command.

James questioned the man's standards. Admittedly Captain Walters was not an aristocrat, but he had been born a gentleman. A younger son, he had rejected both a life in the military and the clergy in favor of roving the seas. James could sympathize with the choices the man had made, but he could not imagine forgoing to bathe when possible.

"Nonsense," James replied with great cordiality. "It is good to see you again. What say you—has it been a good voyage?"

"Fairly so. There was a slight skirmish with a pirate boat just out of Madras, but once I ran the captain through, the others lost heart and jumped overboard to return to their vessel, whereupon we sank it with a round of cannon. The poor fools really overstepped themselves that time."

The threesome laughed, a mixture of amusement and admiration.

"Well done," Wiffey drawled. "It is to be hoped the forthcoming encounter is not beneath your crew." He took out an elaborate cloisonné snuffbox and, after sniffing a generous pinch of its contents, sneezed into a handkerchief lavishly trimmed with lace.

The captain raised a brow in Wiffey's direction, then gave James a questioning look.

James chose not to respond. The captain would learn soon

enough what manner of man Wilfred Carruthers happened to be.

The captain shrugged, then addressed the question. "The easier the fight, the better, I should imagine, Major Carruthers. Prior knowledge should be a great help in that direction."

He turned to James. "Was there any indication as to whether the attack will be at sea or when we dock?"

"None whatsoever. I understand the loose-tongued villain passed out without further elaboration."

"Hmm. In which case I shall put several men on watch in case the ruffians show their ugly faces."

James nodded. "We shall leave the details in your capable hands."

"Good. I shall see to it that none of them sets foot on the *Ocean Queen.*"

"On the contrary, Captain. By all means let them board. We shall have to see to it that they are disarmed before they do any damage."

"Are you sure?"

"Most certainly. How else am I to find out who is behind all this?"

"I thought we had already surmised that it was Simon Fishberry," Rodney interjected.

"I do not call out a man on mere supposition," James replied grimly.

There was a moment of shocked silence, and James saw his friends exchange worried glances. He frowned and shrugged his shoulders. "What other choice does he leave me? If he is the culprit—and at this point I can see it as being no other—unless he is put in his place he will continue to be a threat to my family. This I will not tolerate."

"Oh, quite," said Rodney. "But until it is sorted out I am not leaving your side. Ruysdale is far more likely to settle this with a knife in the back than to risk facing you on a field of honor."

"We shall see."

"In the meantime, might I suggest a glass of cognac and a friendly game of cards?" said the captain, rubbing his hands in anticipation. "It is so seldom I get to enjoy the company of gentlemen. My first mate is an unsociable cove and a very poor card player to boot."

James laughed. "I doubt there is anything wrong with the gentleman's card playing. As I recall, you are uncommonly good at all manner of games. Your fellow officer is merely prudent with his resources."

"Then I take it you do not wish to play?"

"On the contrary. The three of us can offer you fair competition. We had plenty of time to hone our skills on lonely nights on the Peninsula."

Beaming with pleasure, the captain moved toward the cupboard that housed the glasses and spirits. "I think we should forgo the drink, Captain Walters. If it turns out I have to kill a man or two this evening, I prefer to be sober at the time. It is no light thing to dispatch a man to his Maker."

Wiffey yawned delicately behind his hand. "The blackguards we will encounter are more likely to be sent straight to Hades rather than experiencing any side-trips in the other direction."

They played whist and the captain won the first deal and also the first round, each man then winning in his turn. Rodney had just won his second hand when the first mate put in an appearance.

"Begging your pardon gentlemen, but the watch in the forecastle thinks he saw a sail on the larboard side."

"Thinks?" Captain Walters sputtered.

"Aye, sir. The moon went behind the clouds before he could be sure."

"Very well." His words sounded more of a grumble than an assent. Clearly embarrassed, he addressed James. "I suppose we had better look into it."

"I hope the man was not imagining things," James answered. "I would like to get this over with."

As it turned out when the moon broke through the clouds once more, a schooner hove into clear view, and several men were observed being lowered down into a longboat. A couple of them failed to make it and had to be fished out of the water.

"Landlubbers." The captain's voice dripped with contempt.

"Signal the man in the forecastle to turn his back on them," James hissed, "and the rest of us will keep out of sight until I give the signal."

Crouching low on the deck, it seemed an eternity to James before he heard the unsteady rhythm of oars splashing their way through water. They really *are* inept, he thought. The way they are going about it they will be lucky if they get here.

Finally, there was a harsh scraping noise as the approaching boat bumped into the side of the *Ocean Queen*. A yelp of pain accompanied by a string of obscenities rent the air. This was followed by the sound of knuckles against flesh.

"Quiet, you landlubber. You'll give us all away. How many times do you have to be told to keep your hands in the bloody boat?" This admonition, every bit as audible as the previously uttered obscenity, was delivered in slurred tones.

"Would you give credence to it?" James whispered to the captain.

John Walters nodded. "Foxed as mariners," he whispered in reply.

With the poor visibility of nighttime and the close quarters in which they would be forced to fight, it had been decided to fight with swords rather than pistols unless circumstances demanded otherwise.

The crew silently deployed to the positions previously assigned them, with strict instructions not to join in the fray unless ordered to do so. James had decided that too many men running around in the dark brandishing weapons was an invitation to disaster. He and his friends with the aid of the captain, who was reputed to be an excellent swordsman, could take care of a handful of untrained ruffians by themselves.

Nevertheless, James gave the pistols stuck in his belt a reassuring pat. A half-dozen or so of the intruders had their feet unsteadily planted on the deck, and several more were in the process of clambering over the side, when James signaled for his friends to attack.

Wiffey Carruthers reached the enemy first. With a soul-chilling war whoop he downed the first three marauders with ferocious slashes of his blade before they could even get their bearings.

"The man is a bloody whirling dervish," the captain gasped. James flashed him a grin, downed an adversary, and resumed swordplay with a new contender, a villain whose body odor was far more deadly than his skills with a blade. With a bored expression on his face, James toyed with his opponent, parrying his assaults with ease.

One of Wiffey's adversaries let out a howl of anguish. "I hope that answers any questions you might have had on the subject of Major Carruthers," James said as he delivered a playful riposte.

Rendering his opponent's sword arm useless with a cut delivered with the precision of a surgeon, the captain replied, "Indubitably, Lord Northwycke. Indubitably."

"'Ere now," James's opponent remonstrated, his voice filled with indignation. "Is this a fight, or a bloody tea party we're 'aving?"

James shrugged. "If you insist, we will do it your way." With a deft flick of his sword he lofted the man's blade into the air and over the side of the ship.

"Is that better? Ready to give up now?"

The man put his hands up. "Cor blimey. What do you think?" He hiccupped and fell flat on his face.

The battle was over. At any rate, the only two would-be marauders left standing—both bleeding profusely—cast down their weapons. A third was hanging over the side of the ship, vomiting violently enough to rid himself of his toenails.

"Ah, me. What a disappointment, gentlemen," Wiffey declared, delicately dabbing his brow with the infamous handkerchief. He returned the dainty confection to his pocket and with an exaggerated sigh added, "I fear John Barleycorn has to take most of the credit for this dreary little victory. What were they thinking, coming to a fight as drunk as lords?"

"They quite overstepped themselves," said Rodney.

"You can blame Fishberry's agent for that." The voice was

bitter and pain-ridden.

Every one on the deck who was left standing wheeled in the direction from which the voice emanated. Huddled beside a water barrel was a large, dark-haired man sporting a huge gash across his forehead.

James approached him. "Oh? How so?"

"The damned fool gave us half our money in advance with the promise of extra pay for a discreet and successful conclusion to the affair."

He spoke with the well-modulated accent of a gentleman. The son of a servant educated alongside the son of his master? James wondered, and if so, why had he sunk so low? Drink? Or an even worse vice? Perhaps something as mundane as a stint in debtors' prison. James decided to pursue the matter no further. The man was destined for the gallows, and the less he knew about him the better.

"You seem sober enough. Your cohorts must have been a brainless bunch not to see the folly in getting foxed before such an undertaking. No doubt they derived their courage for such a foolhardy adventure from a bottle."

"Ah, my lord. That is not entirely the case, although it would be understandable. These are ordinary little men, worn down and degraded by the hellish life an accident of birth has thrust upon them. In a world where a good meal is nonexistent and a man lies awake at night listening to the cries of his children as they protest the hunger gnawing at their bellies, a drink carries more significance than the mere fostering of false courage."

"Oh? How so?" said James. He was somewhat uncomfortable by the turn the conversation had taken, but he could not let it go. He found it hard to reconcile the educated tones of a gentleman voiced by such a pitiful wretch.

The man coughed before continuing. It was a wracking, painful episode that beaded his forehead with sweat. Blood-tinged foam bubbled between his lips. Consumption would claim him if the hangman did not get to him first, James thought.

The man wiped his mouth on his coat sleeve and said, "My apologies, gentlemen. How so, you ask? Your vision is blinded by your good fortune. How else could you pursue your aimless lives oblivious of the misery that surrounds you?"

His tirade seemingly sapping his strength, he drew a shallow, rale-ridden breath before continuing. "When a man has the price of a couple of drinks the world does not seem such a dreary place. In fact, there is even cause for merriment. Ah, but when a man can afford to get drunk, the world belongs to him and there is no telling what he can accomplish.

"Be not quick to judge this sorry little band of gallows bait. Rather, mourn the plight of their widows and children who shall probably be swift in following them to the gibbet."

He gave James a searching look, as if trying to consign his features to memory. James found it most unnerving.

"Incidentally, my lord, had I known this to be your ship, I would not have joined in this ill-conceived plan." The man punctuated this last remark with a wry little smile, then slumped back onto the deck.

The captain felt his pulse. "Finally we shall get a little peace and quiet—the verbose bastard appears to be dead." He addressed the prisoners, who were herded together. "Anyone know his name? I suppose I should say a few words over him before consigning him to the deep."

"'E goes by the name of Gentleman Joe." The man who uttered the words stepped forward. It was the man James had bested in the fight. "'Is mum was a dancing girl at the opera, and 'e claims 'is dad was some fancy lord wot kept 'er."

He grew silent, as if thinking over what he had said.

"And what might your name be?" James asked, taking advantage of the lull in the conversation. Really, he thought, the denizens of Limehouse are a loquacious lot.

"Michael Dempsey, but I am called Mickey Lightfingers by most as know me."

"Bandying that sort of information about is liable to get you hanged," Rodney interjected with a sniff.

Michael Dempsey shrugged. "I'm already a dead man, ain't I?"

"Do not encourage him, James, I beg of you," Rodney

remonstrated. "By his own admission the man is nothing but a common pickpocket."

James waved him aside. "No. I would like to hear more about this Gentleman Joe. I am sure it is a most interesting tale."

"You 'ave the right o' that. This 'ere Lord dealt well by both of 'em. A nice town 'ouse for 'er. Sent 'im away in the country to a fancy school. Joe and 'is mum would 'ave been set for life if the stupid little cow 'adn't got caught mucking about with a prizefighter. Shame, really. She took to gin and drank 'erself to death."

"And this Joe?"

"Thrown out of the school as soon as the ready was cut off."

"Then?"

"A band of pickpockets got their 'ands on 'im—that's where we joined up. My dad sold me to the bloody thieves when I was a little shaver—they got Joe for nothing.

"Joe did all right for a while, too, until 'e grew too big for the trade." The man shrugged. "Shame really. He was never much cop as an 'ighwayman. Didn't 'ave the stomach for killing. Being as he already owned a horse, he became a rag-and-bone man. Managed to scrape by on that. Then 'e fell sick. This job come along and 'e saw it as a chance to leave something for 'is wife and daughter."

James removed a lantern from a bracket and took a closer look at Gentleman Joe. His hair curled over in a forelock pretty much the same as his own, save there was a sprinkling of gray in the dead man's and his face was pale and gaunt, the skin stretched taut over the skull. The hairs on the back of James's neck stood up. It was the face of a man who had suffered deep privation. He visualized himself being wrenched out of the safe harbor of his life at a very tender age and being exposed to the horror and degradation of life around the less salubrious parts of London. It was a harrowing exercise.

"He seems to be in his late forties," he said.

"Thirty-four 'e was, same as me. A chap grows old before 'is time around 'ere."

"So much for that taradiddle," said the captain, elbowing the pickpocket out of the way. "I may as well proceed with consigning this rogue to the drink."

"No," said James. "I will be responsible for his burial. Kindly see to it that his body is washed and shrouded."

"Very well, my lord, and with your permission I will see that these ruffians are chained and delivered to the proper authorities."

"No. Tend to their wounds first then set them free as soon as we get to port. I have no stomach for any more of this."

He turned to Michael Dempsey. "You may remain free. I have seen you fight and you should present no problem. I wish to talk to you further in the privacy of the Captain's cabin. How do you wish to be addressed?"

"Mickey suits me fine."

"As you wish, Mickey. You may address me as 'my lord,' or 'sir'—whichever you are comfortable with. That should not be too taxing."

Mickey gave him a smile that was most engaging, considering the man had lost most of his front teeth.

"You're all right, sir. That is, for a gent."

James accorded him a slight bow and replied, "Thank you, I suppose."

Early the next morning Emily and Lady Geraldine were calling on an aging parishioner known to her neighbors as "Old Mother Appleby."

To Emily's surprise, the door was opened by Polly, the newly dismissed parlor maid. Apart from a healthy glow on her face, the erstwhile maid's appearance did not betray her pending motherhood, and the beaming smile the girl accorded Lady Geraldine and herself was totally unexpected.

"My ladies," she said, holding out her starched white pinafore for an elaborate curtsey, "Granny will be so pleased you came to see her. She'll be proper proud."

Emily was amused by Polly's performance. Her curtsey could have put many a girl presented at court to shame. Evidently

Lady Geraldine did not share her amusement, for she gave Polly a scathing look through her lorgnette.

"And how *is* Mrs. Appleby?" she asked.

"Right poorly, your ladyship. Took to her bed last week. The rheumatiz finally got the better of her."

"Oh dear," Lady Geraldine replied. "Then Lady Northwycke and I shall not intrude." She handed Polly a basket. "Please be good enough to see that your grandmother gets this. I trust she was able to eat the things I sent over last week?"

"Oh, yes, my lady. She particularly liked the beef broth and the roasted chicken. But please do not go without seeing her. It would break her poor heart, indeed it would."

"In that case," Lady Geraldine replied, signaling Emily to lead the way through the low-set doorway.

"Pray go first," Emily replied.

Her mother-in-law complied, stooping to avoid hitting her head on the lintel.

Once inside, Emily saw that although sparsely furnished with rustic, homemade furniture, the house was clean, the wood plank floor worn smooth from many scrubbings. Curtains fashioned from coarse cotton hung at a window, and a colorful rag rug lay in front of a stone fireplace.

Polly ushered the visitors through the tiny room to one even smaller. There, propped up in a bed that took up most of the available space, was the most wizened old lady Emily had ever seen. It occurred to her that Mrs. Appleby was appropriately named. Framed in a simple cambric nightcap, her face reminded Emily of an apple that had been stored in a cellar too long.

The old woman smiled at her visitors, causing the lines on her face to deepen and confirming the fact that the hollow-cheeked crone lacked for teeth. It did not take Emily long to realize the old woman only had eyes for Lady Geraldine. Her own presence had scarcely warranted a glance.

"Your ladyship, how good of you to visit a poor old woman," she said, her voice wavering and crackling with the ravages of age.

"Not at all, Mrs. Appleby. Lady Northwycke and I are

merely doing our Christian duty."

The old woman glared at Emily. "You ain't Lady Northwycke and don't you be trying to say you are, saucy little madam."

Lady Geraldine shot Emily a mischievous smile. "My apologies," she whispered. "I should have warned you that the old dear is in her dotage."

"It's rude to whisper and don't you forget it," Mrs. Appleby snapped.

"I shall try to remember," said Lady Geraldine.

"Sit down, if you please," Mrs. Appleby commanded, indicating a small wooden chair.

Lady Geraldine complied.

"That's better," she said, then pointed a gnarled finger in Emily's direction. "Tell this little besom to leave the room. It's you I wish to visit with, my lady."

"Now then, Granny," Polly interjected. "That's no way to talk to Lady Northwycke." She looked mortified. "I am truly sorry, your ladyship. Granny doesn't know any better."

"Do not be troubled, Polly. I quite understand. In any case I should like to talk to you in private."

Once back in the small living room, Polly faced Emily, her mouth set in a grim line. "Begging your pardon, my lady, but if this is about the babe I carry I ain't got anything to say on the matter, so please don't ask."

"You have nothing to fear, Polly. Lord Northwycke will protect you."

"I don't need no protecting 'cos I ain't saying anything."

"There are those who think that Lubin Thorpe is the one responsible for all of this unpleasantness."

"But you don't, do you, my lady?"

"I do not know what to think, Polly. I should hate to see the wrong man punished."

"Mr. Hobbes is a sly old codger and will lay the blame at anyone's door just to get the whole thing settled."

Emily looked skeptical. "Surely not."

"Begging your pardon, my lady, but you had dealings with Lubin when you were below-stairs."

"I do not seem to recall him."

"He is the tall, skinny thing with the stutter."

"Oh, yes. He was extremely shy."

Polly nodded. "Do you rightly think he could make a girl toss her petticoats? The only one he could attract was that goose-brained little tweeny, and if he doesn't wed her before she's old enough to know what a ninny he is, he'll lose her for certain."

"I thought Lubin was a nice young man."

"Nice? Yes, your ladyship. But a man?" Polly laughed. "That he'll never be, if you get my meaning."

Emily felt a rush of blood heat her face. She understood all too well. Really, she thought, females of the lower orders are distressingly earthy.

Even as Emily contemplated this thought, Polly became pensive, as if mulling over the situation. Emily watched a gamut of emotions flit across the young girl's face, culminating in doubt and fear. Polly looked very young and achingly vulnerable.

Emily patted her shoulder. "Do not be afraid, Polly, I promise you Lord Northwycke will see to it that you and your babe lack for nothing."

Polly's face broke up and between sobs she choked out, "I do not deserve your kindness, my lady."

Emily handed her a handkerchief. "Am I right in thinking you did not enter willingly into this liaison?"

"Being as you're so kind, this much I'll say. Talk to Alice Barnes. She is about to be delivered of her babe and is poorly. It is feared that both will die. She might be of a mind to set things right."

"Thank you, Polly. I know that was not easy for you."

"Sometimes I think it don't matter one way or t'other, my lady. What kind of a life will the babe have? Labeled a bastard, as it were?"

Emily patted her shoulder once more. They were of an age, but her feelings toward Polly could only be described as maternal. "We shall have to see that he has the best life possible."

Upon hearing these words, Polly burst into tears once more.

Twelve

About the same time Emily and his mother were departing Mrs. Appleby's cottage, James arrived at the Ruysdale mansion. It was the time of day members of fashionable society had usually finished their breakfasts and were either awaiting the arrival of callers or preparing to call on other members of society themselves—a pastime seldom indulged in by Simon Fishberry. That gentleman was inclined to more sordid pursuits—ones best conducted under a veil of darkness.

A somewhat distracted-looking butler opened the door to James and greeted him with a questioning, "Yes?"

This struck James as odd, because whatever else one might say about Simon Fishberry, the man maintained an impeccable staff who usually kept his household running smoothly. He was certain that such cavalier treatment of callers was not the norm in the Ruysdale establishment.

"Kindly inform your master that Lord Northwycke wishes to speak to him." He delivered this imperative with a disdainful look.

The servant granted him entry but left him standing in the hall without so much as offering to take his hat or walking stick, then departed up the stairs muttering to himself. Presently Alfred Fishberry sauntered down the ornately carved staircase and slanted James a smile that bespoke malevolence rather than cordiality.

"What the devil are you doing here, Northwycke?" His voice was curt, totally lacking in the civility that was due a peer of the realm. "Have the goodness to state your business and take your leave. This is dashed inconvenient."

"I informed the manservant that I wished to see Lord

Ruysdale, not his late son's insolent whelp."

Alfred took out his pocket watch and made a show of consulting it. "For your information, to all intents and purposes *I* am Lord Ruysdale and have been for the last hour and a half. My miserable old grandsire finally had the good grace to go to his just reward. Very suddenly, I might add. I should imagine that right about now the filthy old reprobate is getting a very warm reception." He sniggered. "Very warm indeed."

Not deigning to reply, James turned heel and let himself out of the house.

He was somewhat surprised at his reaction to the news of his enemy's demise. To his dismay he felt disappointed that the Grim Reaper had robbed him of the satisfaction of exacting revenge upon the evil Lord Ruysdale. Reason prevailed. He was sensible enough to realize the man's death by natural causes had averted an ugly scandal.

At least, he thought, he can no longer harm my family. His step took on a jaunty air, and for guarding his curricle and horses during his absence, the stableboy was well rewarded.

He visited Mr. Hensley next. The usual pleasantries were exchanged, and the man of affairs was enlightened as to the outcome of the skirmish aboard the *Ocean Queen*.

"I am indebted to you, Mr. Hensley," James said.

"Not at all," he replied with a dismissive gesture. "Happy to oblige in any way I can."

James beamed. "And I am happy to hear you say so, for I would like you to arrange the burial of Gentleman Joe."

Mr. Hensley's heavy, black brows shot up in surprise. "I should think a pauper's funeral would suffice such a personage."

"It probably would," James replied, "but I wish him to have a proper Christian burial in a decent churchyard with a minister of the cloth presiding. The man had his dignity stripped away from him in life. I merely wish to restore it to him in death."

The other man gave him a look of puzzlement.

James smiled. "Just a whim of mine."

"I see," said Mr. Hensley, the expression on his face clearly showing otherwise.

"There is another small matter I would like you to take care of."

"My lord?"

"There is a small estate next to mine which has been vacant for quite some time. The owner died last summer and his heirs have it up for sale. I intend to purchase it."

"A sagacious move. It can only enhance your own holdings. But how may I be of assistance?"

"While I am seeing to the renovations and alterations I would like you to amass a suitable staff for me. Put advertisements in the newspapers and winnow out the applicants, that sort of thing."

"But that is not my sphere of expertise."

"Nonsense. It has not escaped my notice over the years that you are an astute judge of character—one not easily fooled by rascals. You are the ideal person to help me staff an orphanage I intend to establish."

"An *orphanage?*"

"Surprised, Mr. Hensley? So am I, but I cannot stand idly by and do nothing about the plight of innocent children."

He told his man of affairs about the wretched childhood of Gentleman Joe and Mickey Lightfingers. "Of course I cannot right every injustice that takes place in the slums of London, but if I save only a few of these children and give them a chance for decent, productive lives, it will not be in vain."

Emily watched with growing dismay as Miles cultivated Maude's friendship. She knew nothing good could come of it. Warning Miles of the futility of his cause had evidently been to no avail.

Fortunately propriety precluded the young people being alone without a chaperon, but after a couple of days of tight-lipped disapproval on Lady Geraldine's part, she finally took matters into her own hands.

She informed Emily it was time for Maude and herself to visit the waters at Bath. They departed the next morning, with two very exhausted abigails in tow.

The object of his affections clearly out of his grasp for the time being, Miles bade his valet pack his bags. He departed for London the same afternoon.

Suddenly left to her own devices, Emily had time to think about the unsettling things going on about her. There was the matter of Lubin Thorpe and the tweeny, and the more serious problem as to whether he was responsible for the pending increase in the village population.

She even speculated as to whether Mr. Hobbes had a sinister reason for laying the responsibility at Lubin's door. Could Mr. Hobbes be the below-stairs lothario? Common sense dictated otherwise. The man was getting too old for his regular duties, much less the strenuous demands of procreation, and yet...

She blushed. Miles was right. Marriage could be coarsening ... but oh, so delicious. So, so... words could not describe what she was feeling. Three days had gone by. How much longer would James be gone?

She decided to pay Alice Barnes a visit. Mrs. Thatcher made up a food basket to give to the expectant mother, and with Susan for company, Emily went to the Barneses' cottage in a trap and pony.

Like most of the other cottages in the village, the Barneses' was small but quaint, with a heavy thatched roof, diamond-paned windows, and a profusion of hollyhocks and daisies in the garden.

They were greeted at the door by a stony-faced woman who wore her gray hair in a tight little bun on the top of her head.

"If you've come to see our Alice, my lady, you're too late. She died early this morning birthing her babe."

"I am so sorry. You must be her mother."

The woman nodded.

Suddenly the plaintive wail of a baby emanated from the house.

"The boy is hungry and has no mother to feed him." Mrs. Barnes's voice was totally devoid of emotion.

"Surely there is someone in the village who is about to wean a child," Susan interjected. "In the meantime soak a rag in cow's milk and let him suck on that."

"We have no cow."

"I will see to it that some milk is sent over immediately," Emily said.

Mrs. Barnes nodded and took the basket Emily offered. "It is very good of you, my lady."

"May I see the baby?"

Mrs. Barnes nodded once more and moved aside for the two women to enter, then trailed after them into the house.

Once in, she called out to someone in the other room. "Our Mabel, bring the babe out here. Her ladyship wishes to see him."

A girl about twelve years old emerged from the room, carrying the child. It was firmly swaddled in an old blanket. His screams had subsided into muffled little sobs, as if the strength had gone out of him.

Mrs. Barnes took the baby from Mabel and presented it to Emily. She was taken aback by the gesture.

"Ugly little thing," said his grandmother with a sniff. "It would have been better if he'd died, too. Has the mark of the devil on him, that one. Mark my words, no good can come of it."

Emily clutched the child as if to protect him from such a dire prediction. "Do not say such a thing, Mrs. Barnes. He is just an innocent child."

"So was his father at that age, I shouldn't wonder, and look at all the misery that villain has caused in this village."

"Then Alice told you his name?"

Mrs. Barnes shook her head. "Didn't have to. He left the mark of his iniquity on the babe for all the world to see."

She pulled the blanket away from the baby's face to expose a very distinctive birthmark just below his eye.

"Clarence, the groom," Emily said, her voice barely above a whisper.

"May he rot in hell," Mrs. Barnes added.

"You have not taken to the child?"

"Nor will I."

"Then please let me take him home with me. He will be well taken care of."

The woman shrugged. "Suit yourself. When I look at him all I see is the cause of my daughter's death. Angel from heaven was our Alice. The prettiest golden curls."

Her voice broke and the iron facade dissolved into a flood of tears.

Susan tugged at Emily's sleeve. "I think we should leave now, my lady," she said.

Emily nodded in compliance and followed her out of the cottage, still clutching the child.

By the time James arrived home the next afternoon, a wet nurse had been found for the baby boy. His tummy was full and he was sleeping soundly in a cradle that had been brought down from the attic.

James looked at him for a moment, then with a rueful grin, declared him to be the plainest baby he had ever beheld.

"What are you going to call him?" he asked.

"I lean to William. What do you think?"

"It matters not to me. William it is. What do you intend to do with him?"

"What do you mean?"

"You can hardly make him a member of the family. It would not be the thing."

Emily gave him a beseeching look. "Would you have me cast him out to die?"

He gave her a reassuring pat. "Of course not, darling. But the sooner we find a suitable family to foster him, the better."

Emily gave a little murmur of protest.

"It would not do for you to form an attachment for the child—surely you can see that? I shall pay for his support and education. His future will be a lot rosier than he has a right to expect. Every thing will turn out well, just you see."

Emily sighed. "You are quite right, of course, but I do not have to like it."

"There's my girl." He gave her a hug and a kiss.

"James," she whispered, pulling away, "you forget yourself. Not in front of the baby's nurse. You will set tongues to wagging below-stairs if you do not practice a little discretion."

"Then I suggest we depart the nursery in favor of our own quarters, where I shall expect a proper welcome home," he whispered in return.

Silently he mulled over the fact that in the twinkling of an eye, two more babes and their mothers would be committed to his care; and when his plans for the orphanage were put into effect, how many more souls would look to him for succor?

He repeated to Emily what had transpired on the *Ocean Queen*.

"Such a strange tale. It grieves me to think that children are used so cruelly. Why is it allowed?"

"Indifference. The enormity of the task. The cost. Who knows? Many things come into play. It is easier to turn a blind eye."

His mouth formed a grim line as he contemplated the matter. His thoughts turned to the lecherous groom he had incarcerated in the local gaol.

It had come to light that the powerfully built man had threatened to do away with the girls' entire families in the most gruesome ways if they did not submit to his demands.

They were simple, country girls, gullible enough to believe him. Their fears were reinforced when in each case, to drive home the threat, he had forced them to watch while he deliberately tortured one of the stable kittens to death.

What makes a man turn out to be so twisted? James wondered. He thought of his newly deceased adversary, Simon Fishberry. Evil brooked no barriers of class.

Over the next few days, James set about righting the wrongs that had taken place in his household. Mr. Hobbes received a thorough dressing-down for closing his eyes to the matter. It was suggested that if he wished to keep his position he should maintain it with a great deal more integrity. The steward, Mr. Rainey, was also admonished for his overall ignorance of the affair.

Although Mrs. Thatcher was commended for bringing the matter to Lady Northwycke's attention, it was suggested that in future she should confer with the master on such matters rather than burden her ladyship with them.

When Mrs. Thatcher left the room, James heaved a sigh of relief. "I am glad that is over," he said to Emily, whom he had insisted be present while he conducted the lectures.

"After all," he had said when requesting her presence, "when I am absent this burden falls upon your beautiful shoulders; it will not hurt to see how I handle such matters."

Emily nodded.

He smiled in approval. At first Emily had objected to witnessing the servants' humiliation, but she had bowed to his judgment out of respect for his postion as head of the household.

"Now we have to deal with the two expectant mothers. What do you suggest?"

"They are both sorely in need of husbands," Emily replied, pleased to have been asked. "But I suppose that is out of the question. If you could solve that problem, James, everything else would fall into place."

"Husbands. Of course. It should not be too difficult to find a couple of likely fellows for them."

"You think not?" she said, a tiny frown furrowing her brow. "Under the circumstances, I should have thought otherwise."

"The girls in question are both comely. I must say the swine was very discerning in that respect. Also, the poor can be very pragmatic."

"Pragmatic?" The furrow in her brow deepened.

"Yes, darling. Pragmatic. If each girl comes with sufficient coin and a snug little cottage to boot, any number of lusty young lads will offer themselves up to be husbands."

"Like sacrificial lambs. Not unlike certain young men at a come-out."

James laughed. "Precisely. Except that our class prefers, nay, demands that their females be unsullied. We just do not tolerate cuckoos in the nest."

"How horrible. It all sounds so cold-blooded."

He rose and moved toward her. He held her firmly in his arms and whispered, "It does not have to be."

"My first assessment of your character was correct, my

lord," she told him, nestling close.

"And that is?"

"You are a very wicked man."

"And you object to this?" he said between kisses.

"Of course," she replied, returning kiss for kiss.

As it turned out, James was correct in assuming there would be no lack of suitors for the erstwhile chambermaids. Without the incentives he was willing to provide, it would have been years before any of them would be in a position to take a wife.

The expectant mothers had their pick of several, and each selected a very lusty specimen, Polly choosing one of the under-gardeners, the other girl, a muscular ploughboy from one of the farms the Garwoods owned.

Lubin Thorpe was reinstated as under-footman and promised a cottage of his own just as soon as May Smith was of an age to marry. There was one stipulation: no more trysts in the apple cellar or they would both be turned off without a letter of recommendation.

Their obligations fulfilled and the capricious English weather permitting, James and Emily returned to their idyllic pastime of picnicking on the island. James had refined on the matter by seeing to it that servants rowed out there every morning to refurbish the place with fresh linens for the bed and to fill every nook and cranny with vases of flowers culled from the estate gardens.

One sunny afternoon at the beginning of August, James cancelled their visit to the island in favor of an excursion on horseback. It was a pleasant ride along an old bridle path that passed through Garwood land to the next estate.

As they came to a rise that served as a boundary between the two properties, the sound of men's voices could be heard above a clamor of activity. Emily gave James a questioning look. "Has someone bought the old squire's estate, then?" she asked.

"I believe so."

"How exciting," said Emily, urging Syllabub to reach the top of the rise. "I do so hope the new inhabitants are young enough to be sociable."

"I should imagine so," James replied. "I suggest we take a look at what is going on."

When they finally approached the house, Emily was surprised to see that the grounds had been restored to their former glory and the house no longer had an air of neglect. The clamor they had heard came from the outbuildings, where the final repairs were in progress.

"Who would have thought such a transformation could take place?" Emily said.

Several of the workmen doffed their caps as the Garwoods rode around the buildings. "Do you think the new owners will mind us trespassing?" Emily asked as they passed the men.

"I hardly think so. It will be another week before it is occupied."

Emily was wondering how he came by such knowledge when she perceived the most devilish of smiles on his face. She tapped him on the shoulder with her riding crop. "James Garwood, you are up to something and I would be obliged if you would tell me what it is."

He looked wounded. "You cut me to the quick. How could you even *think* such a thing, much less say it?"

"I knew it." Her tone was triumphant. "You would do well to confess, as I will not give you another moment of peace until you do."

He threw up his hands in surrender. "I cede to such a threat. It is to be an orphanage. A haven for abandoned children such as Gentleman Joe and Mickey Lightfingers must have been."

"Who could be responsible for such a generous deed?"

"Lord and Lady Northwycke, I believe."

She leaned over to Tarquin and squeezed James's hand. "There is so much in your character that is worthy of love and admiration."

James was touched to see that both feelings were reflected in her eyes and did not fade for the whole time he showed her around the house. She admired the newly furbished kitchen with its huge fireplace outfitted with a black-leaded oven and hob.

When the sight of narrow cots arranged in neat rows in the

dormitories brought tears to her eyes, he marveled at her tender sensibilities. At the next door, he put his arm around her waist and warned her not to lose her composure before ushering her into the room.

To his consternation, she burst into tears at the sight of four tiny cribs. "Oh, James, it breaks my heart to think of poor innocent babes in such a place. We must do our best to see that they are treated with every possible kindness."

Before he could reply, an ominous clap of thunder warned them it was time to return to Northwycke Hall with all speed. They urged their mounts to a fast gallop, and by the time they handed over the reins to a groom, the first heavy drops of rain began to fall.

A couple of weeks later, James and Emily happened to be looking through the library window and saw an unexpected visitor approaching Northwycke Hall who was not quite so lucky. Even as they watched, a sudden squall unleashed its fury on the hapless rider and his mount.

It was Miles.

What could he want? James thought. Surely not a social visit. The weather was far too sultry to be abroad. Hoping Miles had not got himself enmired in any trouble, he waited with Emily in the reception hall to greet him.

"Miles," said James, vigorously pumping his brother-in-law's hand. "Good to see you, old man. Get into some dry clothes and we shall have a turn with the cards. I have managed to procure some particularly fine cognac I would like you to sample."

Miles looked sheepish. "I have not played cards of late," he owned.

"There is nothing wrong with a game of cards if a man knows what he is about. Come, I can show you a few refinements on several games."

"I should like that," Miles replied. "I must admit that my social life has been a little crimped of late."

When Miles was ushered away to his room, Emily shook her head in disapproval. "Let my brother alone. You really must be starved for entertainment, my lord, for you to lead him down that treacherous road."

He gave her shoulder a reassuring pat. "Miles cannot run away from the world. He has to learn to face it on his own terms, and to that end he has to be armed with all the knowledge possible. Besides, I rather like Miles. He is a very pleasant chap once you get to know him. I highly recommend you do so."

"Recommend what, darling?"

"That you get to know Miles. You really do not know your own brother at all."

Emily did not reply. Her relationship with her brother was a touchy subject.

Later, when Miles and James retired to the library and their first glass of cognac had been consumed, James pointed out the finer points of the game of escarte to Miles. But James could not help but notice that his brother-in-law was ill at ease and was not paying close attention to the cards.

Miles opened his mouth several times as if to say something, only to snap it shut once more. James decided to take matters into his own hands. He put down his cards and pinned the younger man with a penetrating gaze. "It is plain as a pikestaff that something is bothering you, Miles, old chap. Suppose you tell me what it is."

Miles also put down his cards, seemingly relieved to confront whatever was bothering him. "I really do not know how to begin, or if I really should, for that matter. This is a rather delicate subject."

James gave him a reassuring smile. "Come now, Miles. I consider you to be a member of my family, and in case you have not noticed, not too much is considered sacred around here. Especially as far as my mother is concerned."

"Er—yes. Remarkable woman, Lady Geraldine."

"Out with it, Miles. You did not come all the way to Northwycke to play cards. You are a little short of funds, perhaps?"

"Oh, no," he replied hastily. "Nothing of the sort. I would not dream of such a thing." He ran his finger around the inside of his cravat. "This is about Emily."

James's jaw tightened. "Explain yourself."

"There is an ugly rumor spreading all over London that you married my sister because you compromised her. It is said that you did not finish out the season in London because she is with child and was beginning to show. I would have called someone out for it, but dash it all, James, I would not know where to begin—tongues are wagging in every club and drawing room in London."

James was incensed. As far as he was concerned, the identities of the rumor-mongers were not too difficult to deduce. Out loud he said, "Do not fret over it, Miles. That is my prerogative, and damn it, when I get to the bottom of this you may be sure someone will pay for besmirching my wife's honor."

He slammed the table with his fist, causing his cognac glass to crash to the floor, where it shattered into myriad pieces. He rose from the table, threw up his hands in frustration, and began to pace the floor.

"Damned, chattering fools. Always hungry to hear the latest *on dit* without the slightest regard for the truth. Damn, how I despise them!"

"I suggest you get Emily to London as soon as possible. There is to be a Grand Masque in Vauxhall, next week. An affair of great *eclat*. Everyone will be there, and you should be, too. A good opportunity to prove that if anything, my sister has lost, rather than gained, weight."

James stopped pacing. "I hate to dignify this whole affair with a response, but you are quite right, of course. If this thing is not nipped in the bud there will be tales of a hidden baby being whispered behind fans and haunting Emily everywhere she goes for the rest of her life."

He punched his fist into his other hand. "I vow I despise the lot of them!"

"Do not waste your time on it, James. Just find out who is at the bottom of this, demand a retraction, and then dispatch the swine to the devil. You know what they say about revenge."

James smiled. "Rest assured, Miles, I am looking forward to a *very* sweet time."

Thirteen

"But what could I possibly find to wear to the Grand Masque on such short notice?" Emily wailed.

"Anything you choose, darling, as long as it leaves nothing to the imagination."

"*What?* Really, James, surely you jest?"

"That is not exactly what I meant to say. Just choose something that enhances your, er … person."

"I think I know what milor' means," Madame Dupres interjected. "I have the very thing."

With an imperious clap of her hands she summoned one of her long-suffering assistants. A thin, tired-looking young woman answered the call.

"Nancy, *vitement*. The Roman gown for her ladyship, *s'il vous plait.*"

The woman returned with a stream of ivory silk flowing over her arms.

"A trifle voluminous, is it not?" James asked.

"*Mais non.*" Madame Dupres replied, busily dropping the gown over Emily's head. "You see, milor', when it is caught up about milady's divine figure by these golden cords—*voila*. We have the beautiful Goddess, *oui?*"

"Absolutely, Madame Dupres. Venus walks among us."

"I thought you would agree. Gold ribands for her hair, and a jeweled mask to drive mere mortals mad just to get a glimpse of her beautiful face, and you have the most beautiful goddess."

James looked awestruck. "I must agree. A vision straight from Mount Olympus come to grace us mere mortals with her presence."

"For goodness' sake, my lord, try to exercise a little

restraint," Emily protested. "People will think you have gone quite mad."

"And they would be absolutely right. Mad for you, my love."

Emily suffered a little pang. Why did her husband's protestations of love always seem too extravagant to carry any substance?

"Ah! It is so sweet to see the husband adore the wife so," gushed Madame Dupres, wiping an imaginary tear from her eye.

Emily shot her a look. Matters were getting entirely out of hand. "Very well, Madame Dupres. Mark the necessary alterations. I shall be back in the morning for a final fitting." Her manner was deliberately cool.

"*Oui*, my lady," Madame Dupres replied, thoroughly chastened.

As Emily was leaving Madame Dupres's establishment the following morning, she encountered Althea Cross outside. She accorded the countess a brief nod of the head and was about to get into her carriage when the woman put a detaining hand on her shoulder.

Surprised, Emily turned to face her. "You wished to speak to me, madam?"

The other woman smiled, but her expression was far from cordial. Emily wondered how she managed to pull off such a feat. It had to be a unique talent.

"I just wished to bid you good morning," Althea cooed.

Her voice dripped honey, but her eyes were filled with malice. Determined not to be bested by the creature, Emily girded herself for whatever mischief most assuredly would follow.

"How nice to see you in Town once more, Lady Northwycke. I wondered how long it would be before James would tire of the country life."

Knowing full well the woman was implying it was *she* whom James found boring, not the countryside, Emily was sorely tempted to slap the rouge right off her face. Instead, her voice crackling with frost, she replied, "*Lord* Northwycke prefers the country life. He has come to London for my benefit, thinking I might like to attend the Grand Masque at Vauxhall Gardens this week."

She regretted the statement as soon as she had made it. Why am I explaining anything to this dreadful woman? she thought.

"Really?" Althea's tone was skeptical. "The marquess is known to have a large appetite for life. An insatiable craving for variety, one might say. Nothing has been known to hold his interest for very long." She gave Emily's body an assessing sweep. "Nothing."

Emily drew herself up and stared coldly at the shorter woman. "You overstep yourself, madam. My husband is no concern of yours, and I would thank you to remember that."

Althea's lip curled into a sneer. "And *you*, Lady Northwycke, be aware that he can be had by the snap of a finger." She stressed the point by snapping her own fingers.

Emily straightened her spine with all the dignity she could muster and stared the shorter woman down. "You and I have nothing more to discuss," she said.

Once ensconced in her carriage, her facade crumbled. The haughty lady became the heartbroken wife. "She is a liar and a whore," she muttered, gritting her teeth. "If James still wanted her, I would know." She repeated the phrase, "I would know," over and over until the words lost all meaning.

On her return to Mayfair Court, James greeted her with such genuine affection, her doubts receded. She determined that Althea Cross was a jealous, vindictive woman—one who could not accept the fact that she had been rejected by a lover.

Nevertheless, doubting that her husband's regard for her was little more than affection and not the all-consuming passion she had dreamed of all her life, the seeds of mistrust had been sown.

On the evening of the masquerade, Emily walked through Vauxhall Gardens between James and Miles. The enchantment of the place had been somewhat dimmed by her encounter with Althea Cross the previous morning. Wishing to put the incident behind her, she approached each new wonder with determined enthusiasm. Colored lamps twinkled among the graceful elms and lofty poplars, lending an air of magic to the shadowy alcoves and grottoes so convenient for lovers' trysts.

James and Miles were dressed like Roman senators to match the classical theme of Emily's gown. "I declare," she said with false gaiety. "Our costumes are apropos for such a setting."

A girlish giggle came from out of the shadows. James raised a brow. "That is not entirely a good thing. I expect to see a satyr come charging out of the shrubbery in full pursuit of a naughty little bacchante any moment now."

"That is a horrid thing to say. You will make me sorry I chose this dress."

Before the conversation could be continued further, several among their acquaintances stopped to greet the trio. Even as they addressed Emily, some cast sly glances toward her abdomen. A rising anger flooded her being. She could feel her face flush with the heat of it. To think that members of the *ton* could be so rude was beyond belief.

"How charming to see you, Lady Northwycke," said Lady Fotheringham, giving Emily a sweeping glance with a quizzing glass. "Such a rare pleasure," she cooed, her gaze riveted on Emily's middle.

Lord Fotheringham frowned and poked his wife in the elbow, while contributing a "Quite," followed by a "Harrumph!" to the conversation.

Ignoring her husband, Lady Fotheringham turned to James and gave him a playful tap with her mask, a beribboned confection covered with feathers. "It is very selfish of you to keep your lovely wife buried in the country."

"It is her choice, madam. She finds the London season a very tedious affair. As do I."

"Really? How very odd," said the baroness with a sniff. Even so, before she took her leave, she accorded Emily one more sweep with her quizzing glass.

Emily raised her brow and returned the stare, letting her gaze stop for a moment at the older woman's thickening waistline. She held in her own stomach until she thought she would burst.

With an ill-concealed smile the baron gave a slight bow and

walked away. Lady Fotheringham responded with a glare and hastily followed him into the crowd.

"Poor devil. He has to be pitied, married to such an obvious creature," James said, shaking his head. "Well done, Emily dear. You really trimmed her sails."

"Oh dear," said Emily. "I do not know what came over me. I have had to withstand that sort of rudeness all evening. I just could not endure it a moment longer."

"I am not surprised," said James. "Their behavior is probably the result of imbibing too much wine. We have put in our appearance and have been observed by some of the biggest gossips in society. We may leave now, if that is your wish."

Her face fell. "Please let us stay a little longer. We have yet to see the fireworks."

"We shall stay as long as you like, my dear. Come. The roar you hear farther along this path is the Great Cascade. It is quite a spectacle."

"I should like to try some of the arrack punch I have heard so much about."

"Would you now?" James exchanged a smile with Miles.

Miles raised a brow. "Pretty heady stuff for a young lady scarcely out of the schoolroom. Are you sure you are up to it, sister dear?"

"You are both extremely odious, and not fit company for a lady."

James bowed. "We stand corrected. Stay here with Miles, and I shall get us some punch forthwith."

As she waited with her brother, she noticed several couples steal into the shadows of the alcoves. The sounds of coos and giggles emanating from these trysting places formed a background noise to the general festivities.

It seemed to her the arrack punch robbed the revelers of all good judgment, and with masks shielding their identities, far too many of them exhibited appalling behavior.

For Emily, the magic had been stripped away from Vauxhall Gardens. Something ugly and sordid had been revealed, and she no longer wanted to be party to it. The punch had lost all appeal, and even the fireworks display did not sound so tempting.

She stepped aside to avoid colliding with a couple who reeled in her direction, both laughing too loudly, the man taking unbelievable liberties with his partner's physical charms.

"Those doxies should not be allowed in here. Offending the sensibilities of the ladies," said an old gentleman to a female companion as they passed by. Emily observed that as soon as his partner stepped ahead, he turned for one more peek at the gaudily decked courtesan.

She turned to Miles to pass a remark on the incident, and to her dismay she found he was no longer by her side. She felt a moment of rising panic, which faded when she caught sight of him just before a curve in the pathway, conversing with a group of young men.

Fearful of being alone in such a place, she hurried to join him, fully intending to give him a thorough scolding for his lapse. She was diverted from this end by a cowled form that suddenly emerged from the shrubbery and then withdrew into the shadows once more.

A low, feminine voice called out, "Miss Emily, over here, I beseech you."

She had not been called Miss Emily since before her marriage. Suddenly some fireworks illuminated the sky and she caught a glimpse of red hair beneath the cowl.

"Bessy? Is that really you?"

Bessie put a finger to her lips, then withdrew into the bushes. She beckoned Emily to follow.

Emily complied, then said, "Are you all right, Bessie? I have thought about you often, wondering how you were."

A barrage of fireworks rent the air like gunfire.

"Wondering if I was dead in a ditch, don't you mean, Miss Emily?" Bessy said as soon as the noise died down. The irony in her tone was not lost on Emily.

"Yes, that thought has crossed my mind, Bessy, but you do not have to be dead to merit my concern. Why, oh why did you run away? It was such a foolhardy thing to do."

She caught hold of a fold of the other woman's cloak. The

rich satin material slipped through her fingers, giving Emily her answer.

"Begging your pardon, your ladyship, but were you not doing the same?"

"But to run off with a complete stranger."

"And Lord Northwycke was not?"

"Stop this impertinence, Bessy. It is not the same and you know it."

"No, it is not," Bessy conceded. "It was the dressing up and being treated like Quality that was my undoing. Then the gent went and promised me his protection, with a pretty house and servants of my own. I couldn't go back to being a lady's maid. I just couldn't, that's all."

"Lord Ruysdale is kind to you?"

"When it pleases him."

"What do you mean?"

"His Lordship is seldom pleased."

Bessy pulled back her cowl. Even in the dim light Emily could see her jaw was bruised and swollen.

"The monster!"

"He's not that bad. At least not all the time. This bashing will most likely earn me a lovely new gown. In any case, I'd better say my piece and get back before he finds me here, else he'll be taking a riding crop to my backside."

"Say your piece?"

"Yes. You must clear out of here as quickly as possible. He is planning to abduct you."

"But why?"

"To keep the favor of that countess who wants to see you ruined."

"But that is not reason enough to bring ruin on himself. The lady is fast losing her looks. You are much prettier."

"In the dark, my lady, looks don't matter. It is noised in all the brothels that she spent a season in the harem of that Persian gent Prinney is so fond of. Those doxies would part with their teeth to learn all the tricks she keeps up her petticoat."

"Bessy! For shame!"

153

Bessy shrugged. "Merely explaining the situation. Meanwhile, every minute you tarry here puts you in danger."

Emily covered her mouth with her fingertips for a brief moment. "Do they intend to do me physical harm?"

"No. But under the circumstances I think a lady like you would prefer that. They have hired this whore from one of those fancy brothels to wear your costume. By the time she's finished cavorting all over Vauxhall, no decent person will be seen in your company."

"A preposterous plan."

"But it could work. Even your own husband might be convinced of your guilt. Then where would you be?"

"But—"

"I have to go."

Before she could question her further, Bessy turned tail and disappeared into the trees. Emily found it hard to believe such an unlikely tale, but nevertheless a frisson of fear danced in her stomach at the thought of leaving the sheltering bushes.

She remained where she was and peered through the foliage until she saw James come into view. With a cry of relief she rushed to his side and clung to him. The glasses of arrack punch he carried dashed to the ground.

"What on earth has been going on during my absence?" he said, his voice displaying a high level of irritation. "Miles is nowhere in sight, and you come charging out of the bushes like a bedlamite." He cupped her chin and in a much gentler tone added, "You look as if you have seen a ghost."

"In a manner of speaking, I have."

She went on to describe her encounter with Bessy. "But that story is preposterous."

"My words exactly. But it must have taken all the courage Bessy has for her to come here tonight." Her voice broke. "James, the man beats her. You should have seen the bruise on her poor face."

"Perhaps that was at the bottom of all this. She could be seeking revenge against Alfred Fishberry and wants me to call him out."

"I hardly think so. I truly believe that Bessy harbors a genuine regard for me."

"Either way, we are leaving immediately. Never should have come here in the first place." His jaw jutted. "Dammit, Miles can find his own way home."

They left Vauxhall Gardens as the fireworks display lit up the night sky. Very few of the revelers seemed to notice the departure of the Roman goddess and her toga-clad escort.

Once in the haven of Northwycke House, Emily told him of her encounter with Althea Cross.

James swore under his breath. Out loud he said, "I fear the lady has come quite unhinged. This is not the behavior of a rational being."

"Then what she told me is all a hum?"

The look on her face was begging it to be so. One part of him wanted to hold her close and shower her with words of reassurance. Another part felt hurt at the lack of trust in him she displayed. The latter prevailed.

"How can you ask such a thing? I have not seen Althea Cross since the Fotheringhams' ball. Besides, she does not begin to compare with you. She is nothing but a wanton, there for any man to take."

Emily sighed. "According to Bessy, she is the envy of every harlot in the brothels."

"I beg your pardon?" James could not believe that such words could pass from Emily's lips. More to the point, he was outraged that Bessy had spoken thus to her.

"Tell me, James, is it true that she learned how to make love in a Persian harem and has secrets the women in the brothels would sell their souls for?"

James raised a brow. "Their souls?"

Emily gestured. "Their souls, or their teeth. I forget which Bessy mentioned. Which do you think it would be?"

James grinned. "Their souls, I should imagine. I doubt the gaudy little bawds would part with their teeth. Not good for business."

"Oh. Then it is true."

"What is, pray?"

"Do not be so obtuse, James. You know perfectly well what I mean."

"Let me see. The question is, does the Countess of Brookhaven have superior skills in the boudoir that ladies of the demimonde would sell their souls for?" He made a great pretense of considering the question and only answered when he saw a vase in her hand, lofted for the throwing.

"I would have to say no," he replied hastily. He saw by the expression on her face that the answer was insufficient, so he added, "Physical skills are merely exercises. Without genuine affection it is not lovemaking but merely a lewd travesty of the same."

She put down the vase. "And what is it that we do?"

He took her in his arms and kissed her. "Something wonderful," he whispered, and neither one realized he had declared his love for her.

In his bed later that night he held her close but, for once, refrained from delighting himself on her lovely body. His mind dwelt too much on his enemies, Althea Cross and Albert Fishberry, and the problem of how to deal with them.

Fourteen

The next morning James and Emily were enjoying a breakfast of eggs, gammon, and sausages, along with fish, both smoked and fresh. Beef kidneys were braising in a chafing dish next to a platter of melt-in-the-mouth scones.

James was buttering his second scone when the butler informed him Miles had arrived. A few moments later, a very subdued Miles was ushered into the room.

His reaction to being invited to share their breakfast was a mixture of effusiveness and bootlicking gratitude. James regarded him with disapproval, deeming him to be lacking in dignity. Nothing I have taught Miles about gentlemanly conduct seems to have sunk in, he thought.

Then he realized that the younger man was overcompensating for his lapse from grace the previous evening. As if to confirm this theory, Miles apologized throughout the entire meal for not taking better care of his sister the previous evening.

"I am truly sorry, Emily. I caught sight of some chaps who were up at Cambridge the same time I was and went over to speak to them. I thought you had followed me. When I turned around to present them, you were nowhere to be seen."

He ran a finger along the edge of his cravat and glanced down at the table. "I hope you can find it in your heart to forgive me, dear sister."

"Emily might forgive you, young man, but I most certainly will not." James's voice was curt. "As it happens, she was put at considerable risk last evening. There was a plot afoot to ruin her reputation, and I am positive that, had it been carried through, she might also have suffered harm to her person."

Miles groaned. "If such is the case, I neither seek or deserve your forgiveness. Pray tell me what transpired."

When James told him what had happened, Miles pounded his fist on the table. "This cannot go on. Either you call out Fishberry, or I shall."

"Calm yourself, Miles," Emily said. "Neither you or James must pursue such a course."

It was James's turn to pound his fist. "If you think I am going to stand by and let Fishberry do as he pleases with my family…"

"Please, James. If the dreadful creature even so much as suspects Bessy thwarted his plans, he most assuredly will beat her to death."

"I say," Miles remonstrated. "That is a bit thick. Even a bounder like Fishberry would not cross that line."

"In this you are mistaken. I am afraid Bessy is no stranger to the sting of his riding crop upon her… er, person."

"How despicable," Miles replied. "Bessy was such a jolly little girl." He turned to James. "She could climb a tree as well as any boy and, I might add, was a lot more fun to play with than Emily."

James grinned. "Evidently one naughty little boy still thinks so."

"James!"

"I am sorry, darling. I forgot myself."

"Why does she stay with him, I wonder?" Miles asked.

Emily shrugged. "For the same reason married women stay with abusive husbands—security. Having a rich and powerful man as a protector is the equivalent of a brilliant marriage to girls of Bessy's class."

"But to suffer such abuse."

"She considers a house with servants and a wardrobe of beautiful clothes to be well worth the price of a few beatings."

"How do you know so much, young lady?" James asked.

"By listening to Bessy last evening."

He shook his head. "I married a complete innocent, and in no time at all you have become an expert on the human condition. I have not done a very good job of protecting you from the seamy side of life, have I?"

"I do not wish for that kind of protection. How can I be of use in this world if I am kept in ignorance?"

"Do I not have the most marvelous of wives?"

"I am in awe," Miles replied. "And to think I had the temerity to try to tell her what to do."

"She certainly whipped my household into shape when I was away in London supervising things on the *Ocean Queen.*"

"Really? Tell me about it."

James lost no time in the telling.

"Oh, my," said Miles. "You are a most formidable creature, Emily. You suggested finding husbands for the chambermaids and were instrumental in sending Clarence the Cad off to Australia. All the ends neatly tied up, one might say."

"Except a home for baby William. There were plenty of people wanting him. Attracted to the extra money they would get, but none of them suited Emily."

"Never a dull moment at Northwycke Hall."

"If you think *that* is exciting, you should hear of James's adventures in London."

Miles raised a brow. "There is more? Things happen to you two at a dizzying pace."

Miles was thoroughly enrapt at the story, giving little gasps of surprise as it unfolded, but when James got to the part about Gentleman Joe and Mickey Lightfingers, Miles really got caught up in the excitement.

When James came to the conclusion, Miles was quiet for a moment, then said, "There are times I have felt very sorry for myself, but when one considers that two small boys suffered such a fate at the hands of thieves..."

Emily shuddered. "I wonder how many people who are hanged at Newgate could tell a similar story? Life can be cruel." She patted James on the arm. "That is why I am so proud of James. He has started an orphanage for children such as these."

Miles gave his host an admiring look. "How good of you, James, and how unpretentious. You did not say a word about any of this. How long did you intend to keep such a secret?"

"You make too much of it, Miles. Such a trifle scarcely elevates me to sainthood. I suggest we change the subject."

Miles obliged him. "What do you hear from Bath? Are you expecting Lady Geraldine and Maude back any time in the near future?" His voice lingered on Maude's name like a caress.

James picked up on this. "We have no idea," he replied stiffly. "Nothing has been said." He turned to Emily. "I think we should plan on returning to Northwycke in a couple of days. There is nothing more for us to do here, unless you wish to accept some of these invitations we have received."

"I would rather go home," she replied.

Somewhere in the house a clock struck eleven.

"My goodness," Miles said. "It is time I was going. Promised I would go on a picnic in Richmond with a few people."

Once he had taken his leave, Emily turned to James. "Miles has no picnic to attend, he just could not leave this house fast enough. Why were you so curt? You were scarcely civil to him when he inquired after Maude and your mother."

"In this I can scarcely be blamed. May I be so bold as to ask when he fell in love with my sister?"

"The moment he met her, I suspect."

"*What?*" he roared.

"Please do not bellow. You sound like that bull you keep in the far meadow."

"What do you expect to gain by fostering his foolishness?"

"Fostering? How dare you suggest I would do such a thing? I warned him of the hopelessness of his suit."

James clenched his fists. "His suit? By Jove, if that young fool has had the temerity…"

"The temerity?" Emily gasped. "La, but you Garwoods put yourselves right up there on the right hand of God. The blame does not rest entirely with Miles. Maude moons after him like a lovesick calf. She hangs on to his every word as if they were veritable pearls of wisdom."

"By Jove, this nonsense must end here and now."

"Never fear. Your precious sister is safe from my pariah of a brother," Emily said between clenched teeth. "Your mother did not say so, but I am sure that is the reason for her visit to Bath."

"Play fair, Emily," James replied, his voice lowered to a more reasonable tone. "You know I hold Miles in great regard, but I have to do what is best for Maude."

It hurt to see her brother deemed unworthy of a Garwood bride, but logic told her James had no choice in the matter. "You are right, of course," she said. "But I do feel for Miles. In any case, there is no great cause for worry. I am sure your mother will keep Maude well away from here until she is safely betrothed to another." The last sentence was etched in acid. To her surprise, James did not pick up on her tone.

"Of course," he replied, his voice considerably brighter. "My mother can be very resourceful when it suits her fancy."

He bestowed a husbandly peck on her cheek and departed the morning room whistling a cheerful tune, leaving Emily to seethe over the slight dealt her family.

Within the hour he was riding astride his beloved Tarquin, headed in the direction of the London docks. He was accompanied by a particularly burly groom called George, who was adept at fighting with his fists or a pistol.

He had received word from the efficient Mr. Hensley that his ship the *English Lady* was laded with goods bound for India and ready to set sail on the evening tide. It was his habit to give any of his departing ships a final inspection and to share a farewell libation with the captain and crew before wishing them Godspeed.

When they arrived at the *English Lady*'s berth, a small, wiry man with bandy legs came forward and raised his cap as a greeting. "Afternoon. You've come to see your ship off, I see."

It was Mickey Dempsey, the pickpocket.

"Good afternoon, Mr. Dempsey. I see you have managed to avoid going to Newgate. That must be a relief to your wife and children."

"Ain't married. Wouldn't raise kiddies in this cesspool if my life depended on it."

"Really, Mr. Dempsey. You never cease to amaze me."

"Call me Mickey. No one around 'ere calls me Mr. Dempsey."

James grinned. "I believe we have touched on this subject before. If you will oblige me by calling me sir, I think I shall manage to call you Mickey."

For the life of him, he could not understand why he allowed the gap-toothed cockney to take such liberties. Perhaps it was because he had been sold to a pack of thieves as a helpless child, or because he was as chirpy and as cheeky as a London sparrow. In any case, apart from his appalling lack of hygiene, James had to admit that he found the man to be most engaging.

"Word is that you are searching out kiddies in these parts to give 'em shelter. Poor little devils 'ave no one else to look out for them. But I can't 'elp wondering if it's wise of you."

James's eyebrows shot up. "In what way? Kindly explain."

"I mean no disrespect, but what's to become of them when you turn 'em out to face the world? They won't last an afternoon in a place like this."

"You really care about this," said James.

"Yes, sir. I know only too well what they will be up against."

James nodded. "Most commendable of you, Mickey. Let me reassure you, once they are settled in and nourished with good farm food, they will receive educations according to their abilities."

"According to their abilities?"

"When they are old enough, some will be apprenticed to respectable trades. Those who show aptitude will be further educated for loftier endeavors."

"I see." He looked doubtful.

"Do not be troubled. If any return to Limehouse, it will be of their own choosing."

Mickey grinned. "Then I expect quite a few of 'em will be back. Fools will choose damnation over salvation every chance they get."

Really, James thought, Michael Dempsey is full of surprises. "You are quite the philosopher."

"Got that from Joe. He taught me to think for myself."

"How is his family faring since his demise?"

"His wife and daughter 'ave gone to work for one of those fancy dressmakers in your part of London. 'Arriet sews well and Lucy is learning. It's 'ard work, but they're allowed to sleep in the attic over the shop."

"I see."

"Lucy's a good girl, and her mum thought she would have a better chance of staying that way if she got her away from this hellhole."

"No doubt." He hesitated for a moment and then took out a small leather case and removed a card. "This is the address of my man of affairs. If they ever need help, please let me know through him."

It occurred to James that it was doubtful he could read. He was about to give him verbal instructions when Mickey spelled out "Number twenty-four Church Street, St. Martin's-in-the-Fields." The words passed his lips laboriously, but once uttered, his expression was one of triumph.

"It's kind of you, sir, but 'Arriet's far too proud to take charity."

James surmised reading was one of the skills Gentleman Joe had taught Mickey when they were both children. The human spirit is an amazing thing, he mused.

"Take it anyway. One never knows."

"If you say so, sir." Mickey put it in his pocket.

James dismounted, and George quickly followed suit.

Mickey held out his hand. "I'll watch the 'orses for you, sir."

George had been silent up to this point, a look of disbelief on his face while James passed the time of day with the cockney. "Begging your pardon, my lord, but it's to be hoped you won't be putting the horses in his hands. Wouldn't trust him as far as I could throw him."

Mickey looked wounded. "I owe 'is lordship my life. I would not demean myself by stealing 'is bloody 'orses."

"Tarquin is quite spirited. Think you can handle him?"

Mickey's face lit up like a firework display. "Yes, sir. Used to 'elp Joe take care of 'is 'orse, when 'e was 'ighwayman and rag-and-bone man, both."

"He was able to pay you?"

"Nah. I just liked being around old Daisy. Nice little mare, she was. Not much to look at, but the old girl would break 'er back for you."

"I am quite capable of seeing to the horses," George interjected.

"So you are," James replied. "But I thought you might like to come aboard and toast the ship on its way."

George visibly brightened. "As you wish, my lord."

"What's the other 'orse called? Can't rightly see to 'im if I don't know 'is bloody name."

"It's Sampson," James replied.

"Sampson?"

James nodded. "If you notice, he has an unusually long mane."

"Fine name for a fine-looking 'orse. Gelding, ain't 'e?"

"I believe so."

"Not so frisky that way."

He took the reins of both horses, one in each hand. "Come on my lovelies," he crooned. "Old Mickey would give you some nice oats if 'e 'ad some."

Both horses nickered softly and nuzzled him.

James was bemused. "Where on earth did you learn how to handle horses?"

"My dad was a tenant farmer before 'e was turned off. Brought us to London 'oping for a better life. What a joke that was." Mickey gave him a look that was both pleading and defiant. "Do you think my dad wanted to sell me? There was a new baby on the way, and I was the oldest."

James was touched by his defense of his father. He wished his own father had inspired such a love in him. The devil take me, he thought; surely I do not envy this unfortunate little man?

"Quite." It was time for a change of subject. "Both horses seem to have developed a liking for you. Call out if you run into any trouble. George will be here in a trice."

As it turned out, Mickey did not call for help, and when James and the groom came down the gang-plank almost an hour later, it seemed both horses were still lavishing him with affection.

"Ain't natural," George muttered.

"Nonsense," James replied. "It is the way you talk to them, is it not, Mickey?"

"You have the right of it, sir. You can get far more out of 'em with talk than you'll ever get with a whip."

"As I said, you never cease to amaze me. If you ever decide you want to give up picking pockets in favor of looking after horses, please feel free to apply at Northwycke Hall."

Mickey beamed. "Much obliged, but I doubt I'll leave 'ere. Too used to it. By the way, I'm surprised you 'aven't seen fit to 'ire some extra men to guard your cargo. You might not have seen the last of Fishberry's carryings-on."

"So it was the younger Fishberry behind the last fracas? I had thought the old gentleman to be the culprit, but something happened last night which rather points to the grandson. All the same, I am glad to have my suspicions confirmed."

"The old codger was too interested in the wenches to bother with such plottings."

"You may be sure that in future I shall pay more attention to such things." He handed him some coins. "I appreciate the loving care you showed the horses."

Mickey shook his head. "I did not do it for the money. Besides, I owe you my life."

"It will make me feel better if you take it," James said, thrusting the coins once more into his hands. "This way, I will be more inclined to avail myself of your services if the need should arise."

Mickey took the money. "If you put it that way, sir, I am much obliged. I wouldn't want to miss out on tending to such fine 'orses as Sampson and Tarquin 'ere."

James mounted Tarquin and waited for George to mount Sampson; then, with a salute in Mickey's direction, he headed back to Mayfair followed by George, muttering under his breath about the daft antics of the aristocracy.

For most of the journey James's mind dwelt on his two

enemies. However he addressed the problem, he could come to only one conclusion: protecting his wife was his first priority. Bessy Sykes would have to take her chances, for tomorrow he would call on Albert Fishberry and demand satisfaction.

Fifteen

It was a scant half-hour after James had departed for his visit to the *English Lady* that the butler knocked on Emily's bedroom door and informed her that a young person had called, craving an audience with her.

"One could in no way call her a lady, madam, but she was suitably attired and comported herself with decorum. I assumed her to be the daughter of one of those cits who seem to have wormed their way into polite society." He gave a disapproving sniff. "Marie my words, no good can come of condescending to such people."

Emily turned her head to smile. Servants could be bigger snobs than the haughtiest of aristocrats.

"Did she give you her name?"

"Oh, dear," he said. "I was so put out at such a personage darkening our doorstep, I quite forgot to ask."

"Kindly inform the young lady that I shall see her presently."

Emily quickly examined herself in the pier glass that stood over by the window and, deeming herself suitable for presentation, made her way down the curving staircase.

A heavily veiled young woman was standing in the shadow of a Chinese screen in a small anteroom reserved to receive lesser personages. It was not until the woman cried out, "Miss Emily," that she recognized Bessy.

"Bessy, are you all right?" she asked, moving toward her.

"Miss Emily," she uttered once more, her voice filled with anguish, then crumpled to the floor.

Emily darted forward. Bessy's bonnet had fallen from her head. In the position she lay in, only the side of her face could be seen, but what little was exposed made Emily gasp in dismay.

She pulled the bell rope, then ran out into the reception hall and called for help.

A startled footman, followed by the butler, answered her call. "I knew nothing good could come of such goings-on," the latter muttered, panting with exertion from his long run the length of the hall.

The footman went to assist Bessy. He was about to turn her over to a more comfortable position when Emily stayed his hand. "Exercise care," she urged.

The butler peered at Bessy. "My heavens. How did she ever get here? She looks as if she's dying."

"Oh!" Emily put a hand to her mouth in dismay. "Do not move her until you find a cot to carry her, then bring her up to my room. She shall stay in my bed for the present."

The two servants stared at her, frozen where they stood.

"For goodness' sake," she snapped. "Move yourselves!" She pointed to the footman. "*You*, find a cot and someone to help you carry it. *You*, sir," she gestured to the butler, "kindly send someone to summon a doctor, and for heaven's sake, *hurry.*" Both men scurried about their appointed tasks without so much as a bow to their mistress. At that precise moment there was a knocking at the front door.

Oh no, Emily thought, perhaps if no one answers, whoever it is will go away. She signaled the only footman left in attendance not to respond. To her dismay the doorknob turned and a man let himself in.

It was Miles.

Really, she thought, his timing could not be worse. "What do you want, Miles? This is most inconvenient."

"Good Lord, Emily, I just came back to tell you I ran into your friend Cecily Tyndall last evening." He glanced around the hall. "What is going on here? I could hear you all the way to the street, barking out orders to the poor servants like a sergeant major."

She brushed her forehead with the back of her hand. "I am sorry, Miles, I did not mean to be rude. Come, I will show you what has transpired."

Miles turned white at the sight of Bessy's battered face. "My God! Is that Bessy?"

Emily nodded.

"I thought it might be. The red hair, you know. Her face is so swollen it is hard to tell. You must get her off the floor for a start."

"That is what all the commotion was about. I was dispatching the footman to get a cot in order to move her, and charging the butler to send for a doctor." She tapped her foot. "Some men are absolutely no good at all in a crisis."

"I think it would be better were I to carry her to a bed. They are liable to drop her trying negotiate a cot up those stairs."

Emily nodded. "The sooner she is moved the better, I suppose."

Miles cradled Bessy in his arms and straightened up. She let out a groan.

"Careful, Miles, you are hurting her," Emily called out.

"Do not fret, Emily. The poor girl is unconscious and incapable of feeling pain, thank heavens."

Susan was in the bedroom, busily inspecting her mistress's clothes to see if any were in need of repair. She gasped when Emily entered, followed by Miles carrying his burden, and a lacy camisole slipped through her fingers.

"Merciful heavens!" she exclaimed, then dashed forward and pulled back the bedcovers. Miles laid Bessy down on the bed.

"Thank you, Miles. Susan and I will take care of her."

He lost no time in leaving the room.

The two women removed Bessy's clothes, taking care to be gentle in the undertaking. They both caught their breath when they saw the welts on Bessy's body, most of which were on her abdomen.

"Lord-a-mercy," Susan muttered, "may the swine who did this rot in hell."

"No punishment could be too severe for such a creature."

"Most likely her own husband," Susan replied, supporting Bessy under her arms while Emily drew one of her own soft nightrails over her head. "You would be shocked to know which gentlemen of the *ton* beat their wives."

"She has no husband. This is Bessy, my former abigail. It is more than likely that her protector did this to her." She gently pulled the covers over her.

Susan looked affronted. "And you put this little trollop in your own bed? Pardon me for saying so, my lady, you are too good by half. The gutter is where she belongs."

"That will do, Susan," Emily replied. "Kindly remember your place."

"I beg your pardon, my lady," she replied.

Emily nodded. She was about to explain the childhood she had shared with Bessy when Susan exclaimed, "Look! She has opened her eyes."

Emily took Bessy's hand. Bessy recoiled. Her hand was swollen and covered with welts—injuries evidently received when attempting to fend off her attacker.

"Pour some water for her," Emily ordered. "Perhaps it will help."

Susan complied and, evidently atoning for her prior remarks, raised Bessy's head and administered the drink herself. Bessy took a sip, then slumped back on the pillow.

"I hurt really bad, Miss Emily," she moaned.

"Where, Bessy?"

She put her hand on her stomach, let out a shriek, and doubled over in pain.

"What is taking the doctor so long?" Emily asked. A rhetorical question, which no sooner was uttered when there was a knock on the door and the doctor, a portly gentleman with grizzled side whiskers, was ushered in.

"Doctor Henry Ames at your service, my lady. I understand there is a young woman in need of attention."

"Yes. Bessy Sykes, a former servant of mine."

"Really?" He looked about the room as if wondering how a servant merited such grand quarters.

He leaned over the bed and peered at Bessy. She sat up, clutched her stomach, and yowled with pain.

"Her face will heal," the doctor said, ignoring Bessy's cries.

"The swelling makes it look far worse than it really is." He then addressed Bessy. "Come on, my girl. Let me see what all the fuss is about."

He pulled back the bedclothes. Emily and Susan gasped. Bessy was lying in a pool of blood.

"Oh, Bessy. What has that beast done to you?" Emily gasped. She addressed the doctor. "Can anything be done for her?"

At these words, Bessy's howls grew louder.

"For goodness' sake, girl, compose yourself. There's nothing wrong with you that a little bed rest will not cure," he said, palpating her stomach with his hand.

He turned to Emily. "The injuries she has sustained, although painful, are superficial."

"How can you say such a thing?" Emily remonstrated. "All that blood?"

"That, my lady, is the result of something that occurred about three or four months ago. Your erstwhile maid is merely in the throes of a miscarriage."

"What?" Emily and Susan exclaimed in unison, then turned to stare at Bessy. She had the grace to look sheepish.

"His lordship said he would beat the brat right out of me… his words… not mine."

"But why? Most gentlemen provide for the offspring they sire," the doctor said.

"Tha-that's the rub," gasped Bessy, doubling over with another spasm. "The baby took right away and his lordship said it could not possibly be his."

"Let this be a lesson to you, my girl," the doctor pontificated. "This is what comes of leaving good, honest service for life on the primrose path. The next time you may not get off quite so easily."

"If this be easy," she moaned, "then God help me."

Hot water and toweling was sent for, and after the doctor was satisfied the miscarriage had reached a successful conclusion, he left a jar of salve to apply to Bessy's face before taking his leave.

"It's a wonder the pompous old fool did not insist on

bleeding her," Susan remarked. "I wonder how easy he would deem it if he were to receive a thrashing and a miscarriage all in the same day?"

As soon as Bessy was comfortably settled, Emily went downstairs to thank Miles for his help. He was nowhere to be found in any of the public rooms.

She rang for the butler and inquired after him.

"Mr. Walsingham left almost immediately, my lady. Mentioned something about challenging Lord Ruysdale to a duel."

Emily put her hand to her mouth and wondered how to resolve the dilemma. Then she brightened. "Please send someone to summon Mr. Bonham-Lewis. Perhaps he can put a stop to this."

"Very good, my lady." The butler bowed and was about to take his leave when Emily detained him.

"I have changed my mind," she said. "Kindly have a carriage prepared. It will be quicker if I go to him."

She reached the Bonham-Lewis house just as Rodney was about to depart for an airing in Hyde Park. Emily explained the reason for her visit.

"I rather thought so," he replied. "Miles just left here. He asked me to be his second and I agreed. He is to face Ruysdale tomorrow at daybreak on Hampstead Heath."

"Then you must put a stop to it. Miles is no good with a pistol. His aim is terrible. You should see him at a pheasant shoot."

Rodney shook his head. "I cannot. Once a challenge has been issued, a gentleman is honor-bound to follow through."

"Then my brother most assuredly will die." She clenched her hands. "James *would* be away at such a time."

"Emily, dear. Had he been in London, James would have issued the challenge himself. Not over your abigail, of course, but to protect you. In no way would he suggest that Miles play the coward."

"Duels. Men and their misguided idea of what constitutes honor. You would not find two women settling their differences in such an idiotic fashion."

Rodney looked shocked. "I should hope not," he replied.

He was still shaking his head when Emily left.

When James arrived home, Emily literally threw herself into his arms. "Thank heaven you are here. Something terrible has happened."

He untangled himself from her embrace. "Steady on, Emily, darling. Things cannot be that bad. Let us sit down somewhere and you can tell me what has happened."

They retired to the library, and about ten minutes later, James shook his head. "I stand corrected. Things are about as bad as they can be."

He punched the palm of his hand. "Damn that rash young fool. He had no business challenging Ruysdale, that was my prerogative. In fact, it was the very next thing on my agenda. I was going to call him out myself as soon as I had donned some fresh linen. Only I was going to suggest Primrose Hill."

He stroked his chin. "Perhaps Hampstead Heath was the better choice; everyone seems to use Primrose Hill these days."

Emily leapt to her feet with both fists clenched to her sides, shaking with rage. "You silly, silly men. I would like to box both of you on the ears."

His brows shot up in surprise. "What would you have us do, Emily? Look the other way and wait for that unholy pair to do you another injury? I think not. I just wish Miles had not poked his nose where it does not belong."

He went over to the bell rope and gave it a pull.

"What are you doing?"

"Summoning my valet, of course. I shall require him to pack a portmanteau for me."

"Whatever for?"

"It behooves me to spend the rest of this day with your brother, teaching him the finer points of dueling. Then I should be by his side at the actual event to ensure Fishberry does not have any snipers hiding in the shrubbery to do his dirty work for him."

"It will do no good. As I told Rodney, Miles is a terrible marksman. Albert Fishberry's seconds will be in far more danger of being shot than he. More's the pity." She heaved a sigh.

"Rodney was here? I am sorry I missed him."

"No. I thought it would be more expedient to drive over to his house to discuss the matter."

"Are you quite mad, Emily? You must have caused Rodney great embarrassment, behaving in such an unseemly fashion."

She stamped her foot. "You call me mad? My brother will most likely die on the morrow and all you worry about is the sensibilities of Rodney Bonham-Lewis? Fie, sir!"

"Stop it, Emily. One rash act committed by yourself is more apt to damage your reputation than any foul scheme dreamed up by Althea Cross. Just be more circumspect in future."

The argument was left at an impasse. James departed on his mission, leaving Emily with only a brief kiss on the cheek for solace.

"Men," she muttered as she watched him depart for Miles's house in the bottle green carriage. It was the largest conveyance the Garwoods owned. Then she realized it had been chosen in case it was necessary to carry her brother from the field of honor. She promptly burst into tears.

About an hour after dawn the next morning, Miles was carried into the house accompanied by James, Rodney, and an elderly doctor who clucked over his patient like a farmyard biddy. Once the doctor pronounced it safe to visit Miles, Emily entered the room in a somewhat gingerly fashion, as if the very sound of a footfall would send the patient spiraling to his death.

She was relieved to see that his eyes were open, and even more so when Miles managed a smile. "You seem to be all right," she said.

"I am not expected to die, if that is what you mean."

"Count yourself lucky," James interjected. His voice contained not one shred of sympathy. "When did it become the thing to duel over wantons? If such were the case we would be meeting on the grass every hour of the day with time for precious little else."

"I did not have Bessy's welfare in mind. Granted, she had my pity, but no one forced her to run off with Albert Fishberry. I wanted to protect Emily."

"You overstepped yourself, Miles. My wife is *my* responsibility."

"My intentions were good. I thought that if anyone had to get themselves killed, rather it be me. If you were to die, I swear Emily would not know another day of happiness as long as she lived." He winced and sank back into the pillows.

Emily let out a little cry. "Just how badly are you hurt?"

"I took a bullet in the shoulder. The bone was not shattered or anything, but it is beginning to throb like the devil."

"I am sorry Lord Ruysdale had the advantage of you, Miles dear."

"Who said anything about Ruysdale carrying the day?" Miles rejoined, his voice filled with indignation.

"You hit him?"

Miles nodded.

"Did you kill him?"

He grinned. "No, but for a while he will wish I had."

"Oh?"

"I am afraid I got him in a rather delicate place. I have been told that had the bullet been a fraction the right, it is most certain he would be fathering no heirs. As it is, Althea Cross will have to find another champion. This little episode is bound to have dampened any ardor he might have harbored for her."

"*Oh!*" Emily turned pink.

"My apologies, sister. I expect the shock of all this has addled my sense of propriety."

"I would have to concur," James said. "I would also like to add that your choice of target, while effective, could hardly be called sporting, old chap. That was not well done of you, Miles. No, not at all."

Miles sighed. "I have to agree. Actually, I was aiming for his heart."

Sixteen

Miles had been at Mayfair Court for almost a week before he could convince Emily she need not dance attendance to his needs around the clock.

"It is unnerving to wake up in the night to find you hovering over me. I am healing well and have suffered very little fever, so stop neglecting your husband. That is an order."

Emily did as she was asked, albeit very reluctantly, but still spent a good deal of time popping into his room to check up on him. In the meantime, Bessy had been put in one of the smaller guest rooms.

A new mattress was purchased for Emily's bed, but it was not slept on right away. James kept her busy in his own bed. The period of abstinence had sharpened her desire, and to her dismay, she found delight in every subtle nuance of his lovemaking. This confirmed her worst fears. She was one of those depraved women Lady Geraldine held in such contempt.

Bessy made a rapid recovery. After another week had passed, the swellings on her face had gone down. The bruises faded and she took to walking in the garden every afternoon.

"Bessy is looking like her old self," said Emily.

"You know, of course, that she cannot stay here," James replied.

"Surely we can find something for her to do. She sews very well."

"Emily, it would be sheer folly. Once a woman has fallen, she can never be retrieved. Already the younger footmen are casting glances her way, and when she has fully recovered…" He did not finish the sentence.

"Could we not find a husband for her?"

He shook his head. "The other girls were victims. Bessy is a wanton. No man in his right mind would marry her, however well dowered, and I cannot, in all conscience, encourage one of my people to do so."

"Then I suppose her only choices are to starve in the gutter or find another protector."

"I cannot imagine Bessy doing the former, so let us hope she finds in the latter the most generous of benefactors." After giving Emily a husbandly peck on the cheek, he departed for the library to read his newspaper. All afternoon his words echoed in her head. "Bessy is a wanton. No man in his right mind would marry her."

The message was clear. If James found out that she actually enjoyed what they did in the privacy of their boudoir, she would earn his everlasting contempt. This filled her with despair, for it seemed only a matter of time before he discovered the true nature of her character.

It seemed so unfair that it was permissible for a husband to enjoy the rituals of the marriage bed, yet for a wife to do so would make her the object of scorn and revulsion. She sighed. How wonderful it would be if it were otherwise.

She spent the rest of the afternoon brooding over the problem. Later, when Miles actually came downstairs to join them for dinner, she felt a brief moment of elation.

"It is such a relief to see how well you are doing," she said, as the footman removed the soup bowls from the table.

"Yes, it is," he replied. "Now the both of you can return to Northwycke Hall and get on with your lives."

"Only if you agree to accompany us. The country air will do you good," Emily rejoined.

"I am sure the both of you have seen enough of me for quite a time to come. My own servants are perfectly capable of seeing to my recovery."

"Nonsense," James interjected. "Emily and I would not dream of leaving you to the tender mercies of Hotchkiss and his minions. We insist that you come to Surrey with us."

Beaming with pleasure, Miles acquiesced to their wishes.

· · · ·

Two days prior to their appointed departure, James and Emily were enjoying a quiet time together in the small room she liked to use for working on her embroidery. James was reading a book on maritime affairs. Emily was plying a needle to some work stretched on an embroidery frame.

The cozy domestic scene was interrupted when the butler informed James that Mr. Hensley had arrived and craved an audience with him.

"Show him into the library, if you please."

The butler bowed and departed the room. James put his book aside. "He must have news of the *Indian Princess*. It is due in a fortnight or so with a hold full of silks and spices." He smiled in anticipation. "Your brother stands to profit from this venture, as I sold him a small share of the cargo."

Emily looked up from her sewing. "I am most grateful for your kind regard for Miles."

"Nothing would make me happier than to see him become a man of substance. I know you place little faith in him, Emily dear. Granted you have reason for the way you feel, but I truly believe that one day you will be proud of him."

"Do you really think so? It is my fervent wish."

She put aside her needlework and stood up. "While you are receiving Mr. Hensley, I believe I shall take a turn in the garden. The roses are at their peak right now."

"A splendid idea. I cannot remember a time when the garden has looked so lovely."

When she reached the rose arbor she found Bessy seated there. She rose and curtseyed to Emily.

"Please sit down, Bessy. It is so beautiful here, I think I shall join you."

She complied. They were both silent for a minute or two. Bessy's imminent departure weighed on Emily's mind. She was tempted to bring up the subject there and then just to get it over with. However, it was Bessy who spoke first.

"I want to thank you for taking me in, my lady. Had you

not, I know I would be dead by now." She gave Emily a diffident look. "You must think I am very wicked."

"I think you have made some foolish choices, but you have only hurt yourself."

"And the babe." A tear rolled down her cheek. She wiped it away with the back of her hand.

"Of course," Emily said. "I am truly sorry. I should have realized you would mourn your child."

Bessy smiled through her tears. "Do not get too mixed up in my troubles my lady. It's plain to see that you are upset enough, having to turn me away and all."

"Then you know." It was a statement, not a question.

"His lordship told me. Cannot say as I blame him," she said with a shrug. "One of the footmen and a couple of the grooms have already been making sheep's eyes at me. I suppose one day I just might make them back. Although after having a gentleman, I am not so sure."

"Lord Ruysdale may be of gentle birth, but he is in no way a gentleman."

Bessy grinned. "He is lucky he can still call himself a man. I hear that Mr. Walsingham almost gelded him."

"Bessy!"

"I am sorry, madam, my tongue sometimes gets away from me."

Emily shook her head. Albert Fishberry had most definitely not been a good influence on Bessy. Deciding it was safer not to engage her in conversation, Emily attempted not to pursue the subject.

Bessy was in the mood for discussion. "I suppose there is naught for me to do but find myself another gentleman—one, I hope, not so free with his fists."

Emily stared at her, not knowing how to answer. Oblivious to the embarrassment she was stirring up, Bessy sat blithely tapping her foot, a contemplative smile on her face.

"And this gives you no cause for distress?"

"Not if he be young and handsome and generous with his purse." Her smile widened, wrinkling her pert little nose. No doubt some dashing young blood would find her irresistible, Emily thought. But even so…

"Do you not find certain aspects to such an arrangement to be distasteful?"

Bessy responded with a deep, gurgling laugh. "Begging your pardon, Miss Emily, but if ladies of quality were not so squeamish over something meant to be pleasurable, there would be no demand among the gentlemen for girls like me."

Her words filled Emily with dismay. They confirmed her worst fears. She was no better than Bessy or any of the other light-skirts who tossed their petticoats for the gentlemen. She too, delighted in such carnal pleasures.

That night, when James took her in his arms she tried in vain not to succumb to the rising desire brought on by his sweet kisses and tender nibblings. But the love ritual was a long, sensuous affair and when he finally claimed her surrender, she dug her fingers into the palms of her hands, lest she scream out her passion like some depraved creature of the streets.

Emily slept fitfully that night, her dreams invaded by visions of Lady Geraldine pursuing her across the Fotheringhams' ballroom, brandishing her lorgnette screaming, "Fie! Fie, you strumpet." To make matters worse, the distinctive sound of the Countess of Brookhaven's high-pitched laughter could be heard in the background. She woke up several times to find herself trembling.

Two days later, with many assurances from Miles as to his fitness for the journey, they departed for the country. When the iron gates of Northwycke Hall loomed into sight Emily saw a look of contentment come to James's face. They had come home.

He had remarked on several occasions that he did not have the same regard for the house on Mayfair Court. It was just a place to stay when visiting London. In the same way, London was a place to be avoided if at all possible.

When they entered Northwycke Hall, Mr. Hobbes greeted them with news that the Ladies Geraldine and Maude had arrived the day before. Emily insisted on visiting them as soon as possible.

"I wonder if my mother has found a husband for Maude."

"She is far too young," Emily protested.

"Year-long engagements are not unusual."

"But it would not be fair to deprive her of a come-out."

"Did you enjoy yours?"

Emily mulled the question. "At first. But Maude would not encounter the same humiliation I was made to suffer."

He cupped her chin. "But had you not a come-out, my mother would never have recognized you and you would still be a maid, either scorching my sister's dresses with a smoothing iron or breaking vases in the drawing room."

"You beast," she said, softening the words with a beguiling laugh. "I am sure that by now I would be a most proficient maid."

He raised a brow. "You think so? I am of the opinion that I spared Northwycke Hall and its contents from considerable damage by marrying you. Probably the wisest economic decision I ever made." This statement was punctuated by a kiss on her nose.

Emily responded with a playful push. "All the same, I think we should visit the Dower House as soon as possible to find out if Maude has been snapped up."

"At least let us change our clothes, Emily."

Presently they came below-stairs, looking the better for a change of clothes. They were spared a visit to the Dower House by the two ladies showing up on their own doorstep.

As Emily embraced Maude she could not help but notice that her young sister-in-law had the advantage of her by at least an inch. "My goodness, Maude, how could you have grown so much in such a short time?"

"Let me look at you," James said, twirling his sister around. "Yes. You are turning into quite a statuesque young beauty. You will cut quite a dash at your come-out."

"Precious good a come-out will do her," Lady Geraldine snapped, tossing her head like an angry horse.

"Oh? Is there something I should know, Mother?"

"Tell him. Tell your brother what a headstrong little chit

you have become."

"Really, mother, not out here in front of the servants," James admonished. "Let us repair to the drawing room. I will ring for some refreshments and we can discuss this with a little decorum."

The fire left Lady Geraldine eyes. "You are quite right, of course. What could I have been thinking?"

James signaled to Hobbes, who had been studiously studying the angels embellishing the ceiling. "Send for some tea and sandwiches, if you please, Hobbes."

"And some cake, too," Maude interjected, apparently not in the least perturbed by her mother's outburst.

They indulged in small talk until the refreshments were served and the servant had made a discreet exit from the room. As soon as their privacy was assured, James leaned forward in his chair and addressed Maude. "Would you mind explaining what you have done to incur our mother's displeasure?"

"Frederick Howard offered for me and I refused his suit."

"Lord Crestwood's Freddy? Well, did you now?" James chuckled. "Not yet had a come-out and already you have turned down the heir to one of the richest earldoms in the country. My, my. There is no limit to what you might aspire, little sister. A duke? Quite possibly of the blood royal?"

"You are making fun of me and I think it is horrid of you."

"I find no amusement in this matter," Lady Geraldine countered, slanting James a frosty look.

"Let it go, Mother. Maude has plenty of time to find herself a husband. The poor child has yet to see her sixteenth birthday."

"Let it go? Let it go? Do you not care what manner of match your sister makes?"

Emily sensed the hysteria in her voice. She would rather see her married into a family of dull-witted boors, with scarce a chin among them, than with handsome, charming Miles. Just so long as they are flush in the pocket, she thought.

"Do not discommode yourself, Mother. Maude is a comely girl and well dowered to boot. She does not have to snatch the first offer to come her way." He smiled. "Besides, I see no advantage to allying ourselves to the Crestwoods. For the most part they are nigh to being simpletons."

"You exaggerate. Freddy is a charming boy."

"Come now, Mother. Can you possibly imagine having to suffer the company of the Crestwoods at every family gathering? We should all die an early death from sheer ennui."

"Heavens," said Lady Geraldine, tapping her chin with her lorgnette, "I had not thought of that."

Maude beamed. My husband has her undying gratitude, Emily thought.

For the next few minutes nothing was said. The four of them sipped their tea and nibbled on dainty sandwiches and cakes. Maude finally broke the silence by inquiring after Miles.

"He is resting. The trip from London was quite arduous for him," Emily replied.

"Quite arduous?" Maude echoed. "Why should that be? Is he not well?"

James told them about the duel with Albert Fishberry, and the reason for it.

"I cannot understand how you could have allowed this to happen, James," Lady Geraldine said. "It would be far simpler if you were to render Althea Cross harmless, before you are forced to follow in Miles's footsteps. It is not practical to embark on fighting duels with her paramours. You could end up killing or maiming half the young eligibles of the *ton*."

James stood up, and Emily surmised he was about to start pacing. He walked the length of the room twice, then gestured to his mother. "What would you have me do? I can hardly challenge the lady to a duel."

His mother's brows raised like two birds in flight. "What would I have you do? And you call the wits of the Crestwoods to question? Why, 'tis simple. You pay a visit to her father, the Earl of Thirlmere. He will trim her tailfeathers for her."

"What makes you believe she will heed him? She was ever headstrong, even as a young girl."

"Brookhaven named Thirlmere the guardian of his son. The wayward countess might have a love of revenge, but she has an even greater love of luxury." Lady Geraldine laughed. "If her source of funds is threatened she will come to heel readily enough."

James pulled his mother out of her chair and kissed her soundly on the cheek. "Darling, you are absolutely brilliant. How came you by such knowledge?"

His mother straightened her gown and patted her hair. "Really, James, a little restraint would be in order."

"You did not answer my question."

"It was common gossip at all the whist parties at the time. It was the reason for a lot of giggling behind fans. Althea absolutely loathes her father, and well her husband knew it."

James stroked his chin as if savoring the irony. "Sort of a final retribution from beyond the grave. How delicious."

He bent over Emily's chair and kissed her forehead. "The nightmare is over, my dear. The evil cat is about to get her claws pulled."

Emily felt a weight lift from her shoulders.

Seventeen

Lord Thirlmere's country seat was in the Lake District, but the dampness of the weather in those parts aggravated the pain in his arthritic bones, so he retained a small estate in the parish just north of St. Cuthbert's. For this James was grateful. The journey to Lake Thirlmere was long and arduous.

On arriving at the manor house he was ushered into a small anteroom where the elderly lord sat before a roaring fire, a heavy blanket covering his knees. The heat was oppressive. James decided to state his case as quickly as possible, then take his leave.

Lord Thirlmere indicated with an impatient little gesture that James should take the seat opposite his, close to the hearth. James chose to ignore his host and took a small straight-backed chair farther away from the blazing inferno.

"To what do I owe the pleasure of your visit, Northwycke? Let me guess. Heard you discarded my little baggage in favor of matrimony. Making mischief for you, I would hazard."

"One could say that, sir. If she confined her attacks to me, I could handle it. Unfortunately, she has involved my wife. That I will not tolerate."

He went on to enumerate the offenses committed by the Countess of Brookhaven. Her father interjected some remarks of his own into the conversation, such as, "The devil, you say," followed by, "The vindictive little cow."

At the conclusion, Lord Thirlmere stroked his chin as if deep in thought. "Erenow, she has never displayed such venom. Oh, from time to time she has vented that wicked tongue of hers on those who have incurred her displeasure. But this borders on madness." He peered at James over small, wire-rimmed spectacles. "Why do you suppose that is?"

James knitted his brow and looked contrite. "I am afraid I am partly to blame. I paid the lady a visit with the intention of informing her of my marriage. Unfortunately she assumed I had come to pay my addresses and precipitously accepted a proposal that was not offered, embarrassing me and humiliating herself."

"Oh, I say. It is a wonder the hellcat did not rip out your guts with her bare hands." He threw back his head and laughed.

Unfeeling bastard, James thought. No wonder his daughter turned out to be such a monster.

Lord Thirlmere removed his spectacles and wiped his eyes on the edge of his lap robe. "I would have loved to have seen the look on her face. Her mother was quite mad, you know, so I suppose it was to be expected."

"No, I did not know. I had heard that Lady Thirlmere was a frail lady and confined to her chambers at the castle. But mad? No, I had not heard that. I am sorry, sir."

"I suppose you were too young to be aware of all the whisperings and speculation that flew around London at the time. None of the gossip-mongers knew for sure, but it was so."

He gazed into the flames dancing in the grate and seemed to forget that he had a visitor. Then a log cracked from the heat, and he viewed James with a look of surprise.

"Ah, yes," he said. "My wife. She was not what one would call a raving lunatic, but she was quite mad all the same. I discovered she had taken to writing those dreadful stories about monsters lurking in castles, and one unscrupulous publisher actually had the temerity to buy one from her. It cost me a pretty penny to buy it back from him, I can tell you."

"And from this you deduced the poor woman was mad?"

"She had to be. In spite of several beatings she persisted in the endeavor without any consideration as to the scandal it would bring down on the family should it become known. Would you not consider that to be a sign of complete derangement?"

James remained silent. He found it absolutely appalling that his host deemed a beating the best way to make his wife biddable. It dawned on him that Lord Thirlmere had probably raised his daughter with the same degree of violence. No wonder Althea Cross sought love wherever she could find it.

"Finally had to keep her under lock and key when she took to running away."

James began to think the wrong member of the family had been locked up. The man was completely oblivious of the terrible wrong he had done to a defenseless woman. The physical violence was reprehensible. To have carried it to the point where he had crushed the spirit of the very woman he had vowed before God to care for, must assuredly have earned him an entrance into hell.

James determined to put as much distance between himself and the cruel earl as was possible. The fire flared up, intensifying the heat, and he could feel the perspiration trickling down his brow. He felt that he himself stood at the gates of hell.

He took out a handkerchief and wiped his forehead. "I shall take up no more of your time, my lord. I trust you will point out to Lady Brookhaven the disadvantages in pursuing this course. I promise that if she persists I intend to prosecute her to the fullest extent of the law."

"And well you should. However, you need not worry yourself over the matter, Northwycke. It is within my power to remove my grandson from her care and turn her out on the street without so much as a farthing if I so choose."

The look on the old man's face became positively malevolent. James found himself actually pitying Althea Cross. "I should hope it would not come to that, my lord."

He gazed at James through rheumy eyes. "One of those tender-hearted young fools, are you, Northwycke? Have a care, lest the women of your family run roughshod over you. Spare the rod and be prepared to live with the consequences."

He returned his attention to the fire, holding his gnarled hands up to the flames. "Do not concern yourself with my wayward child. The lady will not jeopardize her comfort for revenge."

"The man is beyond the pale," James muttered as he departed the manor. He retrieved Tarquin from the groom. Once mounted, he took a deep breath and headed for home.

• • •

At about the same time James was being ushered into the presence of Lord Thirlmere, Miles was sitting on a bench beside an ornamental pond filled with carp. Waterlilies adorned its surface and a weeping willow swayed gracefully in attendance, its beauty reflected in the water.

Lulled by the balmy weather and the droning of insects, he was on the verge of nodding off to sleep when the sound of footsteps crunching on the gravel path caused his eyes to open wide. He did not have to look up to know it was Maude. The sweet scent of lavender heralded her presence.

"Maude!" He attempted to stand.

She stayed him with a gesture. "Pray be seated, Miles dear. You must not tire yourself. I merely came to see how you were faring."

He made room for her on the bench. Once she was seated he took her hand. "Much better now that you are here, dear girl."

Maude pulled her hand away.

"I beg your pardon, Maude. I did not mean anything untoward. I was so pleased to see you I quite forgot myself." Inwardly he attributed her reserve to a virtuous spirit—a most endearing quality. "I hear you denied the suit of Freddy Howard."

She nodded. "I could not possibly marry such a paperskull. Especially one so lacking in chin."

Miles unconsciously stroked his own strong jaw.

"I did not think you could be swayed into accepting the offer of another."

Her eyebrows arched. "'*Another*'? What mean you by that?"

He reclaimed her hand. "I mean that I love you and I know you feel something for me; I have seen it in your eyes."

She pulled away from him and got to her feet. "Alas, Miles, I fear you are mistaken. What I feel for you is the fondness one has for a good friend. Not quite as deep as the regard for a brother, but similar."

He stood up and faced her, hoping to see in her expression some sign of love requited. Alas, she froze him out.

"You have changed," he said.

"Merely grown up a little more. I now have no need for a hero to worship."

He turned away so she would not see the distress he was feeling.

She touched his shoulder. "But I do have need of a good friend."

He stiffened.

"Please, Miles?"

He forced himself to turn and smile. "Of course, Maude. I would be honored to be considered your friend. I am at your service at all times."

She smiled. "I shall endeavor not to be the cause of any meetings on the grass at dawn, dear friend."

He watched her depart in the direction of the Dower House. Suddenly the lily pond had ceased to be a haven. With shoulders braced as firmly as his wound would allow, he went inside and sought the privacy of his room.

He did not join James and Emily for dinner that evening, choosing to take his meal in his room. Fearing he was not well, Emily checked on him directly after dinner. He was sitting in a chair facing the window.

He invited her to join him. She placed her hand on his uninjured shoulder and they shared the view of the lake. The setting sun washed the waters with fiery ribbons of color and, on the isle, transformed the white marble columns of the folly to a delicate rose.

She looked at the graceful little building with longing. It seemed an eternity since James had made love to her within its confines. *Perhaps tomorrow he will suggest a picnic*, she mused, *and carry me up those steps and—*

Miles coughed. She felt a rush of guilt for exploring such avenues in her brother's presence. She wondered if by engaging him in small talk it were possible to keep such thoughts at bay.

"Is it not a lovely view?" Her voice rose scarcely above a whisper.

He did not reply. Ordinarily he would have responded.

"Are you not feeling well, Miles?"

"I am perfectly all right. Please do not fuss."

He turned away from her.

"I saw you talking to Maude this afternoon by the lily pond. She walked away rather abruptly. Did you quarrel?"

"No. It was not well of you to spy on us, Emily." He was silent for a moment, then took a deep breath. "You might as well know the truth. It will probably come out sooner or later." His voice broke. "The answer is yes. The relationship is strained. I declared my love for Maude and she made it very clear that it was not returned."

She squeezed his hand. "I am truly sorry."

Miles could not mask the grief in his eyes. "I was so sure she was the one. She embodies everything I have ever dreamed of in a woman."

"Maude is a dear, sweet creature, but are you sure you are not deluding yourself in this belief?"

"In what manner?"

She took his hand and gave it a shake. "Think about it. You yourself wondered if you were not taken up with the thought of belonging to this family. It could have colored your judgment."

"If this is delusional, why does it hurt so much?" He ran his hand through his hair. "I am so confused I do not know what to think. In any case, it will not change anything; Maude has just relegated me to a position somewhat less than that of a brother."

He attempted a wry smile. It fell short. "Just let us say that not all the dreams of fools come true."

Emily kissed his cheek. It tasted salty. It had not occurred to her that men were capable of such emotion—in fact, she was sure it was not quite the thing. Poor Miles must really be suffering a broken heart, she thought.

"Dear, dear Miles. One day you will find your true love and she will love you back."

He shrugged. "That remains to be seen. Please do not trouble yourself over the matter. I shall get over it. I now know it is wiser to forget foolish fantasies. I will confine my search for a bride to next season's come-out."

She remained silent as the setting sun hung lower in the sky. The summer twilight seemed to linger even longer than usual, as if loath to cede dominion to the moon. Finally the lengthening shadows darkened the chamber.

Emily rang for Miles's valet and departed for her own chamber. Susan was waiting there to help her prepare for bed. Once settled there, she pulled the covers up to her chin and watched the moonlight gild the most prosaic of objects in the room with its own special magic. What a beautiful place the world can be, she thought.

A gentle rap on her dressing room door, signaling that James sought her company, sent a thrill coursing through her. Her love for him transcended everything else. She held out her arms and welcomed him to her bed.

Eighteen

Autumn triumphed over summer in a series of subtle forays: a chilly evening breeze after a sunny day, an early morning fog lingering until noon, then a night frost signaling the turning of the first leaves. Summer was over.

One morning toward the end of September, a watery sun flirted with a stream of cirrus clouds scudding across the skies—an idyll soon to be broken. Clouds of a more ominous nature were rolling in from the west.

James viewed them as he led Tarquin along the bridle path separating Hope House, the name they had chosen for the orphanage, from Northwycke lands. He urged the horse to a faster gallop, intending to race the storm, Tarquin's pounding hooves crushing a carpet of leaves into the mud as he charged along the path.

James reached the orphanage to find it a hive of activity. On the front lawn children were queued up waiting to return to their studies. Younger ones were being ushered indoors for their naps.

It heartened him to see in the short time the children had been there the change in the way they looked. Pale, pinched faces were fast becoming plump and rosy. Sad expressions were replaced by sounds of childish glee.

James realized he had a difficult road to traverse. Some of the children had to unlearn much of what unscrupulous adults had taught them. In truth, he did not even know if such a thing were possible. All he could do was hope for the best.

He left Tarquin at the stable and, as was his wont, entered the building through the kitchen. The aroma of a hearty stew simmering on the stove permeated the room. Everyone he met, from the housekeeper clad in sturdy black bombazine to housemaids in stiffly starched caps, dropped him a respectful curtsey as he passed through.

He had come to escort his wife home. There was no need to tell him of her whereabouts or give him directions to get there, for invariably she could be found upstairs in the room containing the four tiny cribs.

As he made his way up to the first story, his long legs taking two stairs at a time, he heard the plaintive wailing of a baby. Only two infants occupied the nursery. One was William, the other, a malnourished little girl named Jenny. Jenny looked far younger than the six months she could lay claim to.

He entered the room to find Emily walking back and forth, patting Jenny on the back in a vain attempt to soothe away her tears. Emily acknowledged his presence with a brief smile, then handed the baby over to a nursemaid who sat rocking a crib in which William lay sound asleep, sucking his thumb.

She followed James out to the stair landing. He kissed the top of her head and murmured, "Must you be here every single day? You work too hard. Let these people do their own work. That is what they are paid for."

Emily broke away from him. "I do. I merely come to give the children a little tenderness. If not I, then who? The staff are much too busy for that."

"You are such a love."

She gave a dismissive shrug. "Why are you here so early? Surely it is not time to go home."

"I am afraid so. There is a storm on the way."

Her eyes widened. "How can that be? There was not a cloud in the sky an hour ago."

"Nevertheless."

He offered her his arm and they made their way down the flight of stairs. As they passed through the kitchen, the housekeeper voiced her disappointment at the shortness of the visit, but she was mollified when the pending storm was brought to her notice.

Syllabub and Tarquin were led out of the paddock where

they had been grazing. Once mounted, the Garwoods lost no time in retracing the path to Northwycke Hall.

Miles joined them for a leisurely luncheon prior to the three of them repairing to the library to gather around a cozy fire. The two men played cribbage while Emily worked on her embroidery.

"How are things progressing at Hope House?" Miles asked.

James moved his peg forward before replying. "Quite smoothly now that we know what we are about. Would you not agree, Emily?"

Emily looked up from her sewing. "We gain strength from day to day. Another little boy was delivered to us yesterday—a little chimney sweep called Tim. He will be in the infirmary for a while as his arm was injured when they tried to pull him down from a chimney flue."

Miles clucked in sympathy. "I should like to ride over for a visit before I return to London."

"Surely you are not ready to leave us?" Emily asked.

"I thought to in a couple of days. It is high time. I feel well enough for the trip and thought it would be wise to leave before the weather worsens."

"I insist that one of the grooms take you in a carriage," said James.

"I say, that is awfully kind of you, but I would not dream of such an imposition. If you will just be good enough to give me the loan of a horse…"

"Nonsense, Miles. Not another word," James replied with an expansive smile.

The next morning proved to be the dawning of one of those glorious days that sometimes blaze forth before nature is reconciled to the coming winter chill. As soon as breakfast was over, Emily hurried into the garden to rejoice in the sunshine.

James encountered her as she returned to the house, a basket of showy asters on her arm. Her cheeks were pink from the fresh air, and in her dress of pale lavender muslin, James thought she looked the picture of youth and loveliness. He took the flowers from her and handed them to a footman. Then, walking beside her he slipped an arm about her waist. She smiled and he responded by taking her hand and kissing the inside of her wrist.

"Must you look so beautiful?" he murmured. "I am quite undone."

"La, sir. Pretty speeches trip from your tongue far too easily. But I do thank you for them all the same."

Before James could pursue the flirtation further, Hobbes approached. He prefaced his address with a dry cough. "Begging your pardon, sir, but there are some persons below-stairs requesting an audience with your lordship."

"What are they doing down there? You had better bring them to me."

Hobbes coughed once more and shot a conspiratorial look in Emily's direction. "I am thinking, sir, that it would be better if you received them below-stairs. Mr. Dempsey and his friend are not the sort of people one entertains."

"Nonsense. Mr. Dempsey is here on my invitation. Show him into the library."

"Very good, sir."

The "let the consequences be on your head" expression on the butler's face was not lost on James. Emily merely shrugged and declared her intention of going up to her chamber. James followed her, wishing to change out of his boots before receiving Mickey.

"What could the man want?" Emily mused.

"Employment, most likely. He has a way with horses, so I offered him a job in the stables."

"You offered a common pickpocket employment? Have you taken leave of your senses?"

James stroked his chin. "It has been my experience that Michael Dempsey is the most uncommon of men. He has his own code of honor. I feel our acquaintanceship has progressed to the point where he would consider it demeaning to steal from me."

Emily shook her head. "One can only hope that in this you are not mistaken."

James shrugged his shoulders and went into his own

bedchamber to summon Simpson for help with his boots.

When he finally entered the library, he found Mickey staring out of the large, mullion-paned window. The pickpocket turned to acknowledge his presence.

James was surprised to see that Mickey was freshly bathed and wearing clean clothes. He was touched by the gesture of respect the other man accorded him. It must have been no small thing for a man who was a stranger to soap and water to brave such a venture.

"Good afternoon, Mickey. You are wearing new clothes, I see."

Mickey grinned self-consciously. "Not new, but good enough. Paid for 'em with the money you gave me. I 'ope you realized them was sovereigns, not shillings, 'cos I spent quite a bit. What with a trip to a bath'ouse and the coach fare 'n all."

"You have come to accept the work I offered?"

"Harrumph. Not exactly." Mickey looked at his boots.

"Oh? Then exactly what, pray tell."

"Seeing as her mum died, I was 'oping you would give Lucy a job in the orphanage teaching the kiddies. She can read and write. Joe educated 'er 'imself."

"Where is this Lucy? I would have to see her before making such a decision."

"I am here, sir."

The voice came from the other side of the room. A young girl emerged from the shadows of a bookcase. She was tall for a girl, with auburn hair pulled away from her face in a severe bun. Her thinness was exaggerated by the wearing of a black dress made of heavy cotton.

James wheeled to face Mickey. "Just what are you trying to get away with, you bastard?" He moved toward the small man, his fist clenched. "I have a good mind—"

Mickey backed up until he was abutting the window and had no place further to go, a look of confusion on his face. "I don't rightly know what you mean, sir. You said if Lucy and 'er mum needed 'elp they should come to you."

The young girl placed herself between the two men,

holding her thin arms out as if to protect Mickey. "Please sir, do not harm Mr. Dempsey, I beg of you." She took Mickey's arm. "I told you it was useless to come here. His lordship was merely being polite with his offer of help."

James was stunned. It was not only that Lucy spoke with the well-modulated tones of the *ton*—this could be attributed to the tutelage of her father, the infamous Gentleman Joe. It was the fact that in Lucy he beheld a thinner version of his own sister, Lady Maude Evangeline Garwood.

Could his father be the lord who had died without providing for his son? If so, it would mean that he had acquired a mistress long before he had even married his mother. No wonder his parents' marriage had been devoid of all warmth. He felt a profound pity for his mother. It then occurred to him that being five years older than himself, Gentleman Joe would have been his father's first-born son. He felt a loss of entitlement. This was too much to be borne. But yet he had to know the truth.

"You have nothing to fear from me if you are honest. Tell me, Lucy, what is your full name?"

Lucy curtseyed. "Lucinda Anabel Garwood, my lord"

"And your father's?"

"Josiah James Garwood, if you please."

And if I do not please, James thought. Lucinda and Anabel were the names of his respective grandmothers. Josiah Garwood bore the names of his grandfathers, as did he, only turned around.

He turned to Mickey, noticing that he had maneuvered into a more expedient position aligned to the door. "Why did you wait so long before uncovering this little surprise? What do you hope to gain?"

"I don't know what you mean," he said, his eyes darting to the door. "Lucy and me ain't done nothing wrong. If it's all the same to you, sir, we'll be going back to London."

"I mean why did you not disclose that Gentleman Joe's full name is Josiah James Garwood?"

"Begging your pardon sir, but what 'as that got to do with anything?"

"The matter of his going by my family name has a great bearing on the subject."

"*Your* family name? Now who's trying to be funny? Your name is Northwycke, ain't it?"

"Then you did not know. I am the Marquess of Northwycke, but my name is Garwood. James Josiah Garwood." He took Lucy's hand. "Your father would be my half-brother, so I presume *you* are my niece."

Both visitors regarded him in gape-mouthed amazement. Mickey was the first to recover—at least, to a certain extent. "Cor stone the crows!" he exclaimed, and without so much as a by-your-leave, plopped into a chair.

After motioning for Lucy to also sit, James rang for Hobbes. The butler entered, a pained look on his face.

"Kindly bring some refreshments for my guests. Perhaps a platter of meats and some bread and fruit." He turned to Lucy. "What would you like to drink? Some milk? Perhaps tea?"

Lucy looked diffident. "I should like some milk, if you please, sir. I seldom get the chance to partake of it."

James was touched. Such an easy wish to grant. "Some ale for you, Mickey?"

Mickey nodded. "Much obliged sir."

Once Hobbes had left the room, Mickey addressed James. "Does it mean that Lucy can't work in the orphanage, 'er... being your niece 'n all?"

"It is something to consider."

"If she can't work there, I don't know what's to become of 'er. I really don't." Mickey sounded fretful.

Lucy's lower lip began to quiver.

"Lucy's future is assured. What kind of a monster do you take me for?"

James leaned toward her. "How old are you, Lucy?"

"Almost fifteen, sir."

"Tell me, my dear. When you are old enough, would you not prefer to marry a good country squire and preside over your own household?"

Lucy made a great show of inspecting her fingernails,

which James was pleased to notice were clean and well trimmed. "I—I do not know sir. I suppose if I harbored a deep affection for him. Otherwise…" Her voice trailed off.

"Ah, well, you have plenty of time to consider the matter." A look of relief washed over Lucy's face.

"If you will excuse me for a moment, I should like my wife, Lady Northwycke, to meet you both. Please partake of some refreshments should they get here before I return."

"Begging your pardon, sir, would it be all right for me to look at your books? 'Aven't 'ad one in me 'ands for a long time."

"By all means, Mickey." Surprised by the request, James hastened out of the room.

Mickey went over to the library shelves with the alacrity of a starving man let loose at a Roman banquet. He selected a book bound in fine Corinthian leather and ran his hand reverently over the surface.

Lucy went over to the window and looked outside. "Such a beautiful garden," she said. "Who would dream such a place existed?"

Engrossed in the book, Mickey offered no reply. She fell silent, turning back to look outside. Her attention was broken by the sound of the door opening. She turned and saw a young man enter. He was tall and well favored, though somewhat slender, with hair as sleek as a raven's wing. He smiled at her. Lucy drew in her breath. She thought him to be the most handsome man she had ever beheld.

"Maude, I did not expect to see you here. I was looking for James." Maude, whoever she might be, seemed to cause him great unease.

"I am sorry, sir; you are mistaken. I am Miss Lucy Garwood." She dropped him a curtsey.

"An honest mistake, Miss Garwood. You bear a remarkable resemblance to Lady Maude." He joined her at the window and subjected her to a penetrating stare. Her gaze did not waver. Such beautiful hazel eyes, she thought. They have the look of one who has known sorrow. She longed to stroke his cheek.

"Yes, I can see I was mistaken." He continued his scrutiny,

then pulled up short. "Forgive my rudeness, Miss Garwood, allow me to introduce myself. I am James's brother-in-law, Miles Walsingham."

Lucy inclined her head.

"May I ask what your relationship is to the Garwoods?"

Lucy hesitated. "I think his lordship should be the one to answer that question."

"Oh?"

There was an awkward silence. The young man gave her a searching look. His eyes are flecked with green, she thought. The most perfect color for eyes to be. She stared back, mesmerized.

"Harumph."

The spell was broken. Miles wheeled around.

"The name is Dempsey. Michael Dempsey."

"Michael Dempsey," Miles mused. "The name has a familiar ring. Ah yes. You must be Mickey Lightfingers."

"Some people call me that." This was delivered in a tone that suggested that perhaps Miles would not be part of that select group. "I'll 'ave you know that Miss Lucy is not accustomed to being stared at in such a bold fashion."

Lucy blushed. At that moment, death would have been welcomed. Mercifully, Hobbes returned with a maid, who wheeled in a tea cart laden with refreshments. Miles excused himself and departed.

James and Emily entered just as Mickey and Lucy had finished eating. James had wisely decided that Mickey would be ill at ease eating in front of his betters.

After the unusual guests had been presented to Emily, James invited Mickey to inspect his stables. The little cockney accepted with alacrity, enabling Emily to get better acquainted with the newly discovered member of the Garwood family.

At the stables, Mickey moved from horse to horse, gifting each one from a bunch of carrots James had thoughtfully supplied. He stroked muzzles and patted withers, murmuring sweet nothings to each one in turn.

Eventually he ran out of horses. "Well?" James asked. "Are you still of a mind to return to London? A small cottage with a garden goes with the position."

"A garden? You play rough, my lord. A garden where I can plant vegetables in the back and 'olly'ocks in the front?"

"I believe there is already an abundance of flowers. The previous occupant, the recently expired widow, Mrs. Appleby, was very fond of hollyhocks, roses, and all manner of plants."

Mickey removed his cap and bowed to James. "There's nothing spoiling in London. When do I start, sir? I promise to put my heart and soul into the tending of your 'orseflesh."

James smiled. "I all ready know that, Mr. Dempsey."

Nineteen

Lady Geraldine was gazing pensively into a cabinet filled with figurines when James entered the drawing room. She turned on hearing the door open. "Good morning, James."

"Good morning, Mother. To what do I owe the pleasure of your company so soon after breakfast?"

"I wish to see this girl you tell me is your father's granddaughter. Such a taraddidle."

"Is that wise? You had a right to know about Lucy, but why subject yourself to such a confrontation?"

"Nonsense. I insist on seeing the deceitful little baggage, if only to expose her for the imposter she is. I am not so easily gulled as you seem to be."

James sighed. "As you wish. I would have spared you this." He went over to the bell pull and rang for Hobbes, who as if in anticipation of such a summons, entered the room almost immediately.

At being told to send for Miss Lucy, Hobbes raised a brow. "Very good, my lord."

A few minutes later there was a light rap on the door. James bade Lucy enter. She did so with all the diffidence of a lamb being led to the slaughter. He noticed that with her hair gracefully piled in curls on top of her head, and wearing the black dress of fine muslin (no doubt culled from Emily's wardrobe), she cut a more prepossessing figure.

Lady Geraldine raised her lorgnette to her nose and put Lucy to a thorough scrutiny. Seemingly satisfied, she turned to James. "There is a superficial resemblance to Maude, I suppose, but whoever put this creature up to this has erred. Tell me, miss, how do you explain the color of your hair?"

"The color of my hair? I am led to understand that my grandmother's hair was auburn. I have been told my that my grandpapa admired the color. My own dear papa had black hair, not unlike his lordship's."

"Yes, that is so," James agreed. "I believe now it was a kinship I felt for him that moved me to see that he received a Christian burial."

"I see." Lady Geraldine turned to Lucy. "I am sorry for your bereavement, Miss Garwood. It must have been difficult for you, losing both parents at such a young age."

Tears pooled in Lucy's eyes. "Thank you for your kind words, my lady."

Lady Geraldine nodded and raised her lorgnette once more, subjecting Lucy to yet another scrutiny. She gave a dry little laugh and smoothed her own auburn hair. "And I always thought Maude inherited her good looks from me."

Lucy shot James an agonized look. "If you please, sir, may I be dismissed?"

"By all means, Lucy. I believe Lady Geraldine is finished with you."

His mother made a dismissive gesture with her lorgnette. "Yes, child, run along."

Once Lucy was out of earshot, her eyes sparked with what James could best describe as righteous indignation. "Your father has a lot to answer for."

James braced himself for what he presumed would be a litany of the wrongs his father had perpetrated against her person. He was mistaken.

"When you told me of the story of Gentleman Joe and how he was abandoned as a child, I thought it reprehensible. Knowing the man responsible was my husband does not change anything."

James kissed her on the cheek. "He certainly did not deserve you. You have an honorable and generous spirit, and I am proud to be called your son."

She made a deprecating gesture, but she flushed with pleasure at his praise. Then her face took on a serious expression.

"What do you intend to do with Lucy?"

"We have plenty of time to think of that. I had thought of passing her off as a distant cousin and finding a respectable country squire for her to marry. A handsome dowry would enhance her chances in that direction."

She nodded. "I must say, she certainly comports herself in a genteel manner. Perhaps it will work."

James shrugged. "She did not take to the idea with any degree of enthusiasm. It seems that Miss Lucy will only marry someone for whom she harbors a sincere affection."

Lady Geraldine raised a brow. "Really? Such a ridiculous notion for a penniless waif."

"But it shows a certain purity of spirit."

"Fiddlesticks. You must not encourage her in this nonsense. One has to be practical in such matters."

"I wonder how many lives have been ruined by such thinking?"

Lady Geraldine tapped him on the shoulder with her lorgnette. "Really, James. I do not understand you of late. I am beginning to think that you have taken leave of your senses."

James did not reply. It occurred to him that his mother was better off not delving too deeply into the matter. To invalidate her own life would serve no useful purpose.

She declared her intention of returning to her own house. James offered to escort her there. She accepted his arm and, as if it had been a perfectly uneventful morning, regaled him all the way to the Dower House with the latest *on dits* circulating around the spas and assemblies at Bath.

He returned to the Hall to find Miles about to embark on the return trip to London. His face lit up at the sight of James walking across the lawn. "I was waiting to say good-bye before I left. I cannot begin to thank you for your kindness."

"Not at all," James replied. "Emily and I are going to miss you." He shook Miles by the hand.

"There is something I wish to ask of you," Miles said. "Please do not answer right away, I would deem it a favor if you would give it some thought. At least give me some time to prove myself worthy."

"By all means, Miles old chap. If it is within my power I would be happy to accommodate you."

"It is about Miss Lucy."

"What would that be?" James's tone was guarded.

"You spoke of marrying her off to some country squire. Would you consider me for her husband? In a year or so I will be able to support a wife."

James's lips quirked. "Will you indeed?"

"Oh yes," Miles replied. "I should have enough money from the investments you so kindly allowed me to make, to reopen the family estate in Kent. I am sure I will be able to support a wife by then."

"And you wish to make my niece Mrs. Walsingham? Do you mind telling me why?"

"I find her to my liking. Her person fits my ideal of the girl I would like to marry."

"Good grief, Miles, is that enough? It seems such a flimsy reason to get leg-shackled."

"Of course there is more. I find Miss Lucy to be pleasing in every way. She is modest and demure, virtues I find most desirable. But most important, I find her to be candid, without being unkind. She is a pearl among women."

"I see. You seemed to have engaged her in considerable discourse."

"I went out of my way to converse with her at every opportunity. She is far better educated than any girl I have ever encountered; she would be miserable shackled to a stolid country squire."

"I suppose on any given day, people marry for flimsier reasons."

Miles grabbed him by the sleeve. "Then you agree?"

James pried his sleeve loose. "Steady on, old chap. Let us say that when Lucy has her sixteenth birthday you have my permission to offer for her. I warn you, though, the decision will be entirely up to her."

Miles beamed. "That is all I ask."

James shook him by the hand once more and signaled for the groom to bring the carriage forward. Emily joined them in time to wave Miles on his way. Then she linked arms with James and they went inside.

"Did Miles mention anything about Lucy before he left?"

"He involved you in his doings before talking to me? Really, Emily, I take exception to that."

Emily withdrew her arm from his. "And I take exception to your disagreeable attitude." Her lower lip quivered.

James was unprepared for her reaction to what he had considered to be a perfectly normal objection. "Let us not have a scene over nothing."

"Over nothing? How can you be so horrid?" She burst into tears and dashed up the staircase.

James felt a rising irritation. It was the second time in as many days that Emily had burst into tears over a trifle. He hoped it would not become a regular occurrence, as he had little patience for hysterical females.

Things really came to a head the following weekend. James had organized a fox hunt for the local gentry, but Emily refused to join the festivities, claiming to be indisposed.

Later, Lady Geraldine returned in triumph, the brush having been awarded her. Emily took one look at the bushy red tail and, with eyes glistening, sobbed, "That poor, poor fox." She then turned abruptly and went inside, leaving James's guests to watch her departure in open-mouthed surprise.

As soon as they were alone in their chambers, James laced into her. "How dare you make a scene in front of our guests!"

"I am sorry, James. It was not intentional." She was close to tears once more.

"For goodness' sake, Emily, please control yourself. I cannot take many more of these outbursts. Mother suggests you should consult a doctor."

Emily turned to ice. "Your mother intrudes on my privacy."

"Nevertheless."

Things between them were left at an impasse. That night he did not invite her into his bed. James slept fitfully and awoke the next morning as irritable as a bear with toothache. Their relationship became even more strained as the week progressed, with communication between them practically nonexistent. Emily's eyes were rimmed with red from frequent weeping.

Friday came and James spent the morning conferring with the steward, Mr. Rainey. It was not until Emily failed to show up for luncheon that James realized she was missing. Thinking she had gone over to the orphanage, he checked the stables, but Syllabub was in her stall.

Still not ready to panic, he called at the Dower House. His mother was out on her charitable rounds, but Maude was there to receive him. On hearing Emily was not there, he slumped into a chair.

"Perhaps she has left me. She has been acting very strangely of late."

"I hardly think so, but it would serve you right if she did," Maude said sternly.

James jerked to attention. "How can you say that, Maude? Do I not accord her every affection?"

"When I was a little younger and less discerning I thought so."

"And now?"

"Not now. You lavish the merest kitten in the stables with the same affection you give your wife."

James got to his feet. "How dare you!"

"Because it is the truth. I have heard you refer to her as a darling little poppet when conversing with Miles. And that expression of yours about making women purr like kittens—really James, I blush for you."

"It seems to me, sister, that you spend an inordinate amount of time listening at keyholes."

"When gentlemen are in their cups there is no need to strain to hear what they are saying."

"You say I am incapable of love. Have I ever treated you with less than loving kindness?"

"That is not the point. You have a very loving heart, but you love people in general, not in particular."

"I am afraid you have me confused."

"Think about it, James. You find it in your heart to succor poor orphans, and you really care about the people of Northwycke. No village has a more humane lord. Yet you seem incapable of giving a woman your unconditional love. Unless a man offers me that, I shall live out my days as an old maid."

After a moment James said, "Painful as it is to admit, I think you may be right. But now I must get on with my search for Emily. After our experience in London I do not take anything for granted."

"Shall I come with you?"

"No, Maude dear. This is something I have to do alone."

On returning to Northwycke Hall he searched the gardens to no avail. Now, fear for Emily's safety crawled down his spine like a stalking beast. Maude's words circled in his head, crashing around him like a thunderbolt. Without Emily there would be no reason to go on living. How could he have been so dense and his little sister so wise?

"Dear God," he whispered, "give me one more chance to get things right." He strode past the paddock. Mickey, who happened to be exercising Syllabub, touched his forelock and sang out a cheerful, "Good morning, your lordship."

James nodded, then, grasping at straws, called out, "Would you happen to know the whereabouts of Lady Northwycke?"

"I most certainly would. Lady Northwycke is on that island in the middle of the lake."

"Are you sure?"

"Ought to be. I rowed 'er there meself. S'posed to go back for 'er in a few minutes."

"Keep on with what you are doing. I will go for her instead." James leaped over a stile and sped across the meadow on winged feet. As he rowed out to the island, he pondered the reason for Emily's making the trip without him. They had grown apart of late. He vowed to do all in his power to rectify the situation. He did not want to lose her. Not now. Not after realizing how deeply he loved her.

James found her sitting on the steps of the island

summerhouse, a stalk of wild wheat in her hand. She stared as he approached, a somber expression on her face.

He sat beside her, noticing how cold the marble felt through the sturdy material of his trousers. "There must be a more comfortable place than this to sit."

She did not respond.

"Might I ask what you are doing here?"

"I came for one last look before I say good-bye."

"You mean to leave me, then?"

She nodded. The inevitable tears pooling in her eyes. "You should have our marriage annulled. I am not fit to be a wife."

James took her hand and raised it to his lips. "What nonsense you babble. I will not let you leave that easily. Emily, darling, I love you too much for that."

Her eyes widened. "You do? I had not thought so." Her voice was flat, devoid of emotion.

He clasped her by the shoulders. "Listen to me, Emily. I love you from the depths of my soul. Without you my life would have no meaning. I love you as I have never loved before, or ever hope to love again. Do you find that so hard to believe?"

She searched his eyes. "No, James, I believe you." She began to sob.

He gathered her into his arms and sat rocking her. "You must tell me what is bothering you. You cannot go on like this," he murmured.

"You will hate me."

"It is not in me to hate you."

"Not even if I tell you I am a wanton, fit only for the company of strumpets?"

James released her and sprang to his feet. He felt the blood leave his face, and all he could do was shake, his hands clenched to his side.

"Do you realize what you have done to us?" He walked away from her and did not stop until he came to the other side of the island. There he gazed at the church spire of St. Cuthbert's.

Was it only this spring we vowed to love and honor one another within those walls? he mused. *It seemed more like an eternity. What a smug bastard I was, thinking she would be satisfied with the crumbs I threw her way.*

Emily remained sitting on the steps. She hugged her knees and rocked back and forth, fully aware that she had brought her life crashing down about her head. She did not even bother to look up when she heard James's footsteps coming closer.

To her surprise, he pulled her to her feet. "Tell me, Emily, do you have any regard for me at all?"

She pummeled his shoulder in despair. "I have loved you from the very moment you pulled me up on Tarquin and brought me to Northwycke Hall."

"That is something to build on. I am devastated at the thought of you in another man's arms, but Maude is right, love is unconditional."

Mixed emotions ran through her, warring for supremacy—hurt, bewilderment, shock, outrage. Outrage won out. She swung her arm and slapped him across the face as hard as she could.

"You beast! How *dare* you suggest I would take a lover!"

He stepped back, rubbing his face. She went to slap him again and he grabbed her wrist. "Whoa! Before you loosen my teeth, I think we need to clarify something."

"Unhand me. I have nothing more to say to you," she snapped.

"Unhand me? I believe that was the phrase that started this merry-go-round. Define 'wanton' for me, my lady wife, and I shall cheerfully let go of your wrist."

"You know," Emily countered, not wanting to put her perfidy into words.

He tightened his hold on her, and the look in his eyes boded no good. She wished herself anywhere but there. She hung her head. With his other hand he held her by the chin and forced her to look at him.

"This is important, Emily. Do not choose this moment to turn missish on me."

She knew his look of anguish would haunt her for the rest of her days. "I mean that when you make love to me I want to moan and scream and scratch, just like Bessy and all the other

210

light-skirts."

He raised a brow. "Are you sure that is what they do?"

"I thought so. Bessy says that if ladies allowed themselves to enjoy what after all is supposed to be a pleasurable experience, gentlemen would have no need for mistresses."

He threw back his head and laughed. "That is not necessarily so. Some gentlemen are inordinately greedy. Just let me say that deep in the bosoms of the very best of wives, there is a naughty little Bessy longing to be made love to. And in my case, at least, a husband eager to oblige."

Emily gazed at him in wonder. "Then my confession does not fill you with revulsion?" Emily was confused. "But your mother told me gentlemen scorned wives who behaved in such a wanton manner.

James groaned. "My *mother* told you that? It is most unfortunate, but she is really not to blame. I suspect my father was a very selfish lover who saw only to his own pleasure. Her opinions are colored by her own unhappy experiences."

"But what about Lady Brimstoke? Was she not locked away in the north tower of the family castle for an unseemly display of base passion?"

"Base passion, is it? For a cold fish, my mother has a way with words. I do not suppose she mentioned that Lord Brimstoke was a raving lunatic who ended *his* days locked up in the east tower of the castle?"

"Really? Then you are not shocked by my behavior?"

He gave her a playful kiss. "On the contrary, my love. I am going to take you into our little trysting place and you may scream all you wish. Be as loud as you like, no one will hear you."

She batted her eyes at him and pulled her dress off her shoulder, displaying a scandalous amount of bosom. "Lawks, my lord. I have to agree with her ladyship. You are a very wicked man."

Without another word, he crushed his mouth to hers, scooped her into his arms and carried her inside. He did not end the kiss, until he was ready to take off her clothes.

Afterwards, as they lay nestled together in the afterglow

of their lovemaking, Emily kissed him and murmured, "I must confess, James darling, I love being wanton."

He nibbled her ear. "Let me assure you, not half as much as I enjoy you being so."

She sighed. "I must apologize for the way I have behaved of late. I have not felt well."

James sat up and grabbed her by the shoulder. "What do you mean?" he cried, his voice full of panic.

"You know. I seem to cry over the silliest things, and lately in the mornings, my breakfast has not stayed down."

James hugged her to his breast. "Emily darling, do you not remember what Mrs. Thatcher said about Polly? All these symptoms point to impending motherhood. We are going to have a child."

"Are you sure?"

"Positive. And from this point, having taught you all I know about making babies in the most delicious ways possible, I fear I shall be of no help whatsoever. I have not the least notion of how to raise them."

Emily snuggled closer. "Do not give it another thought, James, darling. We shall learn together."

The Dowager's Daughter

Affairs of the state will soon give way to affairs of the heart.

Althea Markham shoulders many burdens of being an unattached countess—wading through the collection of gold-diggers and rogues to find a suitable husband, providing her family with a male hair, and most of all, protecting her mother, who tends to acts more debutante than dowager. As she sneaks away for illicit meetings with a mysterious stranger, Althea is determined to unveil his identity—and his intentions.

Desperate to escape from beneath the shadow of his older brother, John Ridley takes part in a daring game of espionage against the French. Posing as a smuggler, he engages with the charming Celeste Markham. But despite her winsome allure, it is her daughter, Althea, who seizes John's attention.

As affairs of the state give way to affairs of heart, John must convince Althea that she can trust him with her future, and her love.

A Kiss For Lucy

Could the wrong woman be the right love?

Rescued from a life of hardship by her wealthy uncle, Lucy Garwood can't escape the shadow of her elitist relatives. She longs to be loved and respected in her own right, but it seems that as an orphan, her place amongst her bluebood family is unlikely to improve—that is until a case of mistaken identity leads to a kiss from a dashing stranger...

Robert Renquist, Duke of Lindorough, is determined to win the heart of the lovely Maude. But in an attempt to sweep her off of her feet with a daring act of passion, it isn't Maude he kisses, but her half-niece instead. Though conscious of his standing in society, Robert can't deny his unmistakable attraction to Lucy, and he'll soon discover there is only one thing more powerful than his noble lineage—love.

The Love-Shy Lord

Their match was impossible, but their love was inevitable.

Too tall for a society woman, Clarissa has no potential suitors—not that she needs any. She only has eyes for Marcus, viscount of Fairfax. But as a steward's daughter, Clarissa is hardly a suitable match for Marcus.

Marcus Ridley is far too appealing—and eligible—for his own good. Restlessly pursued by desperate maidens, his view of women and marriage is skewed. But then he meets Clarissa, who steals his heart with a single kiss.

Suddenly, Marcus can't get Clarissa off of his mind, and the high-society lord finds himself desperate to make the steward's daughter his wife.

Printed in the USA
CPSIA information can be obtained
at www.ICGtesting.com
JSHW031713140824
68134JS00038B/3661